D1681841

THE GRAVEYARD BOOK
VOLUME 2

THE GRAVEYARD BOOK Volume 2

Based on the novel by: **NEIL GAIMAN**
Adapted by: **P. CRAIG RUSSELL**

Illustrated by: DAVID LAFUENTE   SCOTT HAMPTON
P. CRAIG RUSSELL   KEVIN NOWLAN   GALEN SHOWMAN

Colorist: LOVERN KINDZIERSKI

Letterer: RICK PARKER

HARPER
An Imprint of HarperCollinsPublishers

The Graveyard Book Graphic Novel, Volume 2

Text copyright © 2008 by Neil Gaiman

Illustrations copyright © 2014 by P. Craig Russell

All rights reserved. Manufactured in China.

No part of this book may be used or reproduced in any manner whatsoever without written permission except in the case of brief quotations embodied in critical articles and reviews. For information address HarperCollins Children's Books, a division of HarperCollins Publishers, 195 Broadway, New York, NY 10007.

www.harpercollinschildrens.com

Library of Congress catalog card number: 2013953799

ISBN 978-0-06-219483-1 (trade bdg.)

Typography by Brian Durniak

14 15 16 17 18 SCP 10 9 8 7 6 5 4 3 2 1

First Edition

To Brooke and Andrew, Jadon and Josiah, and Naomi and Emmeline
(and special thanks to Galen Showman and Scott Hampton for service above and beyond)
—P. C. R.

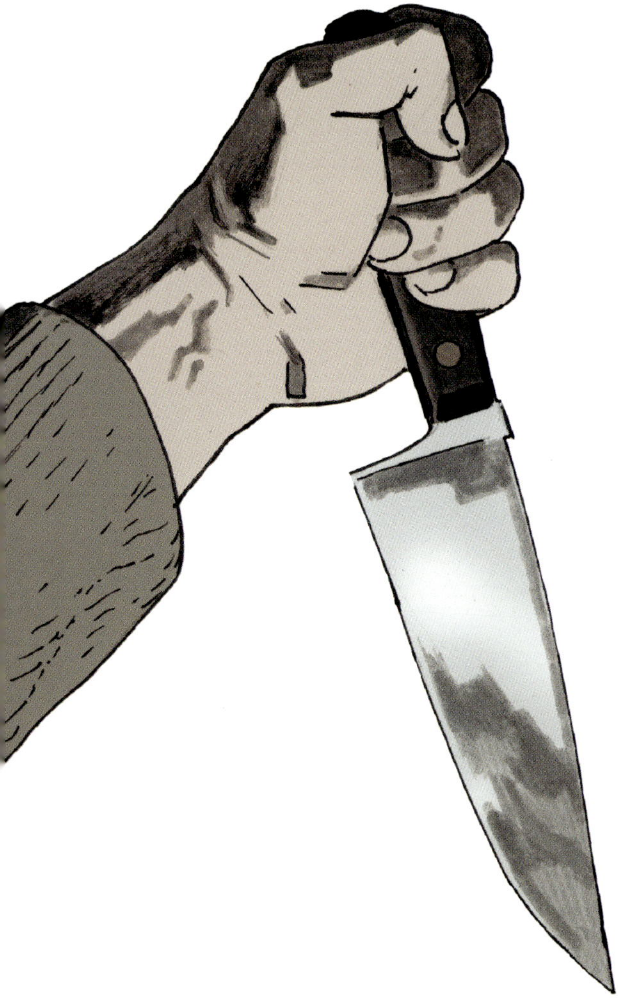

6
Nobody Owens' School Days

Illustrated by David Lafuente

RAIN IN THE GRAVEYARD, AND THE WORLD PUDDLED INTO BLURRED REFLECTIONS. BOD SAT, CONCEALED FROM ANYONE, LIVING OR DEAD, WHO MIGHT COME LOOKING FOR HIM, UNDER THE ARCH THAT SEPARATED THE EGYPTIAN WALK AND THE NORTHWESTERN WILDERNESS BEYOND IT FROM THE REST OF THE GRAVEYARD, AND HE READ HIS BOOK.

DAMM'EE! DAMM'EE, SIR, AND BLAST YOUR EYES!

... 1 ...

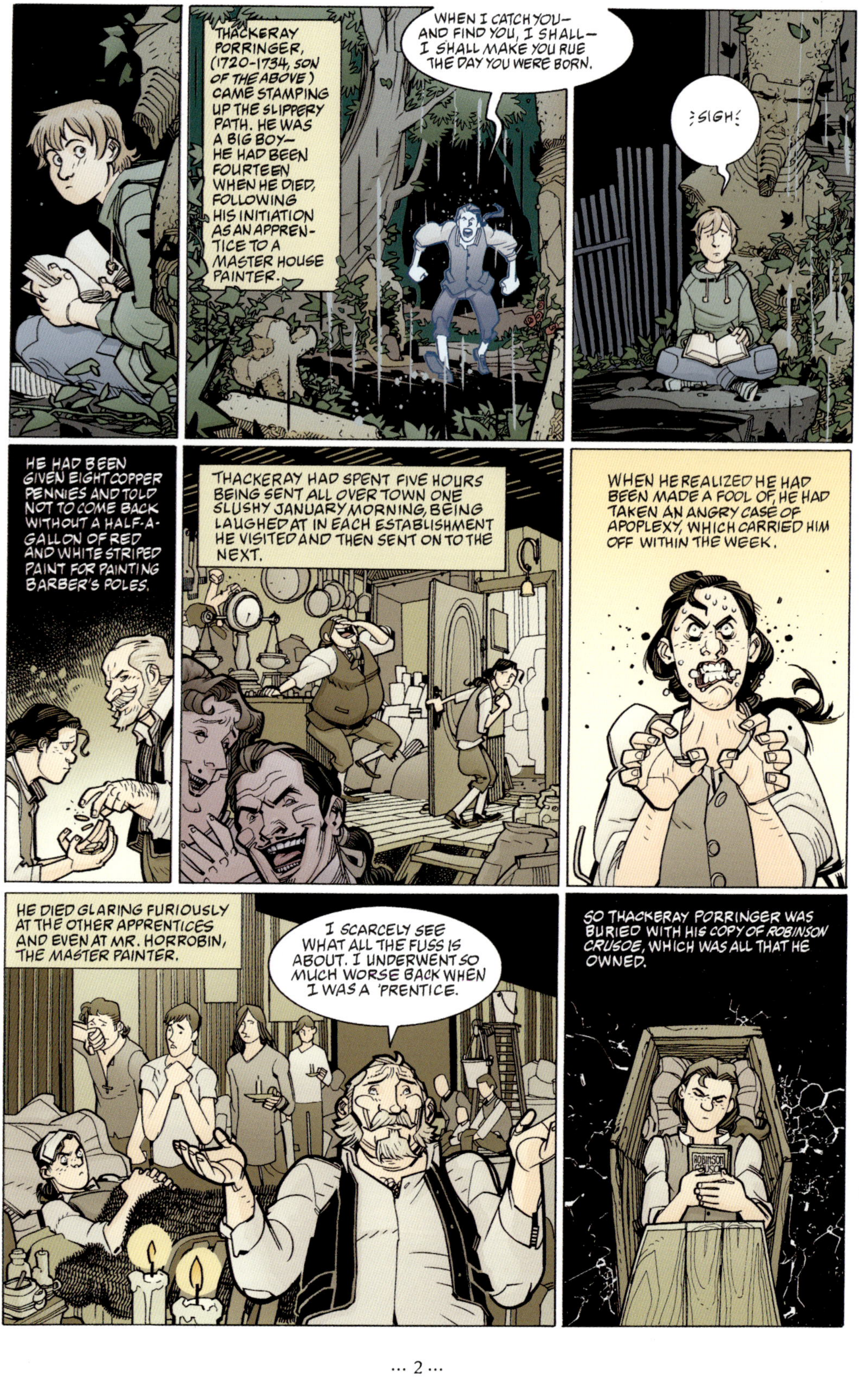
THACKERAY PORRINGER, (1720-1734, SON OF THE ABOVE) CAME STAMPING UP THE SLIPPERY PATH. HE WAS A BIG BOY— HE HAD BEEN FOURTEEN WHEN HE DIED, FOLLOWING HIS INITIATION AS AN APPRENTICE TO A MASTER HOUSE PAINTER.
WHEN I CATCH YOU— AND FIND YOU, I SHALL— I SHALL MAKE YOU RUE THE DAY YOU WERE BORN.
SIGH
HE HAD BEEN GIVEN EIGHT COPPER PENNIES AND TOLD NOT TO COME BACK WITHOUT A HALF-A-GALLON OF RED AND WHITE STRIPED PAINT FOR PAINTING BARBER'S POLES.
THACKERAY HAD SPENT FIVE HOURS BEING SENT ALL OVER TOWN ONE SLUSHY JANUARY MORNING, BEING LAUGHED AT IN EACH ESTABLISHMENT HE VISITED AND THEN SENT ON TO THE NEXT.
WHEN HE REALIZED HE HAD BEEN MADE A FOOL OF, HE HAD TAKEN AN ANGRY CASE OF APOPLEXY, WHICH CARRIED HIM OFF WITHIN THE WEEK.
HE DIED GLARING FURIOUSLY AT THE OTHER APPRENTICES AND EVEN AT MR. HORROBIN, THE MASTER PAINTER.
I SCARCELY SEE WHAT ALL THE FUSS IS ABOUT. I UNDERWENT SO MUCH WORSE BACK WHEN I WAS A 'PRENTICE.
SO THACKERAY PORRINGER WAS BURIED WITH HIS COPY OF ROBINSON CRUSOE, WHICH WAS ALL THAT HE OWNED.
ROBINSON CRUSOE

DEATH HAD NOT IMPROVED THACKERAY PORRINGER'S TEMPER.

I KNOW YOU'RE HERE SOMEWHERE! COME OUT AND TAKE YOUR PUNISHMENT, YOU, YOU THIEF!

I'M NOT A THIEF, THACKERAY. I'M ONLY BORROWING IT. I PROMISE I'LL GIVE THE BOOK BACK WHEN I'VE FINISHED IT.

I TOLD YOU NOT TO!

BUT THERE ARE SO FEW BOOKS HERE. IT'S JUST UP TO A GOOD BIT, ANYWAY. HE'S FOUND A FOOTPRINT. IT'S NOT HIS. THAT MEANS SOMEONE ELSE IS ON THE ISLAND!

IT'S MY BOOK. GIVE IT BACK!

HERE.

I COULD READ IT TO YOU. I COULD DO THAT.

GO AND BOIL YOUR FAT HEAD!

OW!

OW!

⚡#!

... 3 ...

"AH!"

"OW!"

"OH.... HULLO"

MISS EUPHEMIA HORSFALL AND TOM SANDS HAD BEEN STEPPING OUT TOGETHER FOR MANY YEARS. TOM HAD DIED DURING THE HUNDRED YEARS WAR WITH FRANCE, WHILE MISS EUPHEMIA (1861-1883, SHE SLEEPS, AYE, YET SHE SLEEPS WITH ANGELS) HAD BEEN BURIED IN VICTORIAN TIMES. THE COUPLE SEEMED TO HAVE NO TROUBLES WITH THE DIFFERENCES IN THEIR HISTORICAL PERIODS.

"YOU SHOULD SLOW DOWN, YOUNG BOD. YOU'LL DO YOURSELF AN INJURY."

"YOU ALREADY DID. YOUR MOTHER WILL HAVE WORDS WITH YOU."

"AND YOUR GUARDIAN WAS LOOKING FOR YOU."

"BUT IT'S STILL DAYLIGHT."

"HE'S UP BETIMES AND SAID TO TELL YOU HE WANTED YOU. IF WE SAW YOU."

"THANK YOU."

THE CHAPEL DOOR WAS OPEN, AND SILAS, WHO HAD LOVE FOR NEITHER THE RAIN NOR THE REMNANTS OF THE DAYLIGHT, WAS STANDING INSIDE.

"I HEARD YOU WERE LOOKING FOR ME."

... 4 ...

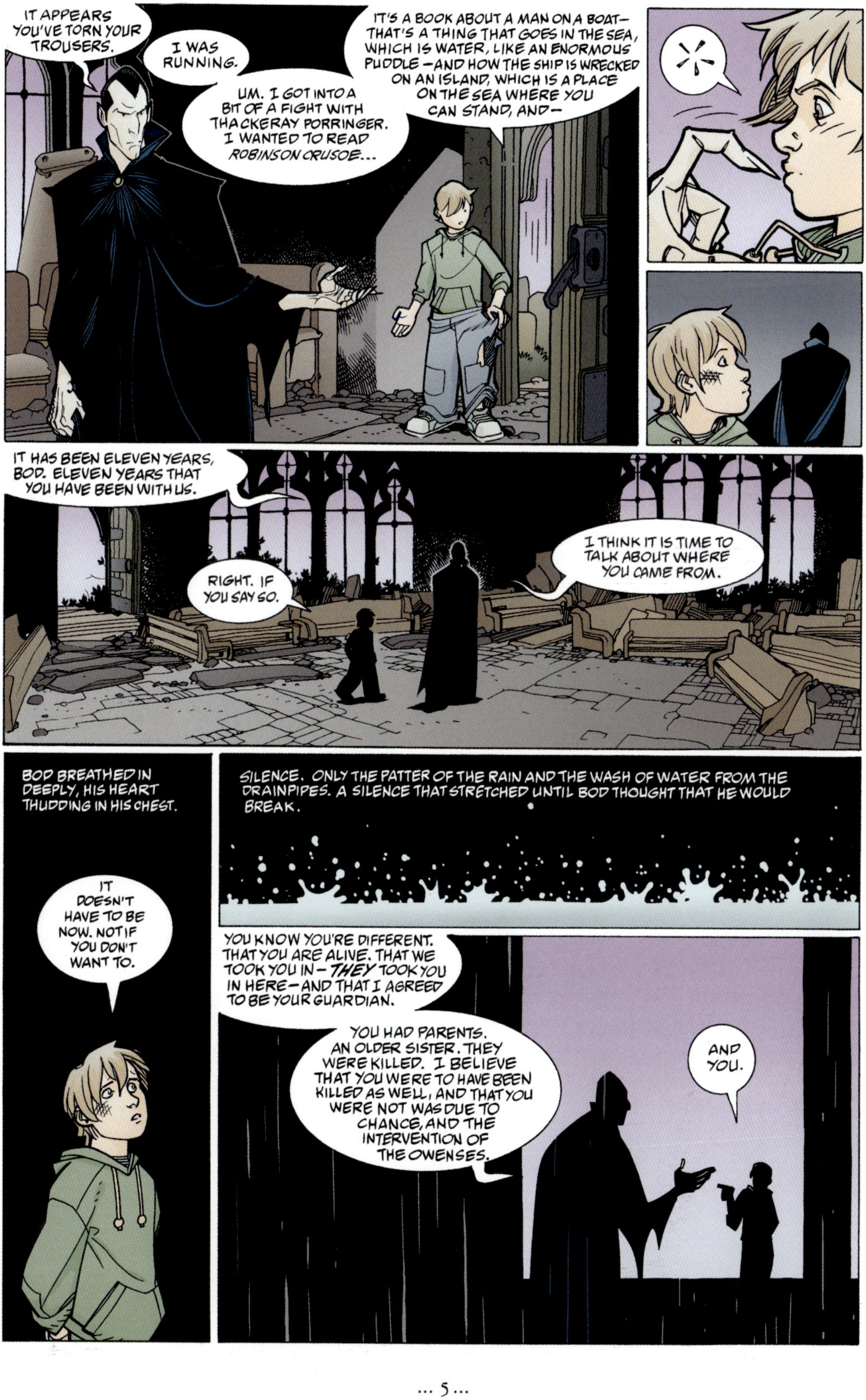
IT APPEARS YOU'VE TORN YOUR TROUSERS.
I WAS RUNNING.
UM. I GOT INTO A BIT OF A FIGHT WITH THACKERAY PORRINGER. I WANTED TO READ ROBINSON CRUSOE...
IT'S A BOOK ABOUT A MAN ON A BOAT— THAT'S A THING THAT GOES IN THE SEA, WHICH IS WATER, LIKE AN ENORMOUS PUDDLE —AND HOW THE SHIP IS WRECKED ON AN ISLAND, WHICH IS A PLACE ON THE SEA WHERE YOU CAN STAND, AND—
IT HAS BEEN ELEVEN YEARS, BOD. ELEVEN YEARS THAT YOU HAVE BEEN WITH US.
RIGHT. IF YOU SAY SO.
I THINK IT IS TIME TO TALK ABOUT WHERE YOU CAME FROM.
BOD BREATHED IN DEEPLY, HIS HEART THUDDING IN HIS CHEST.
IT DOESN'T HAVE TO BE NOW. NOT IF YOU DON'T WANT TO.
SILENCE. ONLY THE PATTER OF THE RAIN AND THE WASH OF WATER FROM THE DRAINPIPES. A SILENCE THAT STRETCHED UNTIL BOD THOUGHT THAT HE WOULD BREAK.
YOU KNOW YOU'RE DIFFERENT. THAT YOU ARE ALIVE. THAT WE TOOK YOU IN—THEY TOOK YOU IN HERE—AND THAT I AGREED TO BE YOUR GUARDIAN.
YOU HAD PARENTS. AN OLDER SISTER. THEY WERE KILLED. I BELIEVE THAT YOU WERE TO HAVE BEEN KILLED AS WELL, AND THAT YOU WERE NOT WAS DUE TO CHANCE, AND THE INTERVENTION OF THE OWENSES.
AND YOU.

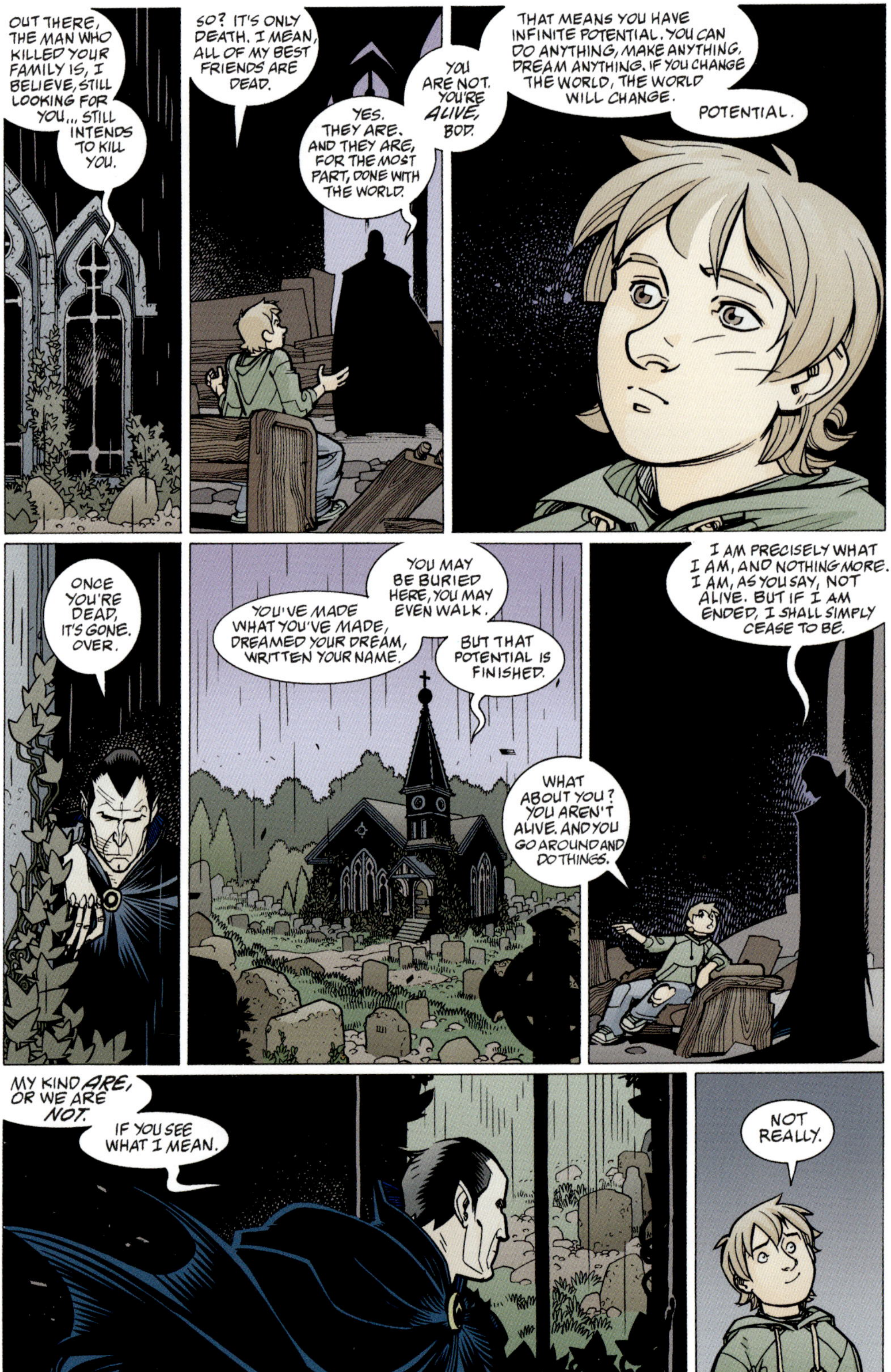
OUT THERE, THE MAN WHO KILLED YOUR FAMILY IS, I BELIEVE, STILL LOOKING FOR YOU... STILL INTENDS TO KILL YOU.
SO? IT'S ONLY DEATH. I MEAN, ALL OF MY BEST FRIENDS ARE DEAD.
YES. THEY ARE. AND THEY ARE, FOR THE MOST PART, DONE WITH THE WORLD.
YOU ARE NOT. YOU'RE ALIVE, BOD.
THAT MEANS YOU HAVE INFINITE POTENTIAL. YOU CAN DO ANYTHING, MAKE ANYTHING, DREAM ANYTHING. IF YOU CHANGE THE WORLD, THE WORLD WILL CHANGE.
POTENTIAL.
ONCE YOU'RE DEAD, IT'S GONE. OVER.
YOU'VE MADE WHAT YOU'VE MADE, DREAMED YOUR DREAM, WRITTEN YOUR NAME.
YOU MAY BE BURIED HERE, YOU MAY EVEN WALK.
BUT THAT POTENTIAL IS FINISHED.
WHAT ABOUT YOU? YOU AREN'T ALIVE. AND YOU GO AROUND AND DO THINGS.
I AM PRECISELY WHAT I AM, AND NOTHING MORE. I AM, AS YOU SAY, NOT ALIVE. BUT IF I AM ENDED, I SHALL SIMPLY CEASE TO BE.
MY KIND ARE, OR WE ARE NOT.
IF YOU SEE WHAT I MEAN.
NOT REALLY.

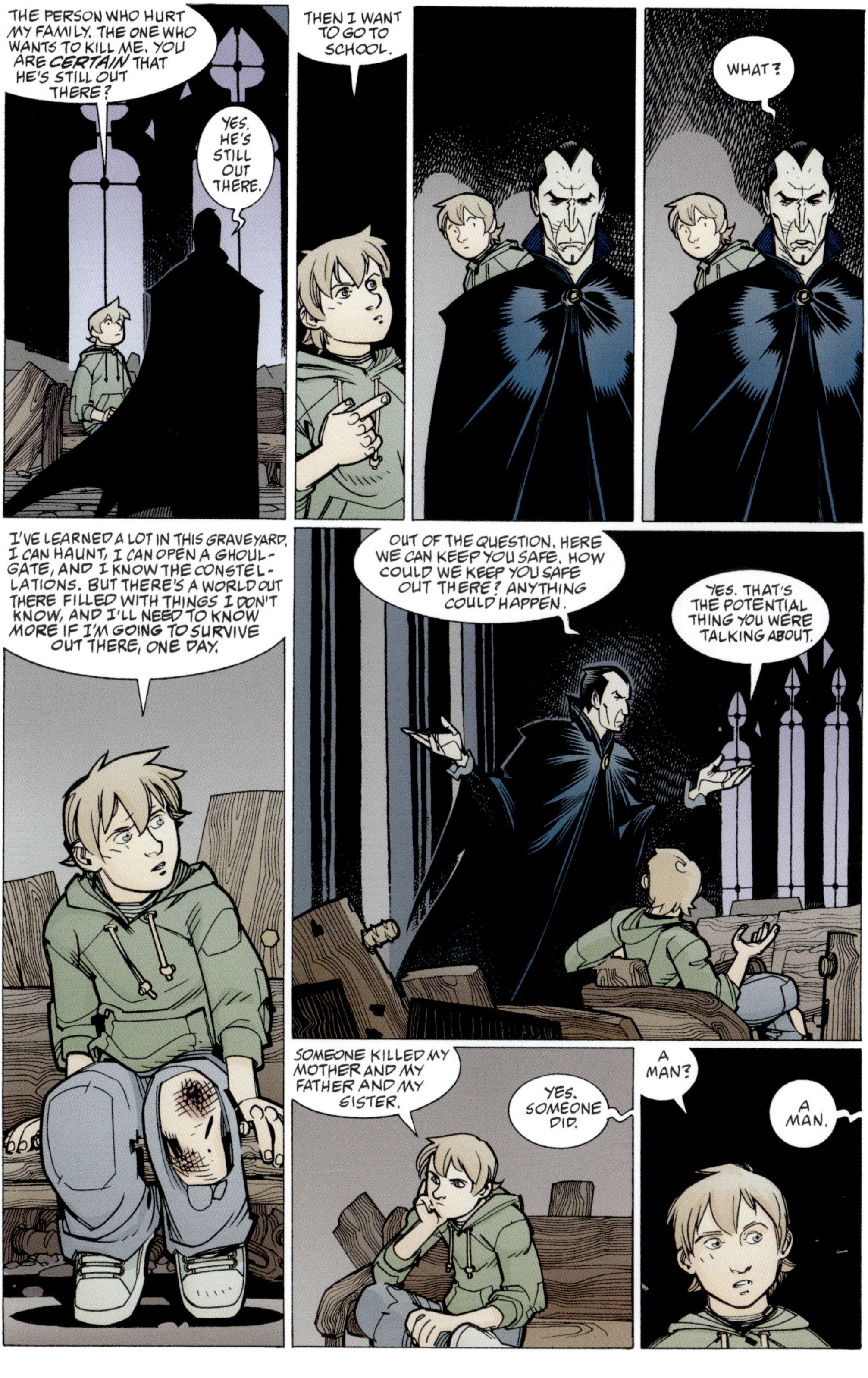
THE PERSON WHO HURT MY FAMILY. THE ONE WHO WANTS TO KILL ME. YOU ARE *CERTAIN* THAT HE'S STILL OUT THERE?
YES. HE'S STILL OUT THERE.
THEN I WANT TO GO TO SCHOOL.
WHAT?
I'VE LEARNED A LOT IN THIS GRAVEYARD. I CAN HAUNT, I CAN OPEN A GHOUL-GATE, AND I KNOW THE CONSTELLATIONS. BUT THERE'S A WORLD OUT THERE FILLED WITH THINGS I DON'T KNOW, AND I'LL NEED TO KNOW MORE IF I'M GOING TO SURVIVE OUT THERE, ONE DAY.
OUT OF THE QUESTION. HERE WE CAN KEEP YOU SAFE. HOW COULD WE KEEP YOU SAFE OUT THERE? ANYTHING COULD HAPPEN.
YES. THAT'S THE POTENTIAL THING YOU WERE TALKING ABOUT.
SOMEONE KILLED MY MOTHER AND MY FATHER AND MY SISTER.
YES. SOMEONE DID.
A MAN?
A MAN.

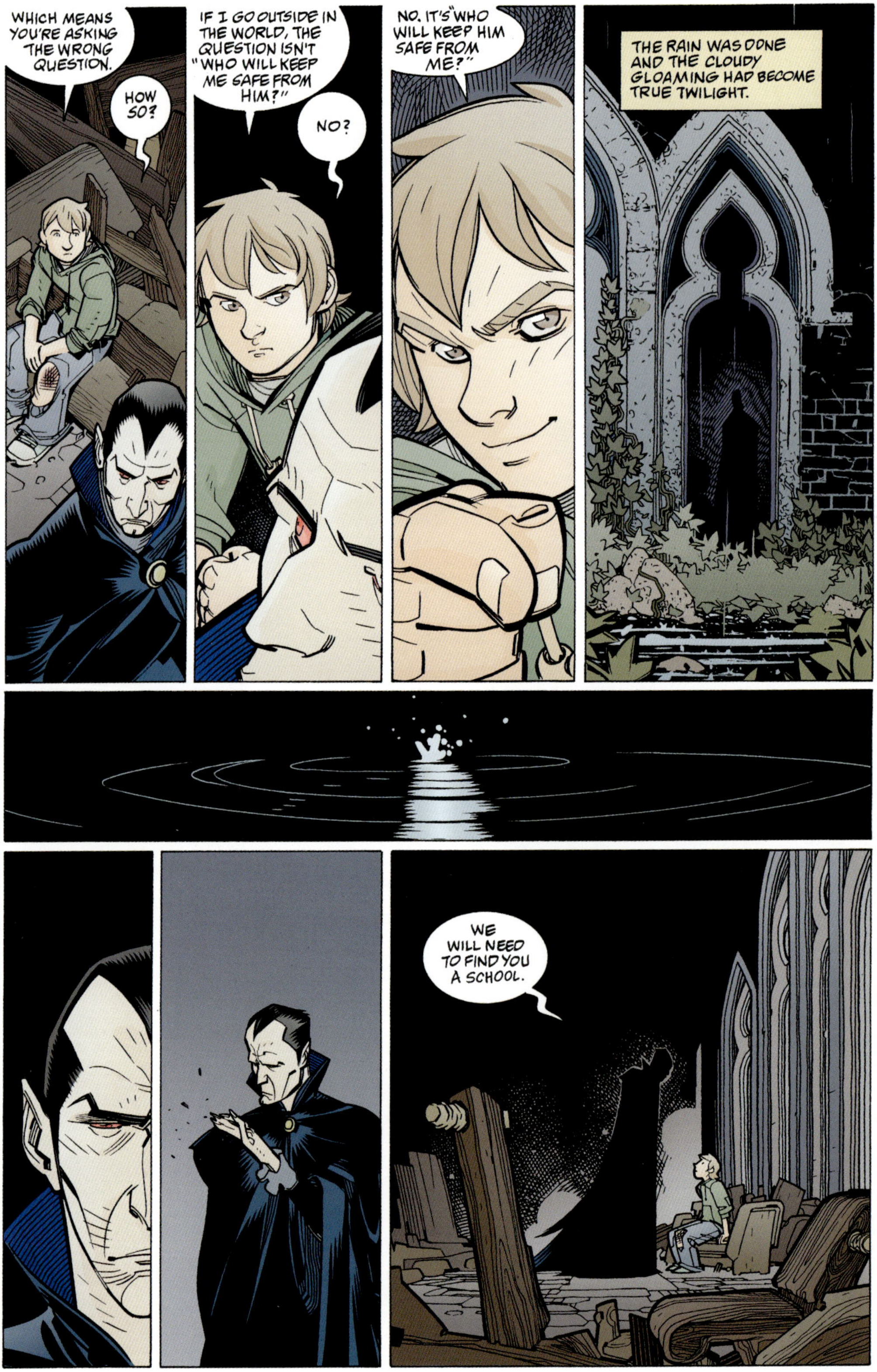
WHICH MEANS YOU'RE ASKING THE WRONG QUESTION.
HOW SO?
IF I GO OUTSIDE IN THE WORLD, THE QUESTION ISN'T "WHO WILL KEEP ME SAFE FROM HIM?"
NO?
NO. IT'S "WHO WILL KEEP HIM SAFE FROM ME?"
THE RAIN WAS DONE AND THE CLOUDY GLOAMING HAD BECOME TRUE TWILIGHT.
WE WILL NEED TO FIND YOU A SCHOOL.

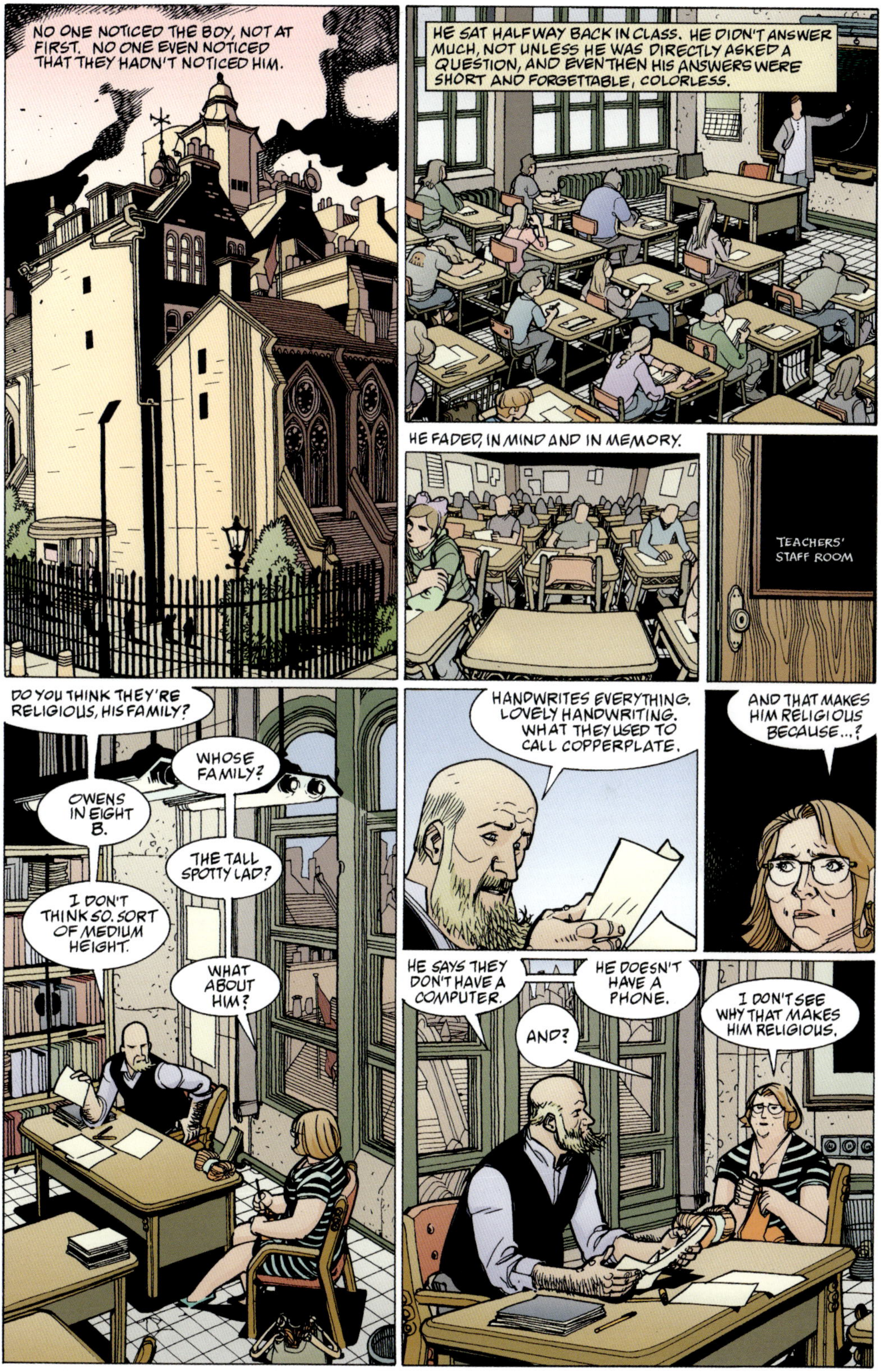

NO ONE NOTICED THE BOY, NOT AT FIRST. NO ONE EVEN NOTICED THAT THEY HADN'T NOTICED HIM.
HE SAT HALFWAY BACK IN CLASS. HE DIDN'T ANSWER MUCH, NOT UNLESS HE WAS DIRECTLY ASKED A QUESTION, AND EVEN THEN HIS ANSWERS WERE SHORT AND FORGETTABLE, COLORLESS.
HE FADED, IN MIND AND IN MEMORY.
TEACHERS' STAFF ROOM
DO YOU THINK THEY'RE RELIGIOUS, HIS FAMILY?
WHOSE FAMILY?
OWENS IN EIGHT B.
THE TALL SPOTTY LAD?
I DON'T THINK SO. SORT OF MEDIUM HEIGHT.
WHAT ABOUT HIM?
HANDWRITES EVERYTHING. LOVELY HANDWRITING. WHAT THEY USED TO CALL COPPERPLATE.
AND THAT MAKES HIM RELIGIOUS BECAUSE...?
HE SAYS THEY DON'T HAVE A COMPUTER.
HE DOESN'T HAVE A PHONE.
AND?
I DON'T SEE WHY THAT MAKES HIM RELIGIOUS.

HE'S A SMART LAD. THERE'S JUST STUFF HE DOESN'T KNOW. AND IN HISTORY, HE'LL THROW IN LITTLE MADE-UP DETAILS, STUFF NOT IN THE BOOKS.
WHAT KIND OF STUFF?
MR. KIRBY FINISHED MARKING BOD'S ESSAY. WITHOUT SOMETHING IMMEDIATELY IN FRONT OF HIM, THE WHOLE MATTER SEEMED UNIMPORTANT.
STUFF.
AND HE FORGOT ABOUT IT.
JUST AS HE FORGOT TO ENTER BOD'S NAME ON THE ROLL. JUST AS BOD'S NAME WAS NOT TO BE FOUND ON THE SCHOOL DATABASES.
STUDENTS
SCHOOL
SEARCH P
NO MATCHES
THE BOY WAS A MODEL PUPIL, FORGETTABLE, AND BASICALLY FORGOTTEN, AND HE SPENT MUCH OF HIS SPARE TIME IN THE SCHOOL LIBRARY, A LARGE ROOM FILLED WITH BOOKS AND OLD ARMCHAIRS, WHERE HE READ STORIES AS ENTHUSIASTICALLY AS SOME CHILDREN ATE.
EVEN THE OTHER KIDS FORGOT ABOUT HIM. NOT WHEN HE WAS SITTING IN FRONT OF THEM: THEY REMEMBERED HIM THEN. BUT WHEN THAT OWENS KID WAS OUT OF SIGHT, HE WAS OUT-OF-MIND.
SUPTU
HIS PRESENCE WAS ALMOST GHOSTLY.
IT WAS DIFFERENT IF HE WAS THERE, OF COURSE.

NICK FARTHING WAS TWELVE, BUT HE COULD PASS FOR SIXTEEN. HE WAS AN EFFICIENT SHOPLIFTER, AND OCCASIONAL THUG WHO DID NOT CARE ABOUT BEING LIKED, AS LONG AS THE OTHER KIDS, ALL SMALLER, DID WHAT HE SAID. ANYWAY, HE HAD A FRIEND. HER NAME WAS MAUREEN QUILLING.

"CALL ME MO."

NICK LIKED TO SHOPLIFT, BUT MO TOLD HIM WHAT TO STEAL.

NICK LIKED TO HURT AND INTIMIDATE, BUT MO POINTED HIM AT THE PEOPLE WHO NEEDED TO BE INTIMIDATED.

THEY WERE, AS SHE TOLD HIM SOMETIMES...

"A PERFECT TEAM."

THEY WERE SITTING IN A CORNER OF THE LIBRARY SPLITTING THEIR TAKE OF THE YEAR SEVENS' POCKET MONEY.

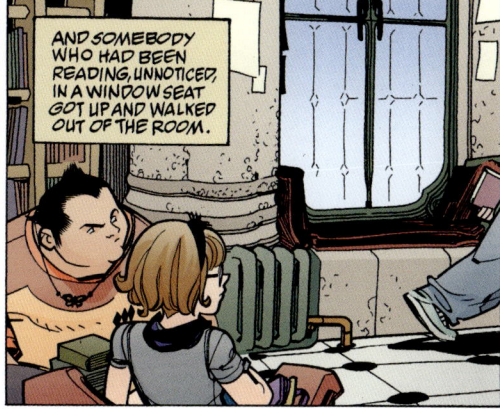

"THE SINGH KID HASN'T COUGHED UP YET. YOU'LL HAVE TO FIND HIM."

"YEAH. HE'LL PAY."

"WHAT WAS IT HE NICKED? A CD?"

"YEH."

"JUST POINT OUT THE ERROR OF HIS WAYS."

"EASY."

"WE'RE A GOOD TEAM."

"LIKE BATMAN AND ROBIN."

"MORE LIKE DOCTOR JEKYLL AND MISTER HYDE."

AND SOMEBODY WHO HAD BEEN READING, UNNOTICED, IN A WINDOW SEAT GOT UP AND WALKED OUT OF THE ROOM.

... 11 ...

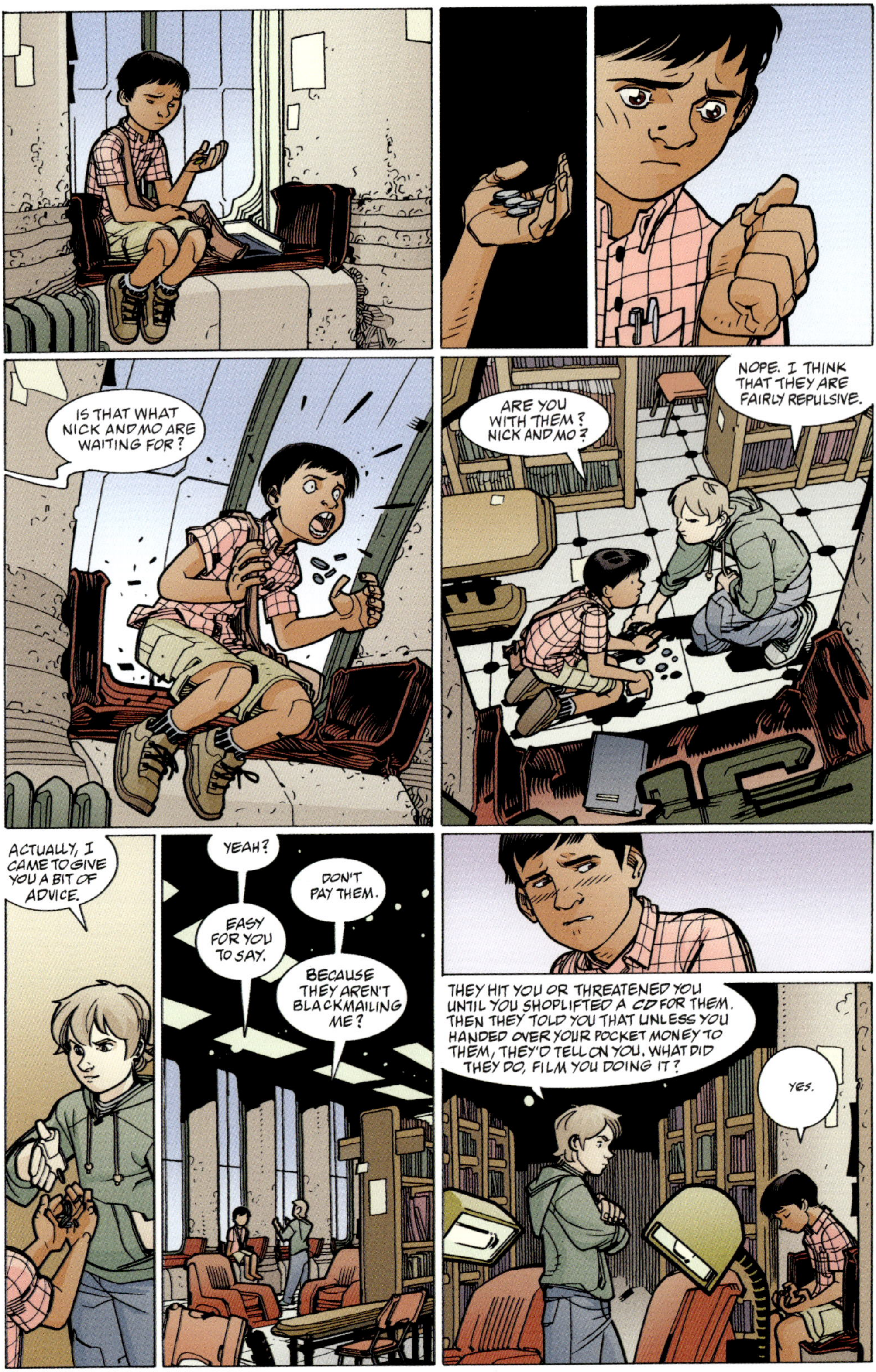
IS THAT WHAT NICK AND MO ARE WAITING FOR?
ARE YOU WITH THEM? NICK AND MO?
NOPE. I THINK THAT THEY ARE FAIRLY REPULSIVE.
ACTUALLY, I CAME TO GIVE YOU A BIT OF ADVICE.
YEAH?
DON'T PAY THEM.
EASY FOR YOU TO SAY.
BECAUSE THEY AREN'T BLACKMAILING ME?
THEY HIT YOU OR THREATENED YOU UNTIL YOU SHOPLIFTED A CD FOR THEM. THEN THEY TOLD YOU THAT UNLESS YOU HANDED OVER YOUR POCKET MONEY TO THEM, THEY'D TELL ON YOU. WHAT DID THEY DO, FILM YOU DOING IT?
YES.

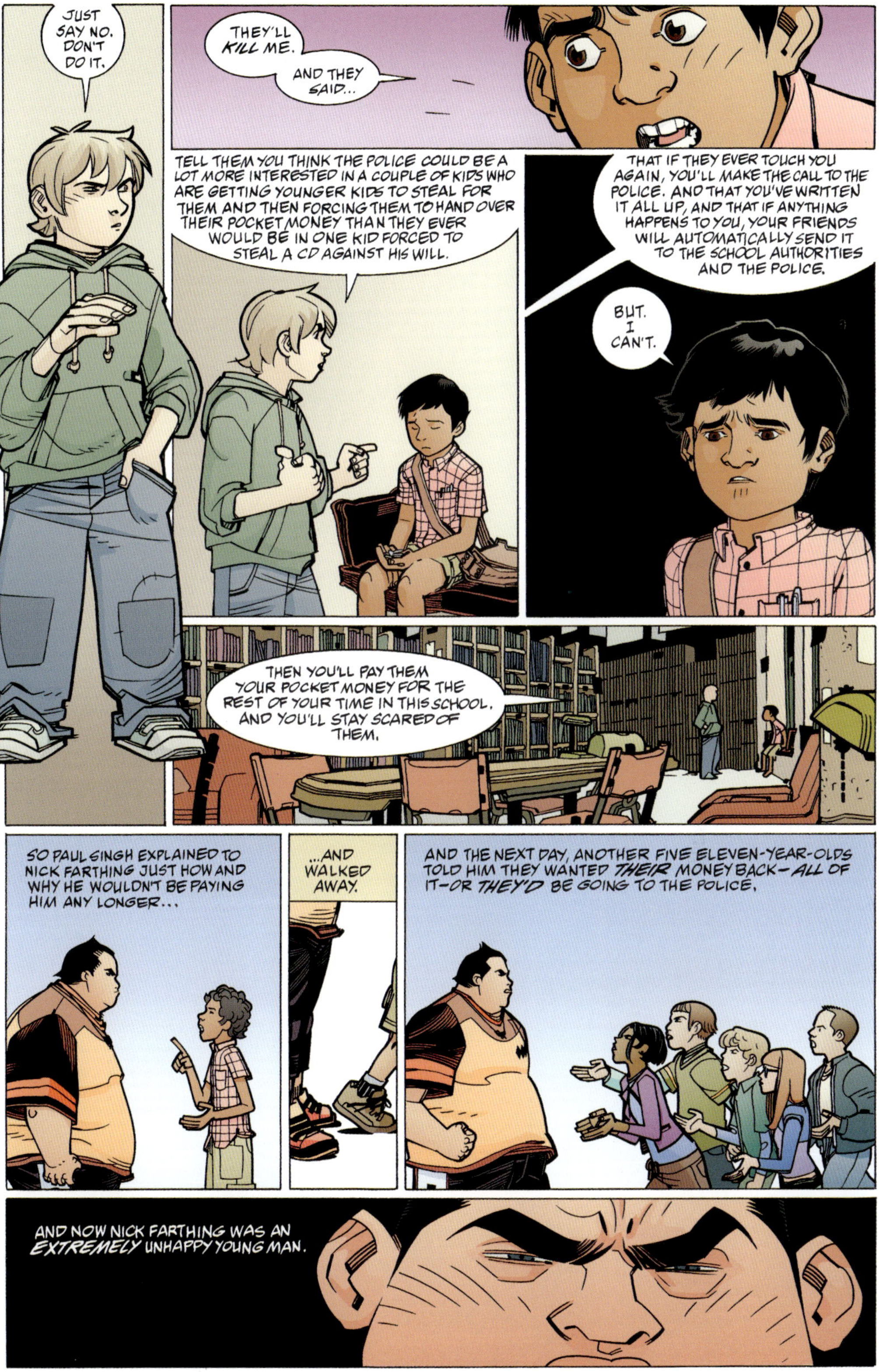
JUST SAY NO. DON'T DO IT.
THEY'LL KILL ME.
AND THEY SAID...
TELL THEM YOU THINK THE POLICE COULD BE A LOT MORE INTERESTED IN A COUPLE OF KIDS WHO ARE GETTING YOUNGER KIDS TO STEAL FOR THEM AND THEN FORCING THEM TO HAND OVER THEIR POCKET MONEY THAN THEY EVER WOULD BE IN ONE KID FORCED TO STEAL A CD AGAINST HIS WILL.
THAT IF THEY EVER TOUCH YOU AGAIN, YOU'LL MAKE THE CALL TO THE POLICE. AND THAT YOU'VE WRITTEN IT ALL UP, AND THAT IF ANYTHING HAPPENS TO YOU, YOUR FRIENDS WILL AUTOMATICALLY SEND IT TO THE SCHOOL AUTHORITIES AND THE POLICE.
BUT. I CAN'T.
THEN YOU'LL PAY THEM YOUR POCKET MONEY FOR THE REST OF YOUR TIME IN THIS SCHOOL. AND YOU'LL STAY SCARED OF THEM.
SO PAUL SINGH EXPLAINED TO NICK FARTHING JUST HOW AND WHY HE WOULDN'T BE PAYING HIM ANY LONGER...
...AND WALKED AWAY.
AND THE NEXT DAY, ANOTHER FIVE ELEVEN-YEAR-OLDS TOLD HIM THEY WANTED THEIR MONEY BACK—ALL OF IT—OR THEY'D BE GOING TO THE POLICE.
AND NOW NICK FARTHING WAS AN EXTREMELY UNHAPPY YOUNG MAN.

IT WAS HIM. HE STARTED IT. THEY'D NEVER HAVE THOUGHT OF IT ON THEIR OWN. HE'S THE ONE WE HAVE TO TEACH A LESSON. THEN, THEY'LL ALL BEHAVE.
WHO?
THE ONE WHO'S ALWAYS READING. THE ONE FROM THE LIBRARY. BOB OWENS. HIM.
WHICH ONE IS HE?
I'LL POINT HIM OUT TO YOU.
BOD WAS USED TO BEING IGNORED, TO EXISTING IN THE SHADOWS. WHEN GLANCES NATURALLY SLIP FROM YOU, YOU BECOME VERY AWARE OF EYES UPON YOU, OF GLANCES IN YOUR DIRECTION, OF ATTENTION.
THEY FOLLOWED HIM OUT OF THE SCHOOL AND UP THE ROAD...
...PAST THE CORNER NEWSAGENT AND ACROSS THE RAILWAY BRIDGE.
HE TOOK HIS TIME, MAKING CERTAIN THAT THE TWO WERE FOLLOWING HIM.
HE WALKED INTO THE TINY GRAVEYARD AT THE END OF THE ROAD AND WAITED.

"YOU'RE THAT KID. BOB OWENS. WELL, YOU'RE IN REALLY BIG TROUBLE, BOB OWENS."

"IT'S *BOD*, ACTUALLY."

"WITH A *D*."

"AND YOU'RE JEKYLL AND HYDE."

"IT WAS *YOU*. YOU GOT TO THE SEVENTH FORMERS."

"SO WE'RE GOING TO TEACH YOU A LESSON."

"I QUITE LIKE LESSONS. IF YOU PAID MORE ATTENTION TO YOURS, YOU WOULDN'T HAVE TO BLACKMAIL YOUNGER KIDS FOR POCKET MONEY."

"YOU'RE *DEAD*, OWENS."

"I'M NOT, ACTUALLY. *THEY* ARE."

"WHO ARE?"

"THE PEOPLE IN THIS PLACE. LOOK, I BROUGHT YOU HERE TO GIVE YOU A CHOICE."

"YOU DIDN'T BRING US HERE."

"YOU'RE HERE."

"I WANTED YOU HERE. I CAME HERE. YOU FOLLOWED ME."

"SAME THING."

"YOU'VE GOT FRIENDS HERE?"

"YOU'RE MISSING THE POINT, I'M AFRAID. YOU TWO NEED TO STOP THIS. STOP BEHAVING LIKE OTHER PEOPLE DON'T MATTER."

"FOR HEAVEN'S SAKE..."

"...HIT HIM."

... 15 ...

"I GAVE YOU A CHANCE."

"#@!⚡"

"WHERE DID HE GO? HE WAS HERE. YOU KNOW HE WAS."

NICK HAD LITTLE IMAGINATION.

"MAYBE HE RAN AWAY."

"HE DIDN'T RUN. HE JUST WASN'T THERE ANYMORE."

MO HAD AN IMAGINATION, AND THE HAIRS ON THE BACK OF HER NECK WERE PRICKLING.

"SOMETHING IS REALLY, REALLY WRONG."

"WE HAVE TO GET OUT OF HERE."

FEAR IS CONTAGIOUS. YOU CAN CATCH IT. MO WAS TERRIFIED, AND NOW NICK WAS TOO.

THEY RAN UNTIL THEY REACHED NICK'S HOUSE...

...AND THEY WENT INSIDE AND TURNED ON ALL THE LIGHTS...

...AND MO CALLED HER MOTHER AND DEMANDED, HALF CRYING, TO BE PICKED UP AND DRIVEN THE SHORT DISTANCE TO HER OWN HOUSE, BECAUSE SHE WASN'T WALKING HOME THAT NIGHT.

... 16 ...

THAT WAS GOOD, DEAR. A NICE FADE FIRST, THEN THE FEAR.
THANK YOU. I HADN'T EVEN TRIED THE FEAR OUT ON LIVING PEOPLE. I MEAN, I KNEW THE THEORY, BUT. WELL...
IT WORKED A TREAT. I'M AMABELLA PERSSON.
BOD. NOBODY OWENS.
THE LIVE BOY? FROM THE BIG GRAVEYARD ON THE HILL? REALLY?
UM...
RODDY?
PORTUNA?
COME AND SEE WHO'S HERE!
MASTER OWENS, HERE WAS FRIGHTENING SOME CHILDREN WHO DOUBTLESS DESERVED IT.
GOOD SHOW. BOUNDERS GUILTY OF REPREHENSIBLE BEHAVIOR, EH?
THEY WERE BULLIES. MAKING KIDS HAND OVER THEIR POCKET MONEY. STUFF LIKE THAT.
A FRIGHTENING IS CERTAINLY A GOOD BEGINNING. AND WHAT HAVE YOU PLANNED IF IT DOES NOT WORK?
I HADN'T REALLY THOUGHT-
I SHOULD SUGGEST THAT DREAMWALKING MIGHT BE THE MOST EFFICIENT REMEDY. YOU CAN DREAMWALK, CAN YOU NOT?
I'M NOT SURE.
MISTER PENNYWORTH SHOWED ME HOW, BUT I HAVEN'T REALLY- WELL, THERE'S SOME THINGS I ONLY REALLY KNOW IN THEORY...

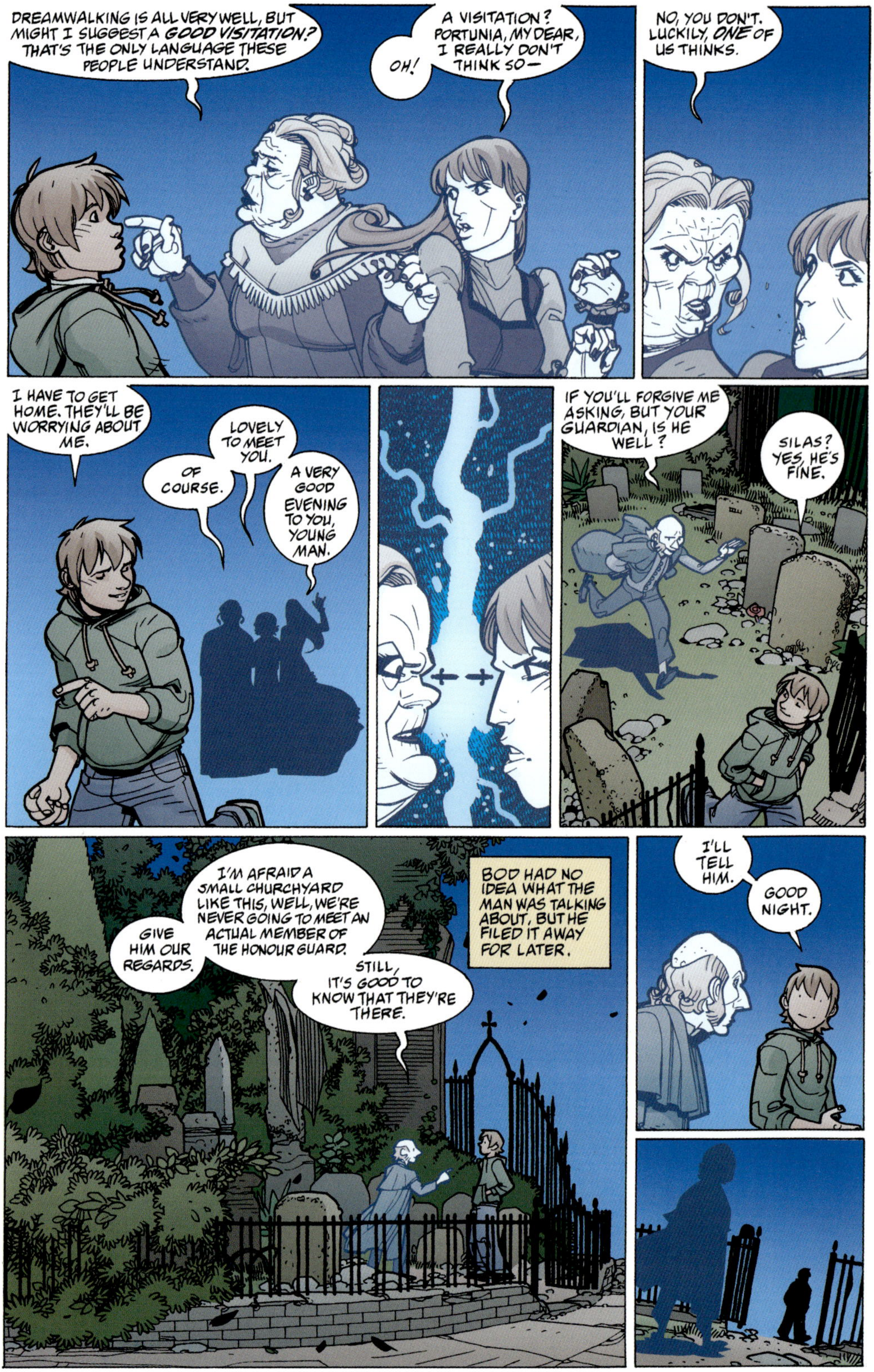
DREAMWALKING IS ALL VERY WELL, BUT MIGHT I SUGGEST A GOOD VISITATION? THAT'S THE ONLY LANGUAGE THESE PEOPLE UNDERSTAND.
OH!
A VISITATION? PORTUNIA, MY DEAR, I REALLY DON'T THINK SO—
NO, YOU DON'T. LUCKILY, ONE OF US THINKS.
I HAVE TO GET HOME. THEY'LL BE WORRYING ABOUT ME.
OF COURSE.
LOVELY TO MEET YOU.
A VERY GOOD EVENING TO YOU, YOUNG MAN.
IF YOU'LL FORGIVE ME ASKING, BUT YOUR GUARDIAN, IS HE WELL?
SILAS? YES, HE'S FINE.
GIVE HIM OUR REGARDS.
I'M AFRAID A SMALL CHURCHYARD LIKE THIS, WELL, WE'RE NEVER GOING TO MEET AN ACTUAL MEMBER OF THE HONOUR GUARD.
STILL, IT'S GOOD TO KNOW THAT THEY'RE THERE.
BOD HAD NO IDEA WHAT THE MAN WAS TALKING ABOUT, BUT HE FILED IT AWAY FOR LATER.
I'LL TELL HIM.
GOOD NIGHT.

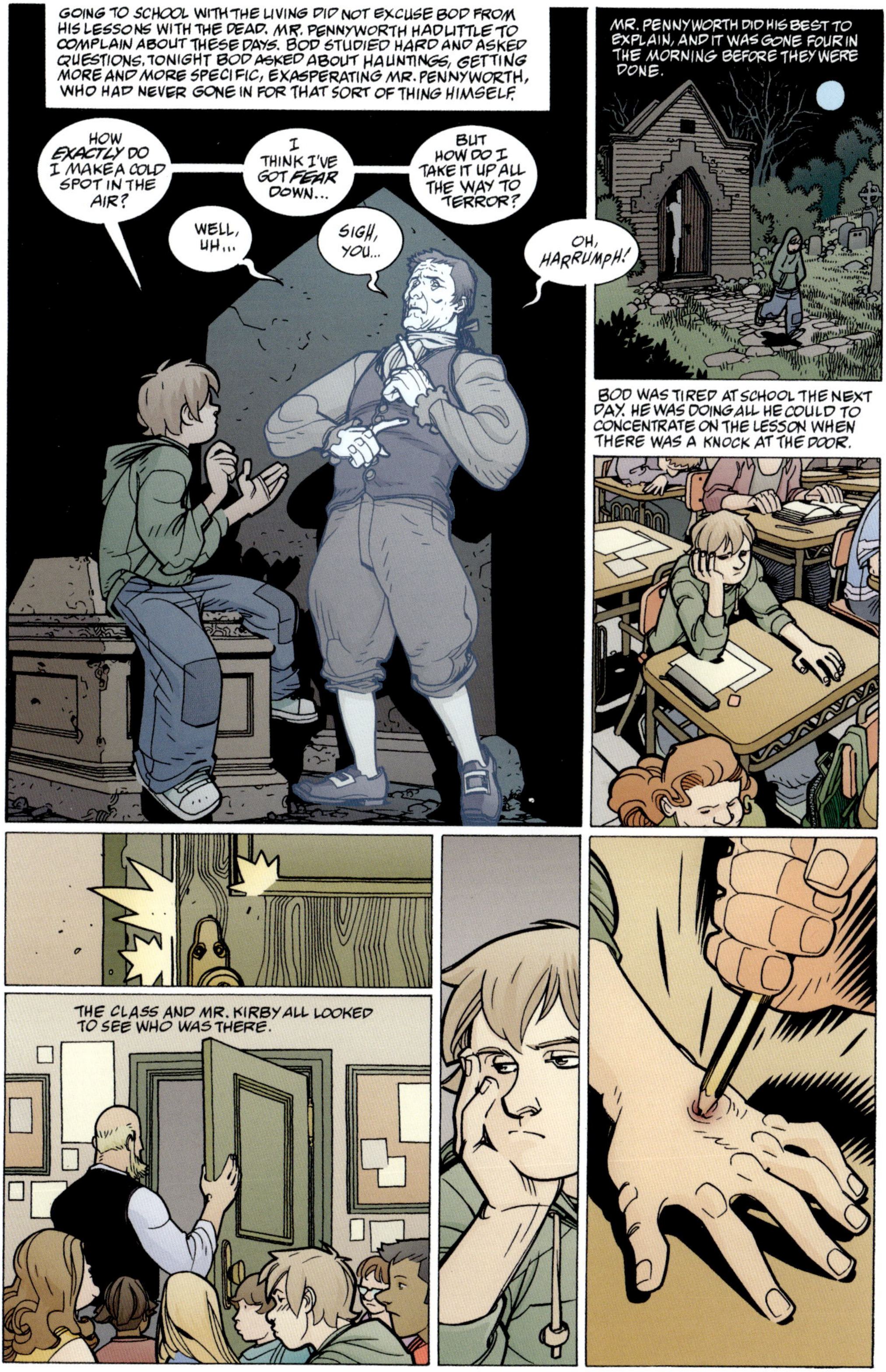
GOING TO SCHOOL WITH THE LIVING DID NOT EXCUSE BOD FROM HIS LESSONS WITH THE DEAD. MR. PENNYWORTH HAD LITTLE TO COMPLAIN ABOUT THESE DAYS. BOD STUDIED HARD AND ASKED QUESTIONS. TONIGHT BOD ASKED ABOUT HAUNTINGS, GETTING MORE AND MORE SPECIFIC, EXASPERATING MR. PENNYWORTH, WHO HAD NEVER GONE IN FOR THAT SORT OF THING HIMSELF.
HOW EXACTLY DO I MAKE A COLD SPOT IN THE AIR?
WELL, UH...
I THINK I'VE GOT FEAR DOWN...
SIGH, YOU...
BUT HOW DO I TAKE IT UP ALL THE WAY TO TERROR?
OH, HARRUMPH!
MR. PENNYWORTH DID HIS BEST TO EXPLAIN, AND IT WAS GONE FOUR IN THE MORNING BEFORE THEY WERE DONE.
BOD WAS TIRED AT SCHOOL THE NEXT DAY. HE WAS DOING ALL HE COULD TO CONCENTRATE ON THE LESSON WHEN THERE WAS A KNOCK AT THE DOOR.
THE CLASS AND MR. KIRBY ALL LOOKED TO SEE WHO WAS THERE.

MO QUILLING PASSED BOD IN THE CORRIDOR.

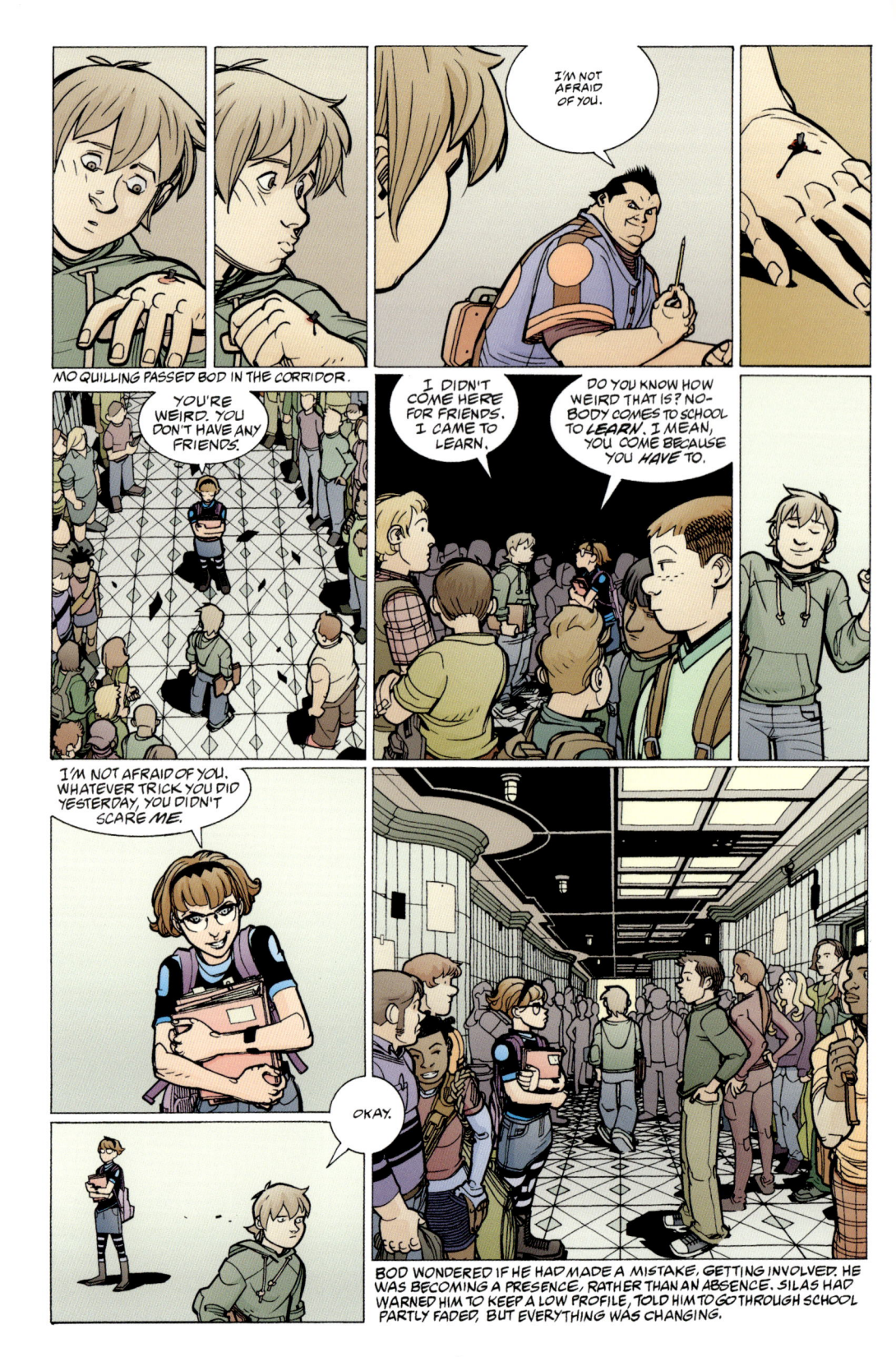

"I'M NOT AFRAID OF YOU."

"YOU'RE WEIRD. YOU DON'T HAVE ANY FRIENDS."

"I DIDN'T COME HERE FOR FRIENDS. I CAME TO LEARN."

"DO YOU KNOW HOW WEIRD THAT IS? NOBODY COMES TO SCHOOL TO *LEARN*. I MEAN, YOU COME BECAUSE YOU *HAVE* TO."

"I'M NOT AFRAID OF YOU. WHATEVER TRICK YOU DID YESTERDAY, YOU DIDN'T SCARE *ME*."

"OKAY."

BOD WONDERED IF HE HAD MADE A MISTAKE, GETTING INVOLVED. HE WAS BECOMING A PRESENCE, RATHER THAN AN ABSENCE. SILAS HAD WARNED HIM TO KEEP A LOW PROFILE, TOLD HIM TO GO THROUGH SCHOOL PARTLY FADED, BUT EVERYTHING WAS CHANGING.

I CANNOT BELIEVE THAT YOU COULD HAVE BEEN SO... SO STUPID. EVERYTHING I TOLD YOU ABOUT REMAINING JUST THIS SIDE OF INVISIBILITY, AND NOW YOU'VE BECOME THE TALK OF THE SCHOOL?

WELL, WHAT DID YOU WANT ME TO DO?

NOT THIS. IT'S NOT LIKE THE OLDEN TIMES. THEY CAN KEEP TRACK OF YOU, BOD.

WHAT SHOULD I DO?

DON'T GO BACK. THIS SCHOOL BUSINESS WAS AN EXPERIMENT. LET US SIMPLY ACKNOWLEDGE THAT IT WAS NOT A SUCCESSFUL ONE.

IT'S NOT JUST THE LEARNING STUFF. IT'S THE OTHER STUFF. DO YOU KNOW HOW NICE IT IS TO BE IN A ROOM FILLED WITH PEOPLE, AND FOR ALL OF THEM TO BE BREATHING?

IT'S NOT SOMETHING IN WHICH I'VE EVER TAKEN PLEASURE.

SO.

YOU DON'T GO BACK TO SCHOOL TOMORROW.

I'M NOT RUNNING AWAY. NOT FROM MO OR NICK OR SCHOOL. I'D LEAVE HERE FIRST.

YOU WILL DO AS YOU ARE TOLD, BOY.

OR WHAT? WHAT WOULD YOU DO TO KEEP ME HERE?

KILL ME?

... 21 ...

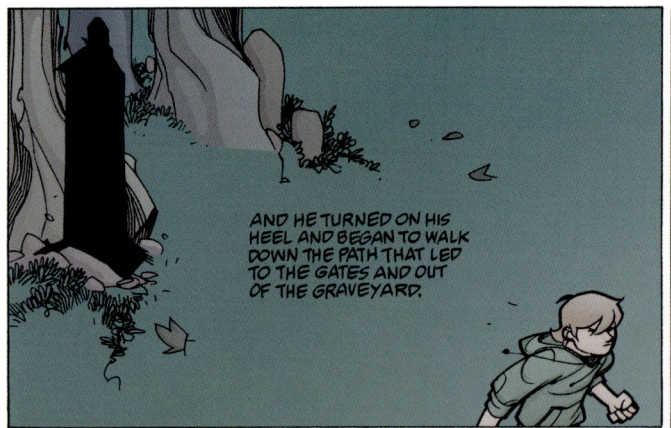

AND HE TURNED ON HIS HEEL AND BEGAN TO WALK DOWN THE PATH THAT LED TO THE GATES AND OUT OF THE GRAVEYARD.

SILAS WRAPPED THE SHADOWS AROUND HIM LIKE A BLANKET, AND STARED AFTER THE WAY THE BOY HAD GONE, AND DID NOT MOVE TO FOLLOW.

NICK FARTHING WAS IN HIS BED, ASLEEP AND DREAMING OF PIRATES ON THE SUNNY BLUE SEA, WHEN IT ALL WENT WRONG.

ONE MOMENT HE WAS THE CAPTAIN OF HIS OWN PIRATE SHIP — A HAPPY PLACE, CREWED BY OBEDIENT ELEVEN-YEAR-OLDS, EXCEPT FOR THE GIRLS, WHO WERE ALL A YEAR OR TWO OLDER THAN NICK.

AND THE NEXT...

AND THEN, IN THE WAY OF DREAMS, HE WAS STANDING ON THE BLACK DECK OF THE NEW SHIP.

YOU'RE NOT AFRAID OF ME.

DO YOU THINK YOU'RE A PIRATE, NICK?

YOU'RE THAT KID.

BOB OWENS.

... 23 ...

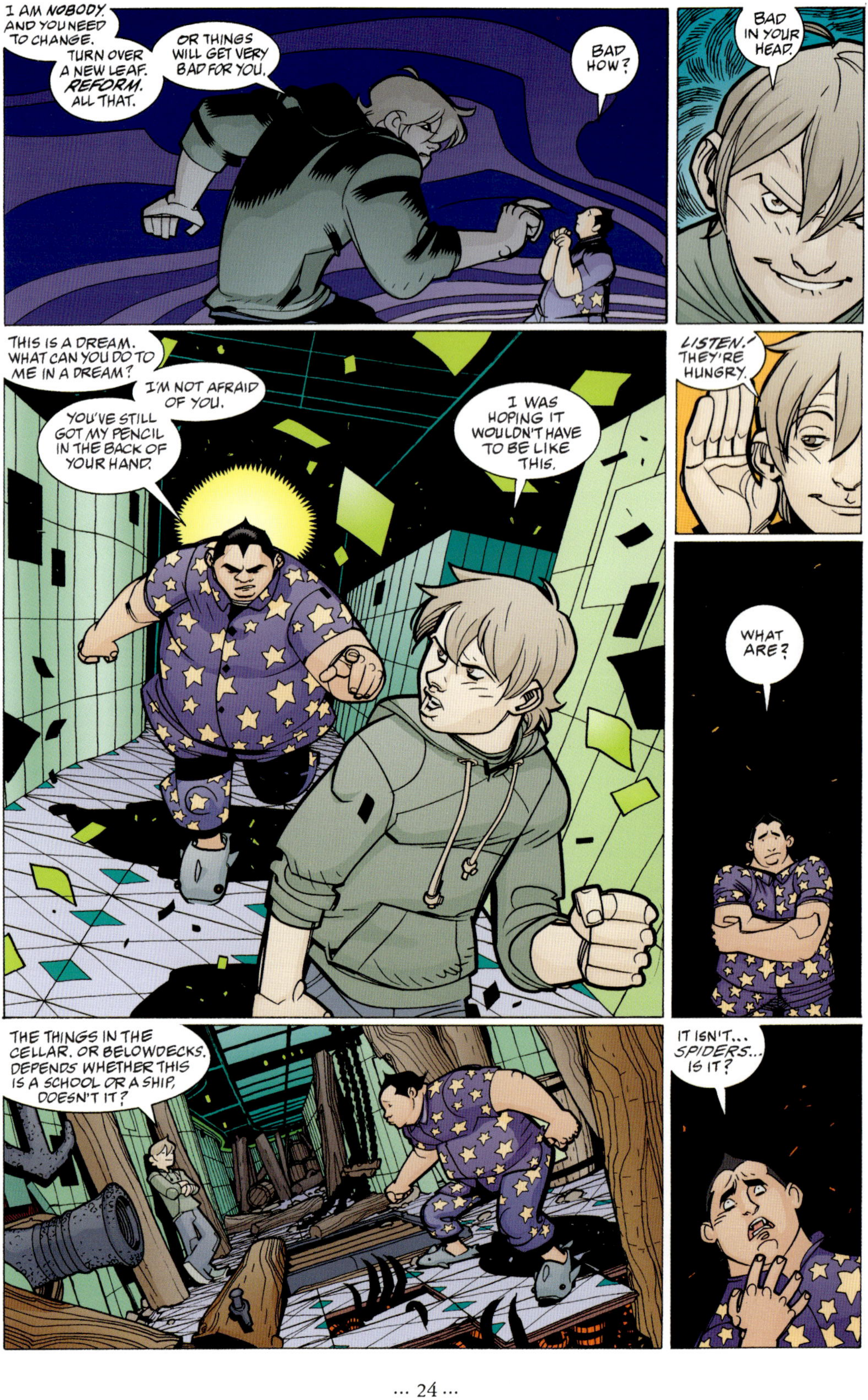
I AM NOBODY. AND YOU NEED TO CHANGE.
TURN OVER A NEW LEAF. REFORM. ALL THAT.
OR THINGS WILL GET VERY BAD FOR YOU.
BAD HOW?
BAD IN YOUR HEAD.
THIS IS A DREAM. WHAT CAN YOU DO TO ME IN A DREAM?
I'M NOT AFRAID OF YOU.
YOU'VE STILL GOT MY PENCIL IN THE BACK OF YOUR HAND.
I WAS HOPING IT WOULDN'T HAVE TO BE LIKE THIS.
LISTEN! THEY'RE HUNGRY.
WHAT ARE?
THE THINGS IN THE CELLAR. OR BELOWDECKS. DEPENDS WHETHER THIS IS A SCHOOL OR A SHIP, DOESN'T IT?
IT ISN'T... SPIDERS... IS IT?

IT MIGHT BE. YOU'LL FIND OUT, WON'T YOU?
NO. PLEASE NO.
IT'S ALL UP TO YOU, ISN'T IT? CHANGE YOUR WAYS ...
...OR VISIT THE CELLAR.
THERE WAS A SORT OF A SCUTTLING NOISE, THEN...
...AND NICK WOKE UP SCREAMING.
BOD FELT THE SATISFACTION OF A JOB WELL DONE.
THE OTHER BOY WOULD HESITATE BEFORE TORMENTING SMALLER KIDS.

I LEFT THE GRAVEYARD, I CAN LEAVE THE SCHOOL.
I'LL GO SOMEWHERE NO ONE KNOWS ME AND I'LL SIT IN A LIBRARY ALL DAY AND READ BOOKS.
I WONDER IF THERE ARE STILL DESERTED ISLANDS IN THE WORLD, LIKE THE ONE ROBINSON CRUSOE WAS SHIPWRECKED ON.
OPEN
I COULD GO AND LIVE ON ONE OF THOSE.
ARE YOU RUNNING AWAY, THEN?
THAT'S THE DIFFERENCE BETWEEN THE LIVING AND THE DEAD, ENNIT?
HULLO, LIZA.
THE DEAD DUN'T DISAPPOINT YOU. THEY'VE HAD THEIR LIFE, DONE WHAT THEY'VE DONE. WE DUN'T CHANGE.
THE LIVING, THEY ALWAYS DISAPPOINT, DUN'T THEY? YOU MEET A BOY WHO'S ALL BRAVE AND NOBLE, AND HE GROWS UP TO RUN AWAY.
THAT'S NOT FAIR!

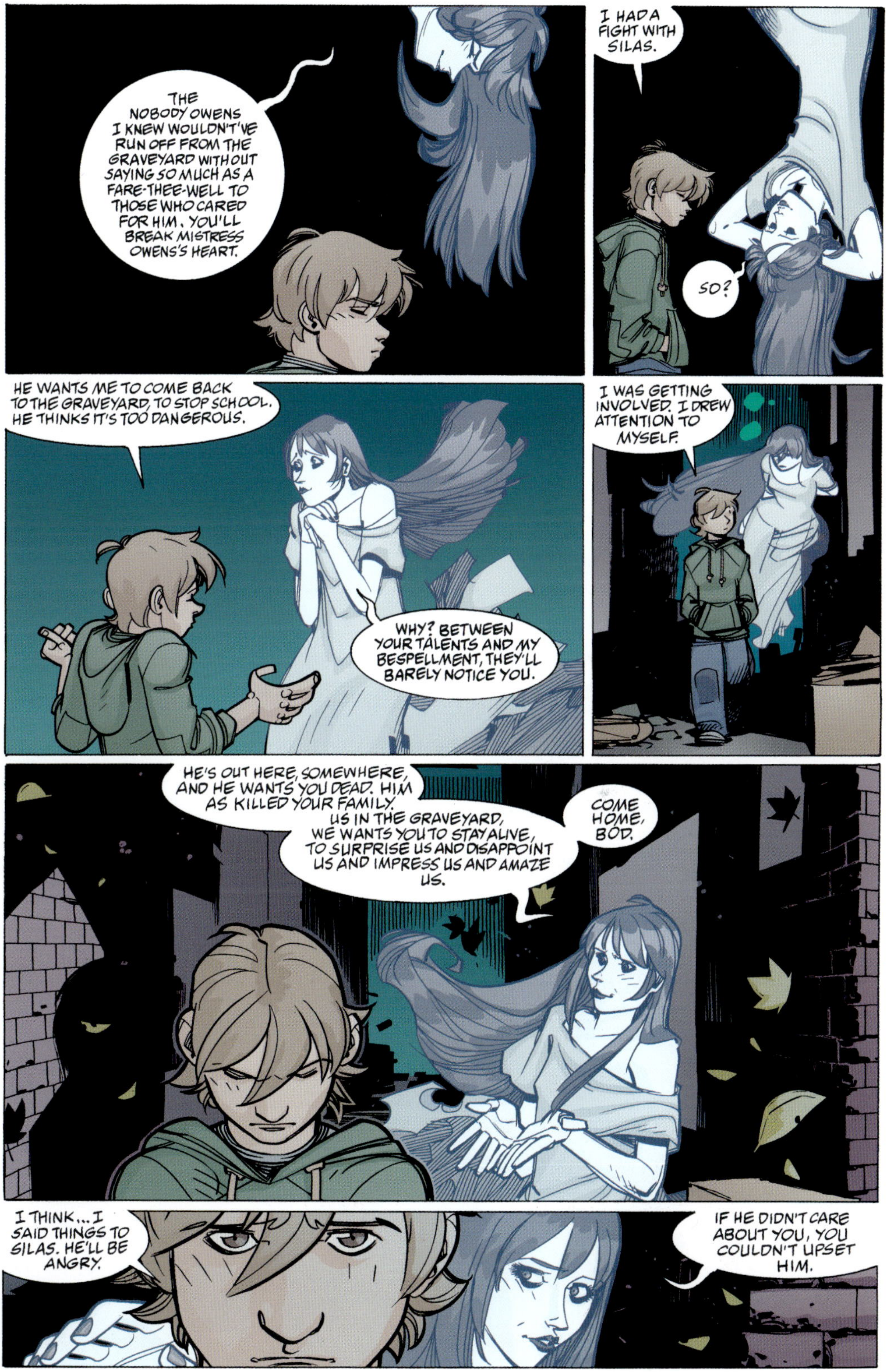
THE NOBODY OWENS I KNEW WOULDN'T'VE RUN OFF FROM THE GRAVEYARD WITHOUT SAYING SO MUCH AS A FARE-THEE-WELL TO THOSE WHO CARED FOR HIM. YOU'LL BREAK MISTRESS OWENS'S HEART.
I HAD A FIGHT WITH SILAS.
SO?
HE WANTS ME TO COME BACK TO THE GRAVEYARD, TO STOP SCHOOL. HE THINKS IT'S TOO DANGEROUS.
WHY? BETWEEN YOUR TALENTS AND MY BESPELLMENT, THEY'LL BARELY NOTICE YOU.
I WAS GETTING INVOLVED. I DREW ATTENTION TO MYSELF.
HE'S OUT HERE, SOMEWHERE, AND HE WANTS YOU DEAD. HIM AS KILLED YOUR FAMILY. US IN THE GRAVEYARD, WE WANTS YOU TO STAY ALIVE, TO SURPRISE US AND DISAPPOINT US AND IMPRESS US AND AMAZE US.
COME HOME, BOD.
I THINK... I SAID THINGS TO SILAS. HE'LL BE ANGRY.
IF HE DIDN'T CARE ABOUT YOU, YOU COULDN'T UPSET HIM.

THE FALLEN AUTUMN LEAVES WERE SLICK BENEATH BOD'S FEET, AND THE MISTS BLURRED THE EDGES OF THE WORLD. NOTHING WAS AS CLEAN-CUT AS HE HAD THOUGHT IT, A FEW MINUTES BEFORE.

I DID A DREAMWALK.

HOW DID IT GO?

GOOD. WELL, ALL RIGHT.

YOU SHOULD TELL MR. PENNYWORTH. HE'LL BE PLEASED.

YOU'RE RIGHT. I SHOULD.

WHAT ARE YOU DOING?

GOING HOME LIKE YOU SAID.

THAT'S GOOD.

?!

BOD! RUN! OR FADE!

SOMETHING'S WRONG!

... 28 ...

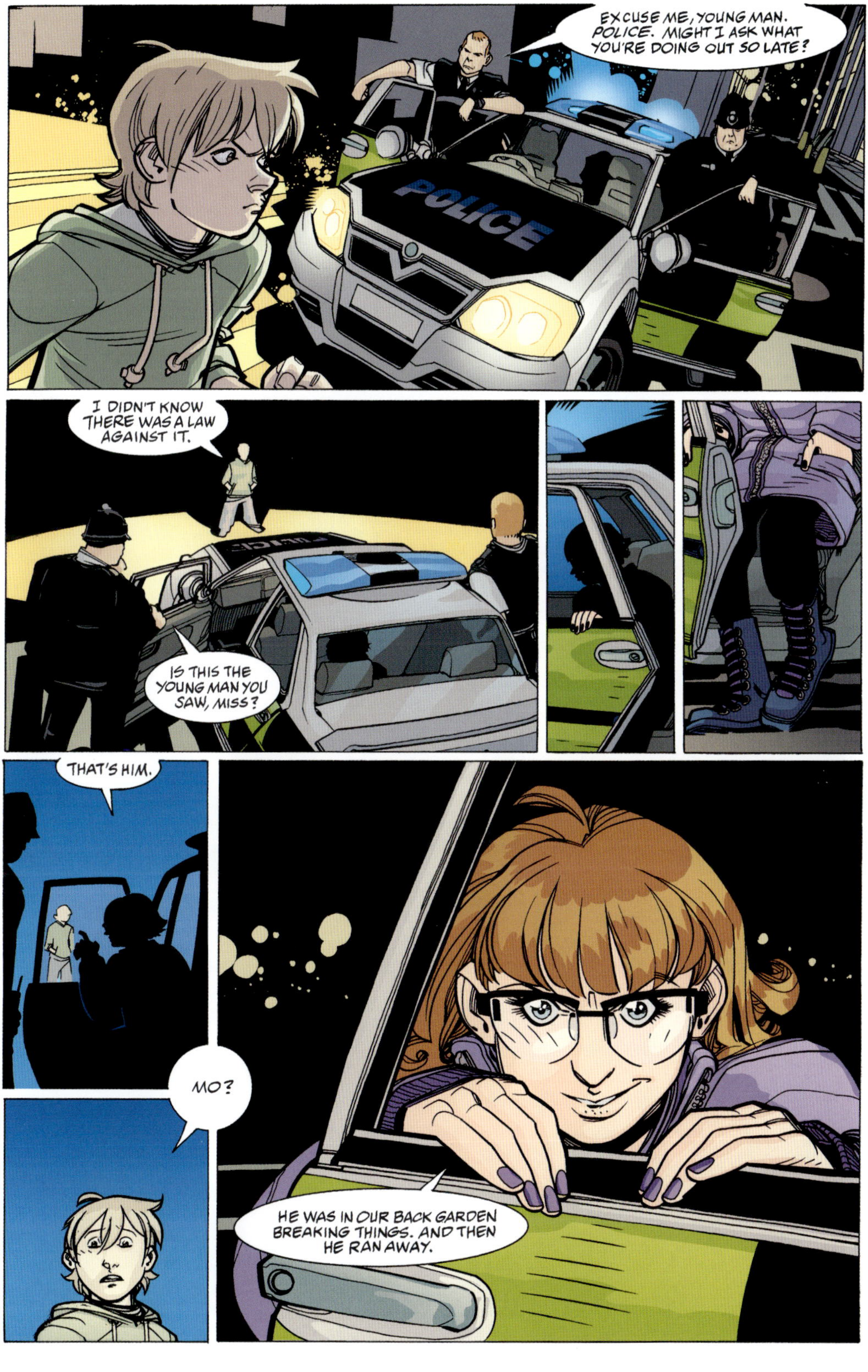
EXCUSE ME, YOUNG MAN. POLICE. MIGHT I ASK WHAT YOU'RE DOING OUT SO LATE?
POLICE
I DIDN'T KNOW THERE WAS A LAW AGAINST IT.
IS THIS THE YOUNG MAN YOU SAW, MISS?
THAT'S HIM.
MO?
HE WAS IN OUR BACK GARDEN BREAKING THINGS. AND THEN HE RAN AWAY.

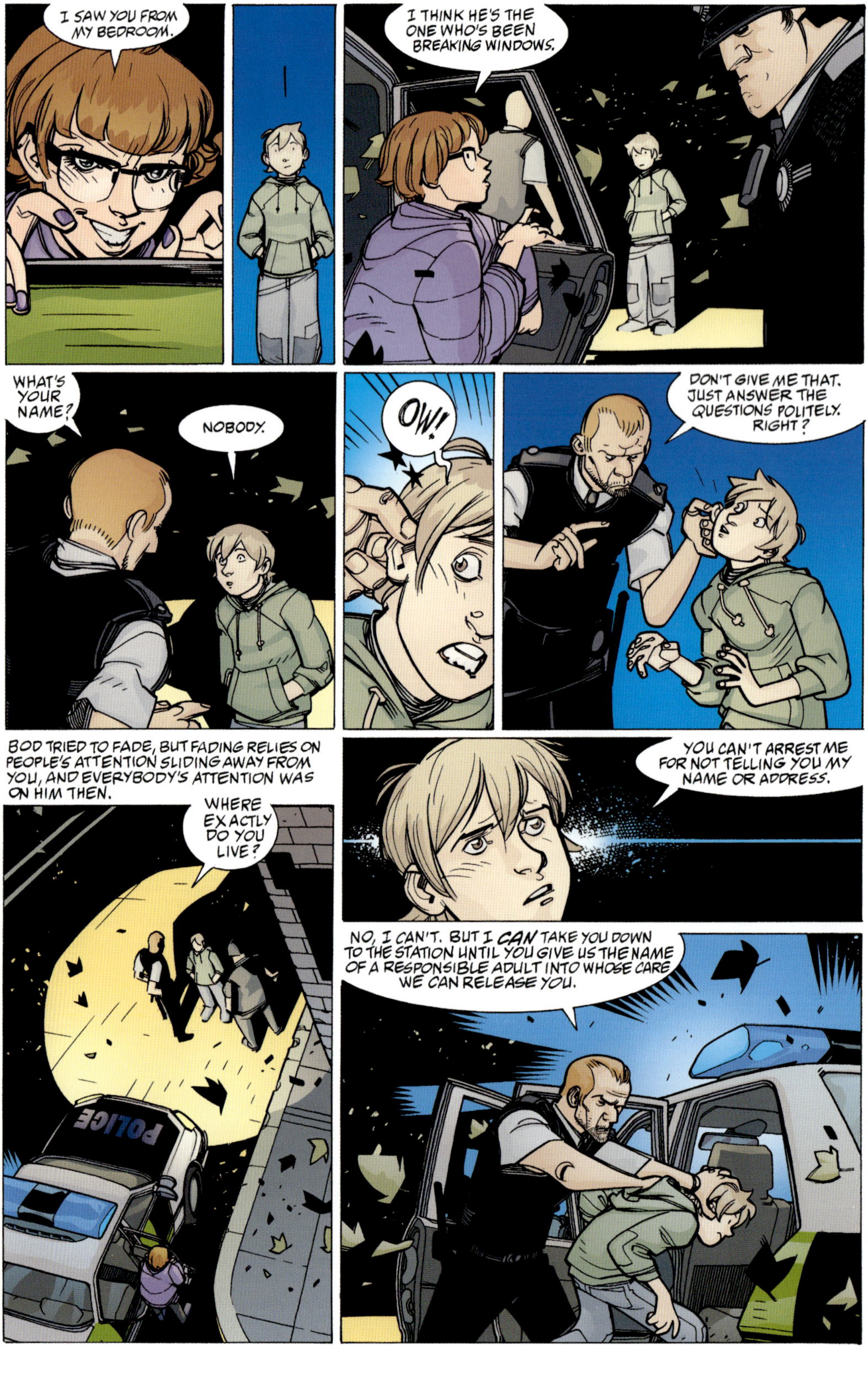
I SAW YOU FROM MY BEDROOM.
I THINK HE'S THE ONE WHO'S BEEN BREAKING WINDOWS.
WHAT'S YOUR NAME?
NOBODY.
OW!
DON'T GIVE ME THAT. JUST ANSWER THE QUESTIONS POLITELY. RIGHT?
BOD TRIED TO FADE, BUT FADING RELIES ON PEOPLE'S ATTENTION SLIDING AWAY FROM YOU, AND EVERYBODY'S ATTENTION WAS ON HIM THEN.
WHERE EXACTLY DO YOU LIVE?
POLICE
YOU CAN'T ARREST ME FOR NOT TELLING YOU MY NAME OR ADDRESS.
NO, I CAN'T. BUT I CAN TAKE YOU DOWN TO THE STATION UNTIL YOU GIVE US THE NAME OF A RESPONSIBLE ADULT INTO WHOSE CARE WE CAN RELEASE YOU.

I SAW YOU FROM THE FRONT WINDOW, SO I CALLED THE POLICE.
I WASN'T DOING ANYTHING.
I WASN'T EVEN IN YOUR GARDEN. AND WHY ARE THEY BRINGING YOU OUT TO FIND ME?
QUIET BACK THERE!!!
WE'LL CALL YOU TOMORROW, LET YOUR MOM AND DAD KNOW WHAT WE FOUND.
THANKS, UNCLE TAM.
JUST DOING MY DUTY.
THEY DROVE BACK THROUGH THE TOWN IN SILENCE, BOD TRYING TO FADE AS BEST HE COULD, WITH NO SUCCESS. HE FELT SICK AND MISERABLE.
IN ONE EVENING, I HAD MY FIRST REAL ARGUMENT WITH SILAS.
I TRIED TO RUN AWAY, FAILED, AND NOW I CAN'T GET BACK.
I CAN'T TELL THE POLICE MY NAME, OR WHERE I LIVE. I'LL SPEND THE REST OF MY LIFE IN A POLICE CELL, OR IN A PRISON FOR KIDS.
DO THEY HAVE PRISONS FOR KIDS?
EXCUSE ME? DO THEY HAVE PRISONS FOR KIDS?
GETTING WORRIED, NOW, ARE YOU? I DON'T BLAME YOU. YOU KIDS. RUNNING WILD. SOME OF YOU NEED LOCKING UP, I'LL TELL YOU.

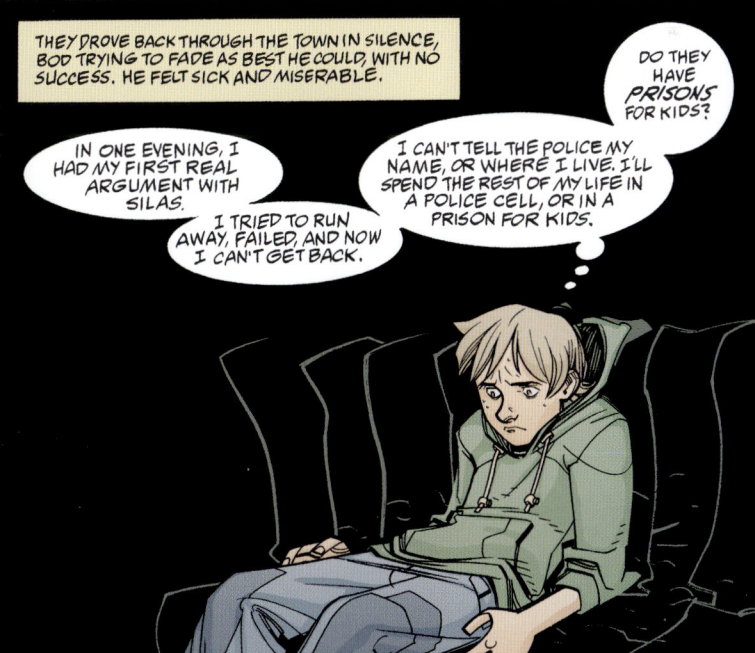

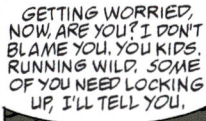

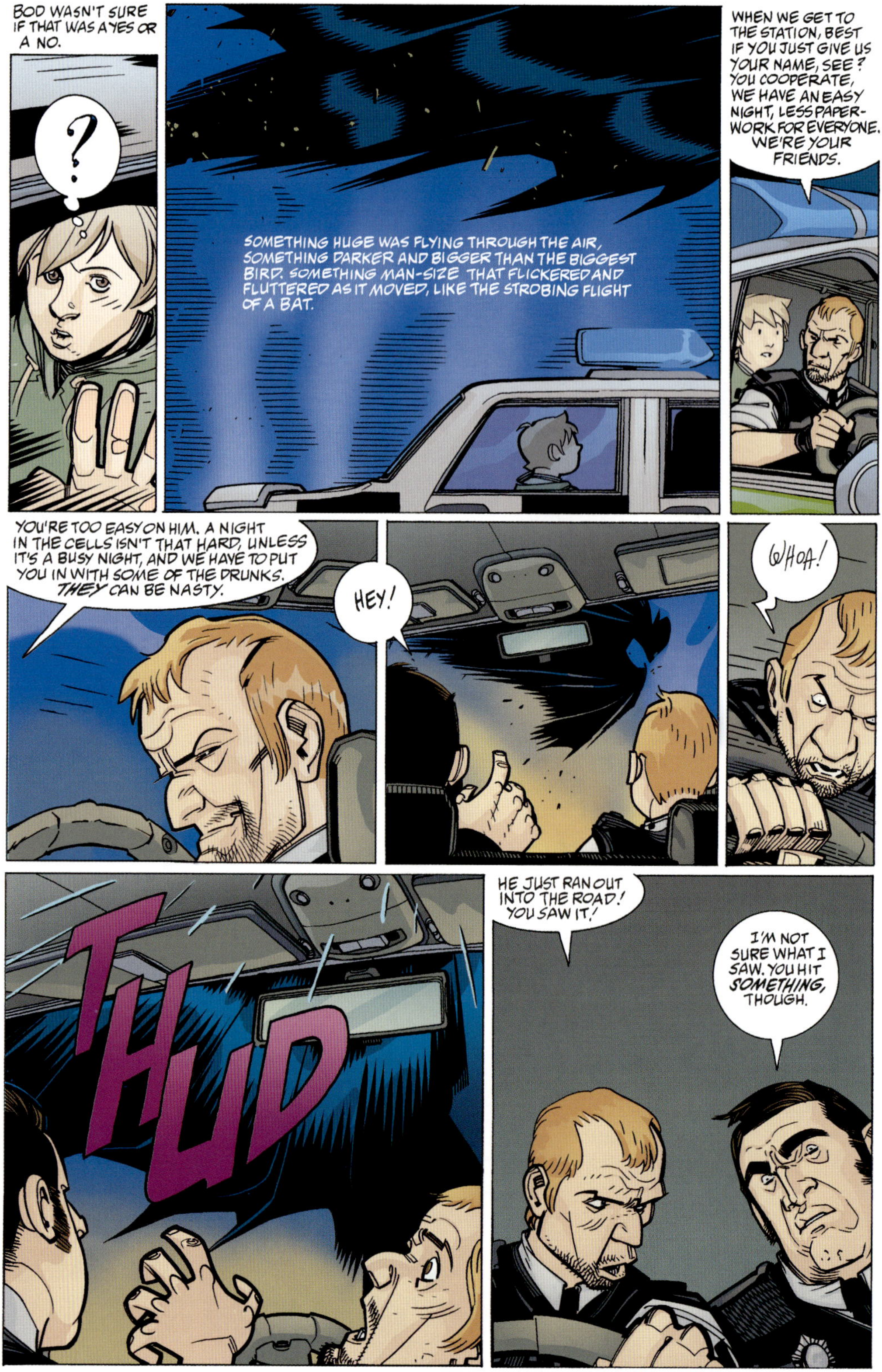
BOD WASN'T SURE IF THAT WAS A YES OR A NO.
?
SOMETHING HUGE WAS FLYING THROUGH THE AIR, SOMETHING DARKER AND BIGGER THAN THE BIGGEST BIRD. SOMETHING MAN-SIZE THAT FLICKERED AND FLUTTERED AS IT MOVED, LIKE THE STROBING FLIGHT OF A BAT.
WHEN WE GET TO THE STATION, BEST IF YOU JUST GIVE US YOUR NAME, SEE? YOU COOPERATE, WE HAVE AN EASY NIGHT, LESS PAPERWORK FOR EVERYONE. WE'RE YOUR FRIENDS.
YOU'RE TOO EASY ON HIM. A NIGHT IN THE CELLS ISN'T THAT HARD, UNLESS IT'S A BUSY NIGHT, AND WE HAVE TO PUT YOU IN WITH SOME OF THE DRUNKS. THEY CAN BE NASTY.
HEY!
WHOA!
THUD
HE JUST RAN OUT INTO THE ROAD! YOU SAW IT!
I'M NOT SURE WHAT I SAW. YOU HIT SOMETHING, THOUGH.

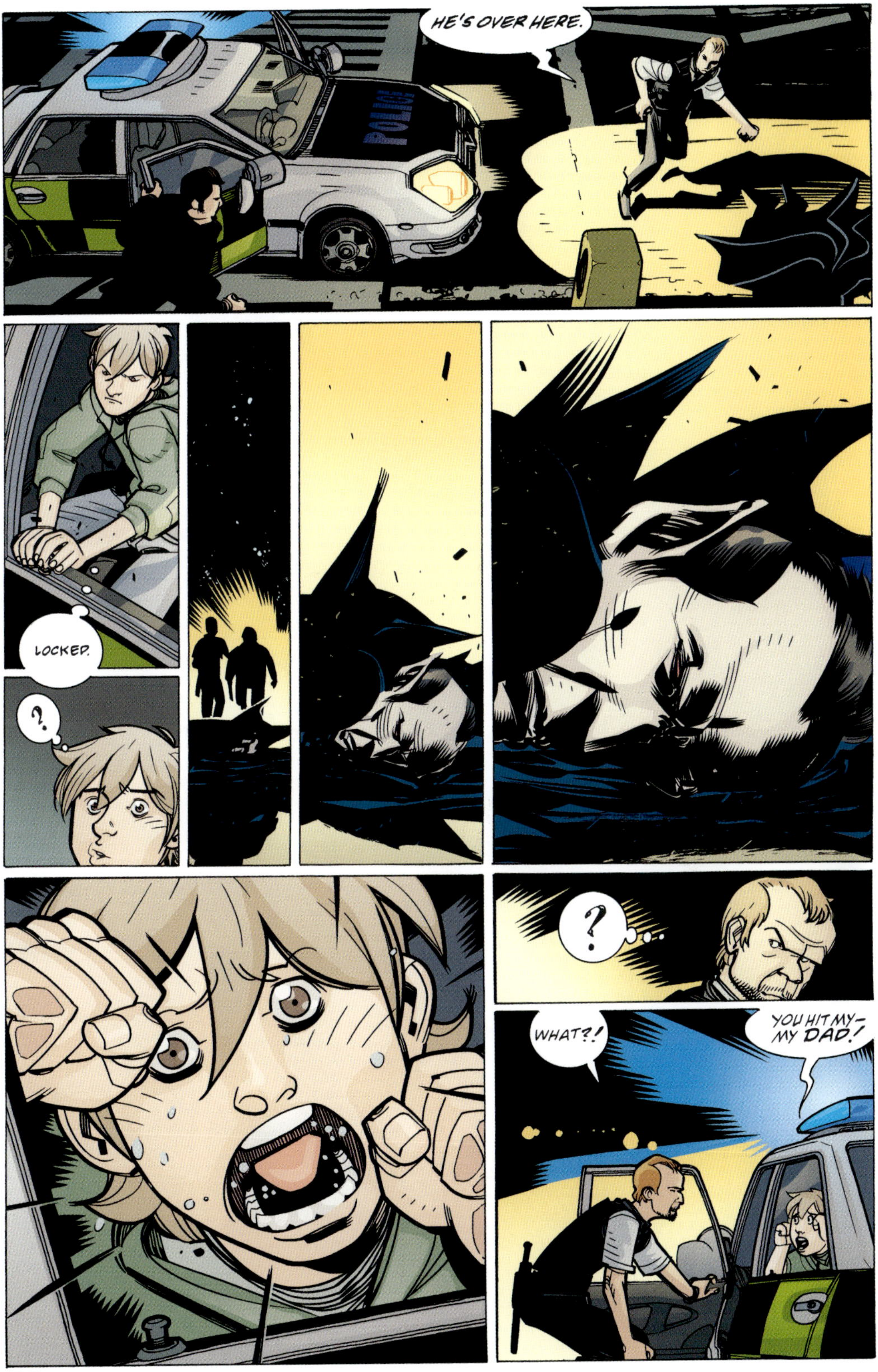

HE'S OVER HERE.
LOCKED.
?
?
WHAT?!
YOU HIT MY—
MY DAD!

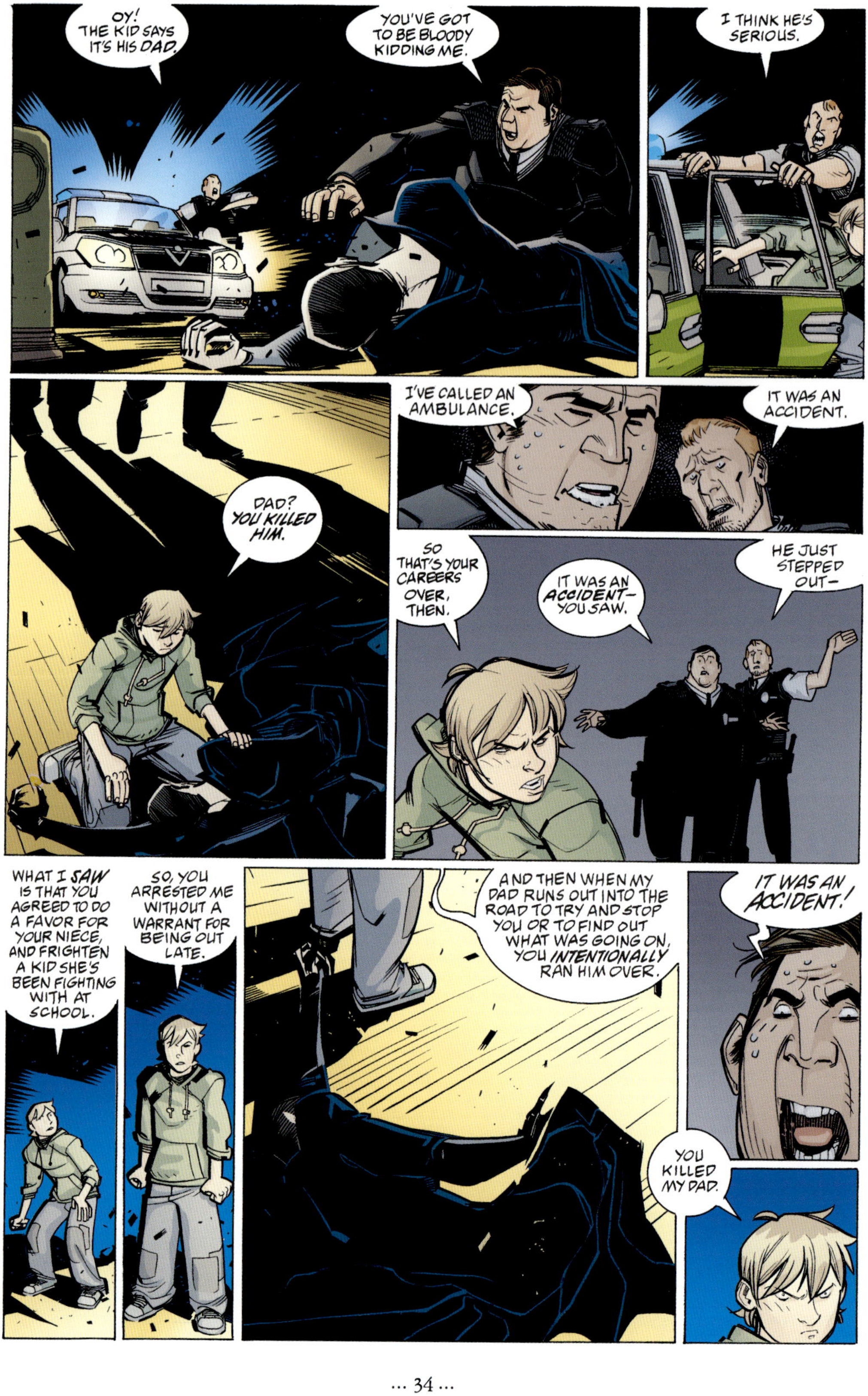
OY! THE KID SAYS IT'S HIS DAD.
YOU'VE GOT TO BE BLOODY KIDDING ME.
I THINK HE'S SERIOUS.
DAD? YOU KILLED HIM.
I'VE CALLED AN AMBULANCE.
IT WAS AN ACCIDENT.
SO THAT'S YOUR CAREERS OVER, THEN.
IT WAS AN ACCIDENT— YOU SAW.
HE JUST STEPPED OUT—
WHAT I SAW IS THAT YOU AGREED TO DO A FAVOR FOR YOUR NIECE, AND FRIGHTEN A KID SHE'S BEEN FIGHTING WITH AT SCHOOL.
SO, YOU ARRESTED ME WITHOUT A WARRANT FOR BEING OUT LATE.
AND THEN WHEN MY DAD RUNS OUT INTO THE ROAD TO TRY AND STOP YOU OR TO FIND OUT WHAT WAS GOING ON, YOU INTENTIONALLY RAN HIM OVER.
IT WAS AN ACCIDENT!
YOU KILLED MY DAD.

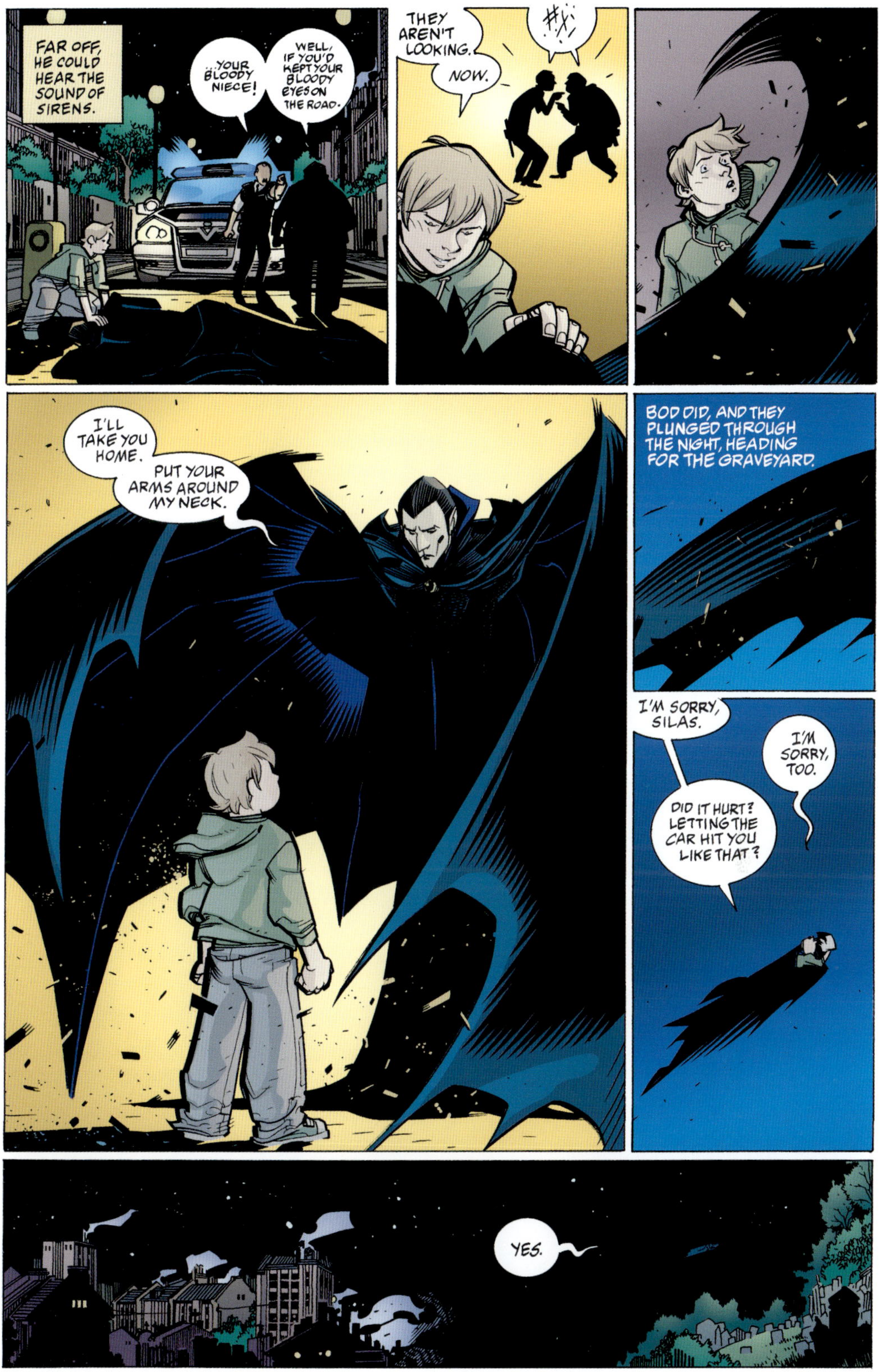
FAR OFF, HE COULD HEAR THE SOUND OF SIRENS.
...YOUR BLOODY NIECE!
WELL, IF YOU'D KEPT YOUR BLOODY EYES ON THE ROAD.
THEY AREN'T LOOKING.
NOW.
#%!
I'LL TAKE YOU HOME.
PUT YOUR ARMS AROUND MY NECK.
BOD DID, AND THEY PLUNGED THROUGH THE NIGHT, HEADING FOR THE GRAVEYARD.
I'M SORRY, SILAS.
I'M SORRY, TOO.
DID IT HURT? LETTING THE CAR HIT YOU LIKE THAT?
YES.

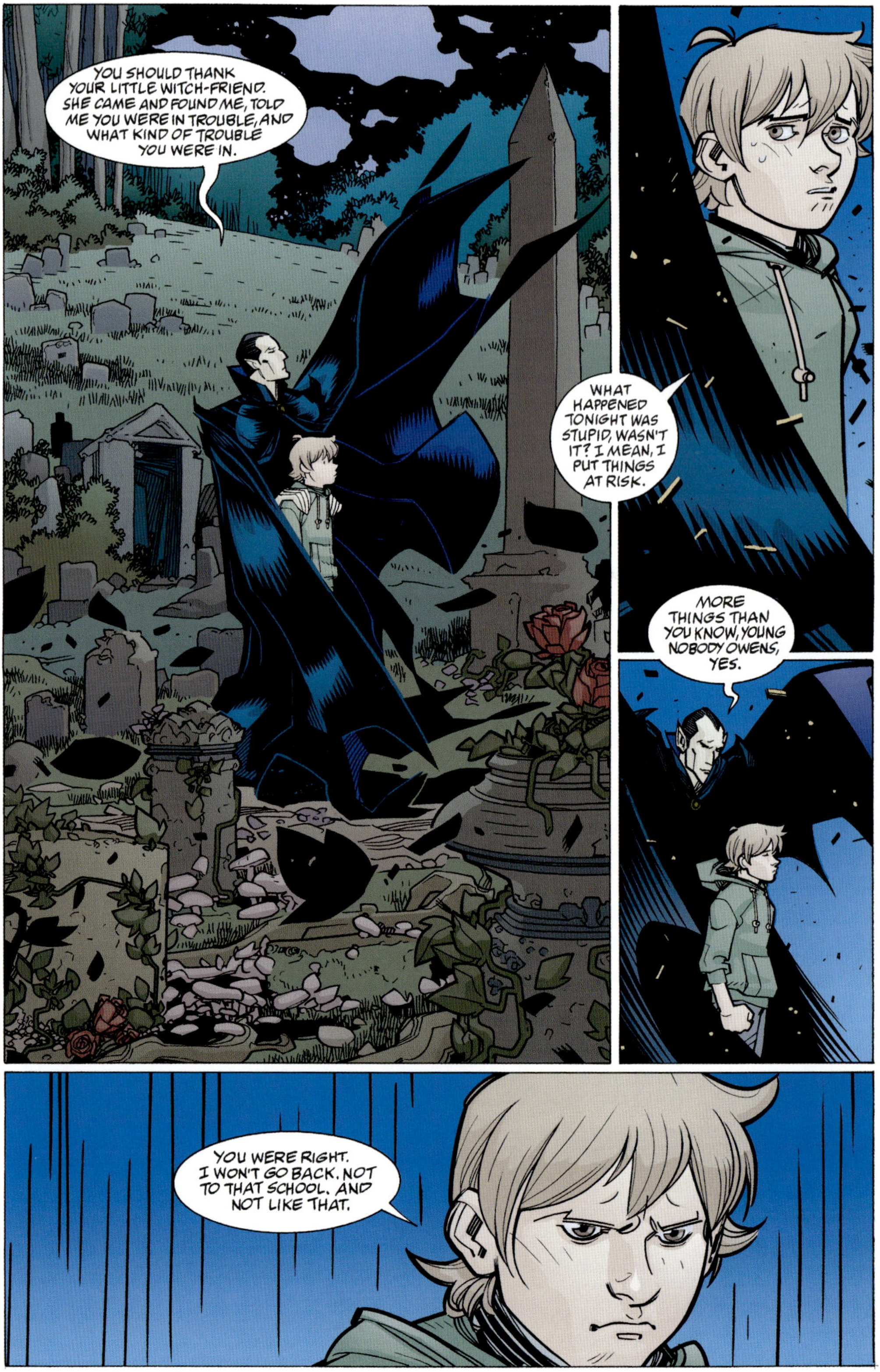
YOU SHOULD THANK YOUR LITTLE WITCH-FRIEND. SHE CAME AND FOUND ME, TOLD ME YOU WERE IN TROUBLE, AND WHAT KIND OF TROUBLE YOU WERE IN.
WHAT HAPPENED TONIGHT WAS STUPID, WASN'T IT? I MEAN, I PUT THINGS AT RISK.
MORE THINGS THAN YOU KNOW, YOUNG NOBODY OWENS, YES.
YOU WERE RIGHT. I WON'T GO BACK. NOT TO THAT SCHOOL. AND NOT LIKE THAT.

MAUREEN QUILLING HAD HAD THE WORST WEEK OF HER LIFE.
NICK FARTHING WAS NO LONGER SPEAKING TO HER.
HER UNCLE TAM HAD SHOUTED AT HER ABOUT THE OWENS KID THING.
AND IF YOU EVER MENTION ANYTHING ABOUT THAT EVENING TO ANYONE, I COULD LOSE MY JOB AND I WOULDN'T WANT TO BE IN YOUR SHOES IF THAT HAPPENS.
EVEN THE YEAR SEVENS WEREN'T SCARED OF HER ANYMORE.
IT WAS ROTTEN.
SHE WANTED TO SEE THAT OWENS KID WRITHING IN MISERABLE AGONY. SHE WOULD CONCOCT ELABORATE REVENGE SCHEMES IN HER HEAD, COMPLEX AND VICIOUS. THEY WERE THE ONLY THING THAT MADE HER FEEL BETTER.
AND EVEN THEY DIDN'T REALLY HELP.
IF THERE WAS ONE JOB THAT GAVE MO THE CREEPS, IT WAS CLEANING UP THE SCIENCE LABS. IT STOOD TO REASON THAT HERE, IN THE WORST WEEK OF HER LIFE, IT WOULD BE HER TURN.
AT LEAST MRS. HAWKINS WAS THERE, COLLECTING PAPERS AT THE END OF THE DAY. HAVING HER THERE, HAVING ANYBODY THERE, WAS COMFORTING.
YOU'RE DOING A GOOD JOB, MAUREEN.
THANKS.

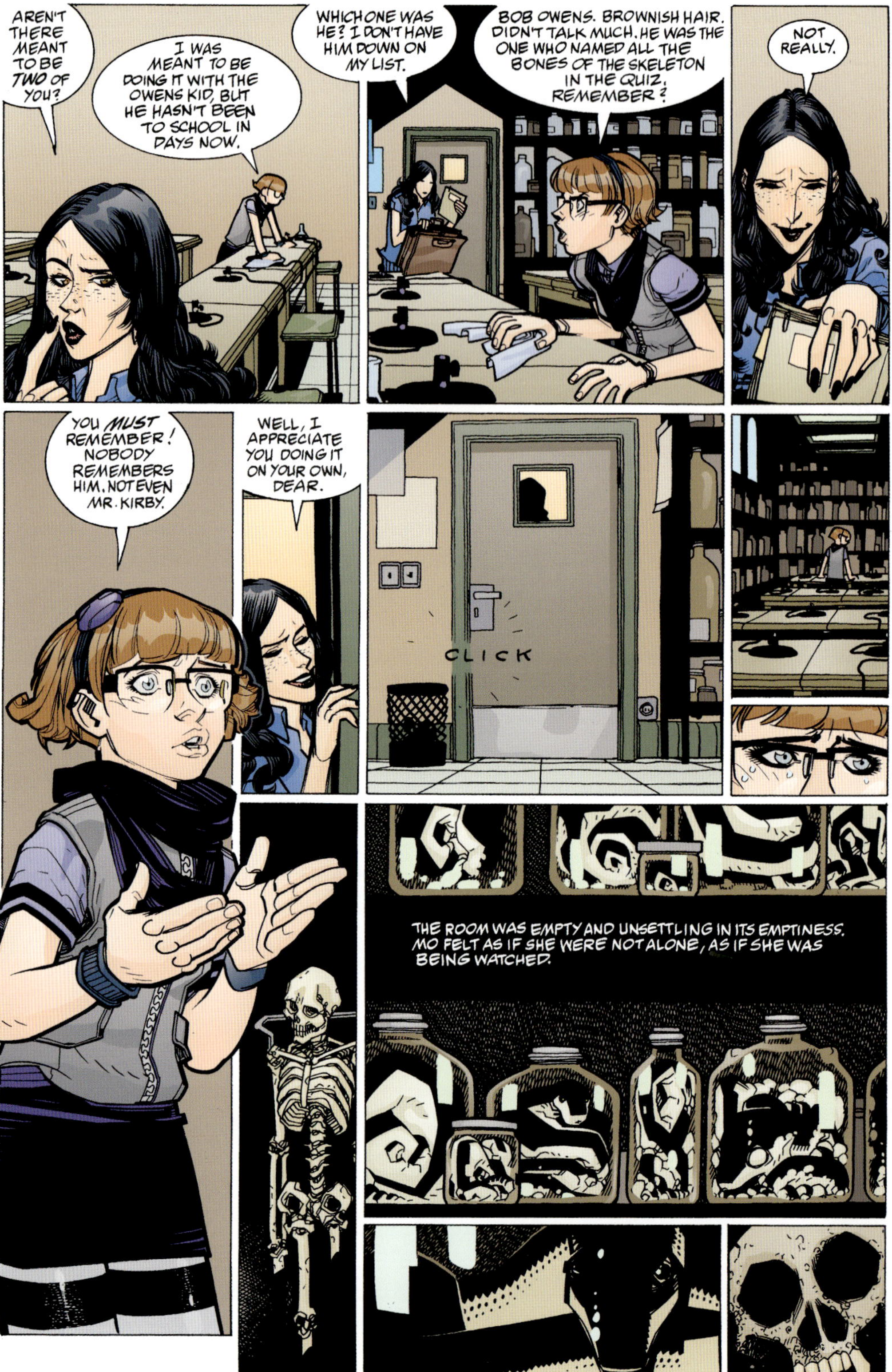
AREN'T THERE MEANT TO BE TWO OF YOU?
I WAS MEANT TO BE DOING IT WITH THE OWENS KID, BUT HE HASN'T BEEN TO SCHOOL IN DAYS NOW.
WHICH ONE WAS HE? I DON'T HAVE HIM DOWN ON MY LIST.
BOB OWENS. BROWNISH HAIR. DIDN'T TALK MUCH. HE WAS THE ONE WHO NAMED ALL THE BONES OF THE SKELETON IN THE QUIZ, REMEMBER?
NOT REALLY.
YOU MUST REMEMBER! NOBODY REMEMBERS HIM. NOT EVEN MR. KIRBY.
WELL, I APPRECIATE YOU DOING IT ON YOUR OWN, DEAR.
CLICK
THE ROOM WAS EMPTY AND UNSETTLING IN ITS EMPTINESS. MO FELT AS IF SHE WERE NOT ALONE, AS IF SHE WAS BEING WATCHED.

WELL, OF COURSE I'M BEING WATCHED. A HUNDRED DEAD THINGS IN JARS ARE ALL LOOKING AT ME. NOT TO MENTION THE SKELETON.
THAT WAS WHEN THE DEAD THINGS IN THE JARS BEGAN TO MOVE.
THIS ISN'T HAPPENING. I'M IMAGINING IT.
I'M NOT FRIGHTENED.
THAT'S GOOD. IT SERIOUSLY SUCKS TO BE FRIGHTENED.
NONE OF THE TEACHERS EVEN REMEMBER YOU.
BUT YOU REMEMBER ME.
HOW'S NICK?

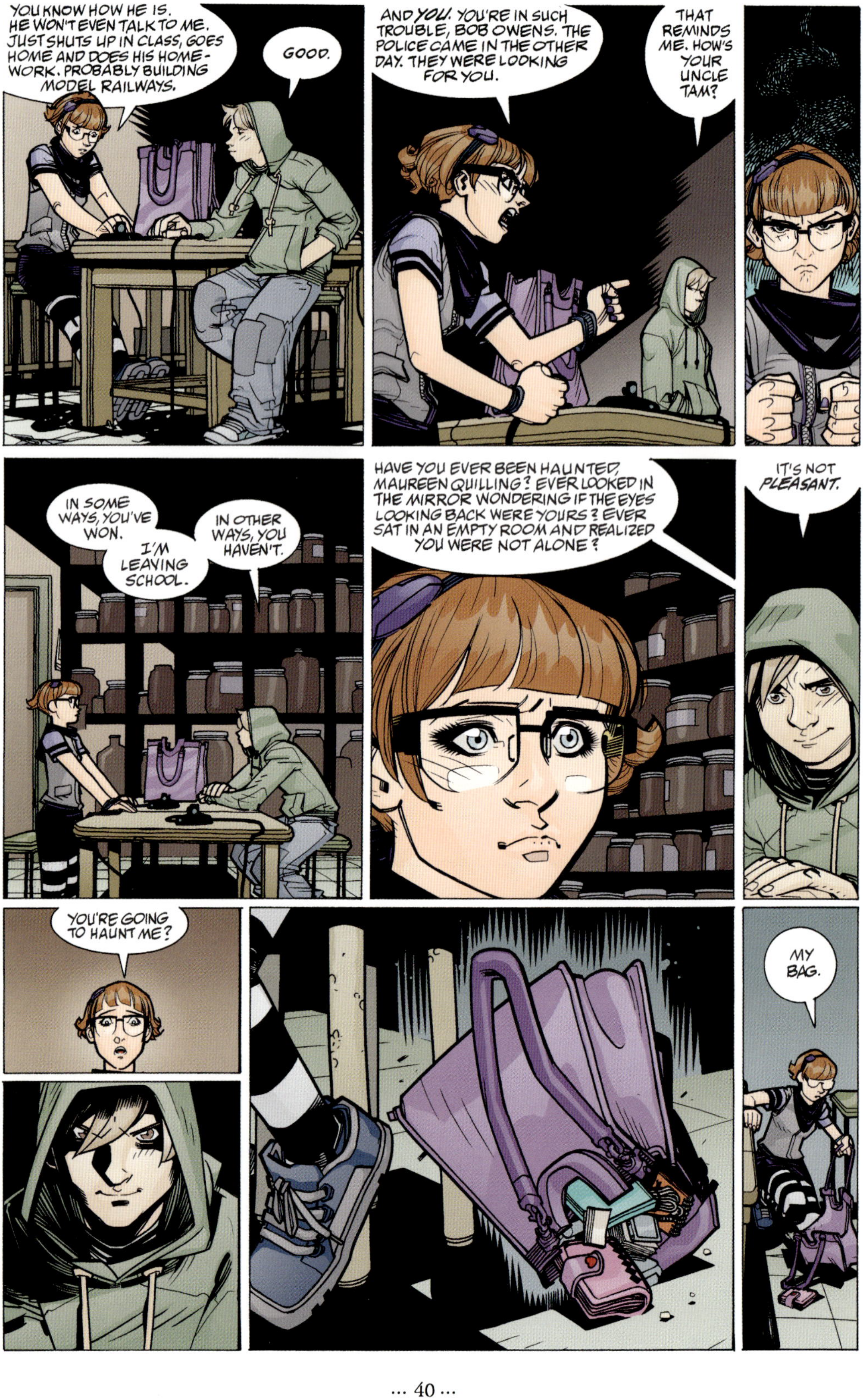
YOU KNOW HOW HE IS. HE WON'T EVEN TALK TO ME. JUST SHUTS UP IN CLASS, GOES HOME AND DOES HIS HOME-WORK. PROBABLY BUILDING MODEL RAILWAYS.
GOOD.
AND *YOU*. YOU'RE IN SUCH TROUBLE, BOB OWENS. THE POLICE CAME IN THE OTHER DAY. THEY WERE LOOKING FOR YOU.
THAT REMINDS ME. HOW'S YOUR UNCLE TAM?
IN SOME WAYS, YOU'VE WON.
I'M LEAVING SCHOOL.
IN OTHER WAYS, YOU HAVEN'T.
HAVE YOU EVER BEEN HAUNTED, MAUREEN QUILLING? EVER LOOKED IN THE MIRROR WONDERING IF THE EYES LOOKING BACK WERE YOURS? EVER SAT IN AN EMPTY ROOM AND REALIZED YOU WERE NOT ALONE?
IT'S NOT *PLEASANT*.
YOU'RE GOING TO HAUNT ME?
MY BAG.

DID YOU...?
BOB?
HER WAY HOME WAS GOING TO BE VERY LONG AND VERY DARK.
DOES IT STILL HURT?
A LITTLE. BUT I HEAL FAST.
COULD IT HAVE KILLED YOU? STEPPING OUT IN FRONT OF THAT CAR?
THERE ARE WAYS TO KILL PEOPLE LIKE ME, BUT THEY DON'T INVOLVE CARS.
I WAS WRONG, WASN'T I? THE WHOLE IDEA WAS TO DO IT WITHOUT ANYBODY NOTICING. AND THEN I HAD TO GET INVOLVED WITH THE KIDS IN THE SCHOOL, AND THE NEXT THING YOU KNOW, THERE'S POLICE AND ALL SORTS OF STUFF.
BECAUSE I WAS SELFISH.
YOU WEREN'T SELFISH. YOU NEED TO BE AMONG YOUR OWN KIND. IT'S JUST HARDER OUT THERE IN THE WORLD OF THE LIVING.
I WANTED TO KEEP YOU PERFECTLY SAFE. BUT THERE IS ONLY ONE PERFECTLY SAFE PLACE FOR YOUR KIND, AND YOU WILL NOT REACH IT UNTIL ALL YOUR ADVENTURES ARE OVER, AND NONE OF THEM MATTER ANY LONGER.

HE'S STILL OUT THERE, THE MAN WHO KILLED MY FIRST FAMILY. I STILL NEED TO LEARN ABOUT PEOPLE. ARE YOU GOING TO STOP ME FROM LEAVING THE GRAVEYARD?
NO. THAT WAS A MISTAKE, AND ONE THAT WE HAVE BOTH LEARNED FROM.
THEN WHAT?
THOMAS R. STOUT 1817 - 1851 DEEPLY REGRETTED BY ALL WHO KNEW HIM.
THERE ARE OTHER WAYS TO SATISFY YOUR INTEREST IN STORIES, AND BOOKS, AND IN THE WORLD, AND MANY SITUATIONS IN WHICH THERE MIGHT BE OTHER LIVING PEOPLE AROUND YOU, LIKE LIBRARIES, THE THEATER, OR THE CINEMA.
WHAT'S THAT? IS IT LIKE FOOTBALL?
FOOTBALL. HMM. THAT'S USUALLY A LITTLE EARLY IN THE DAY FOR ME. BUT MISS LUPESCU COULD TAKE YOU TO SEE A FOOTBALL MATCH THE NEXT TIME SHE'S HERE.
I'D LIKE THAT.
WE HAVE BOTH LEFT TOO MANY TRACKS AND TRACES IN THE LAST FEW WEEKS.
THEY ARE STILL LOOKING FOR YOU, YOU KNOW.
YOU SAID THAT BEFORE. HOW DO YOU KNOW? AND WHO ARE THEY? AND WHAT DO THEY WANT?
LAFUENTE
BUT SILAS ONLY SHOOK HIS HEAD AND WOULD BE DRAWN NO FURTHER, AND WITH THAT, FOR THE TIME BEING, BOD HAD TO BE SATISFIED.

7
Every Man Jack

Illustrated by Scott Hampton

SILAS HAD BEEN PREOCCUPIED FOR THE PREVIOUS SEVERAL MONTHS. HE HAD BEGUN TO LEAVE THE GRAVEYARD FOR DAYS, SOMETIMES WEEKS, AT A TIME. OVER CHRISTMAS, MISS LUPESCU HAD COME OUT FOR THREE WEEKS IN HIS PLACE, AND BOD HAD SHARED HER MEALS IN HER LITTLE FLAT IN OLD TOWN. SHE HAD EVEN TAKEN HIM TO A FOOTBALL MATCH, AS SILAS HAD PROMISED THAT SHE WOULD, BUT SHE HAD GONE BACK TO THE PLACE SHE HAD CALLED "THE OLD COUNTRY" AFTER SQUEEZING HIS CHEEKS AND CALLING HIM HER PET NAME FOR HIM...

NIMENI.

NOW SILAS WAS GONE, AND MISS LUPESCU ALSO. MR. AND MRS. OWENS WERE SITTING OUTSIDE THE JOSIAH WORTHINGTON TOMB TALKING TO JOSIAH WORTHINGTON. NONE OF THEM WAS HAPPY.

YOU MEAN TO SAY THAT HE DID NOT TELL EITHER OF YOU *WHERE* HE WAS GOING OR HOW THE CHILD WAS TO BE CARED FOR?

NO!

WELL, WHERE *IS* HE?

HE'S NEVER BEEN GONE FOR SO LONG BEFORE. AND HE PROMISED, WHEN THE CHILD CAME TO US, HE WOULD BE HERE TO HELP US CARE FOR HIM. HE *PROMISED*.

I WORRY THAT SOMETHING MUST HAVE HAPPENED TO HIM.

THIS IS TOO BAD OF HIM! IS THERE NO WAY TO FIND HIM, TO CALL HIM BACK?

NONE THAT I KNOW. BUT I BELIEVE THAT HE'S LEFT MONEY IN THE CRYPT, FOR FOOD FOR THE BOY.

MONEY! WHAT USE IS *MONEY*?

BOD WILL BE NEEDING MONEY IF HE'S TO GO OUT THERE TO BUY FOOD.

YOU'RE ALL AS BAD AS EACH *OTHER!*

... 44 ...

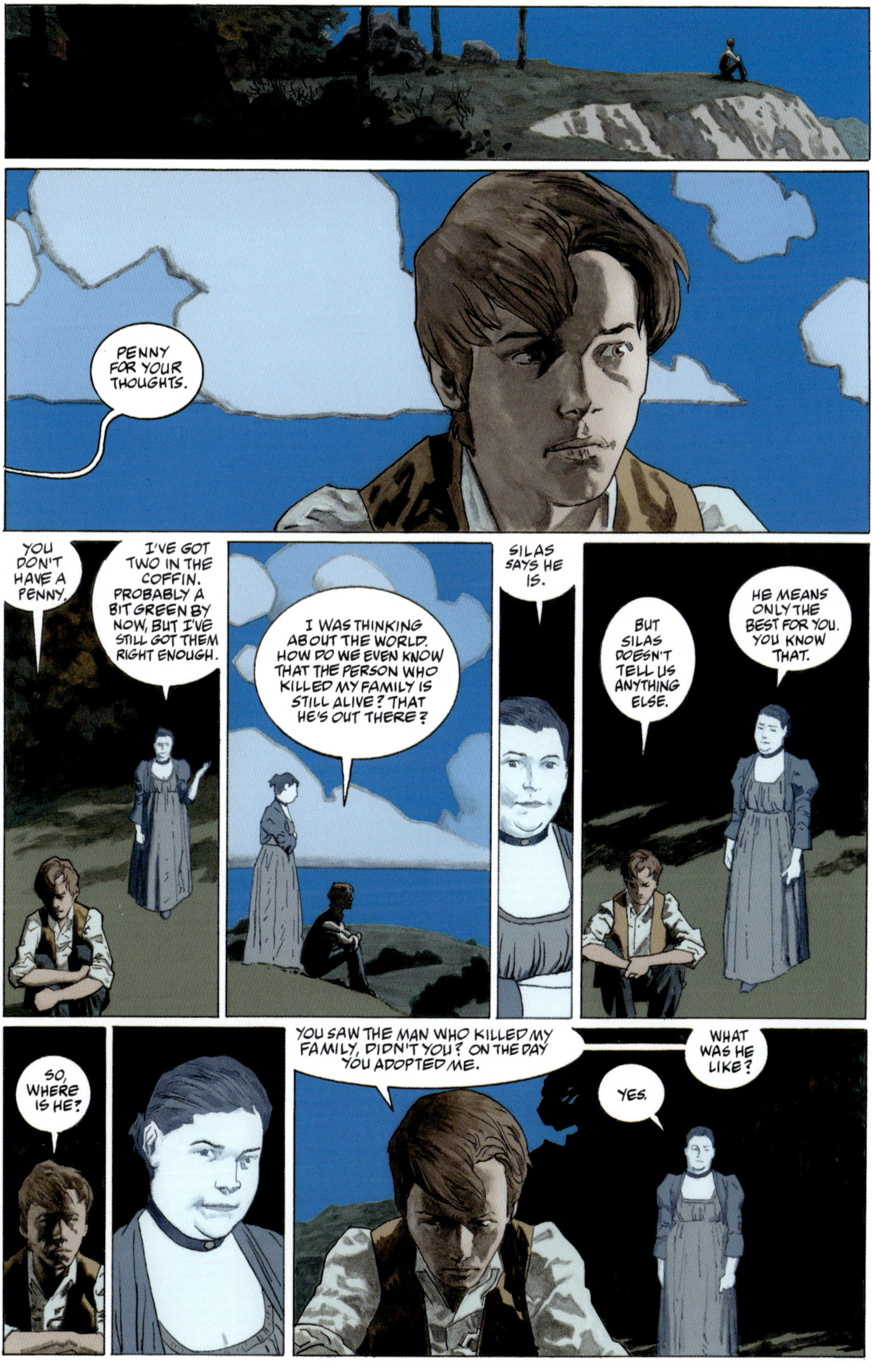
PENNY FOR YOUR THOUGHTS.
YOU DON'T HAVE A PENNY.
I'VE GOT TWO IN THE COFFIN. PROBABLY A BIT GREEN BY NOW, BUT I'VE STILL GOT THEM RIGHT ENOUGH.
I WAS THINKING ABOUT THE WORLD. HOW DO WE EVEN KNOW THAT THE PERSON WHO KILLED MY FAMILY IS STILL ALIVE? THAT HE'S OUT THERE?
SILAS SAYS HE IS.
BUT SILAS DOESN'T TELL US ANYTHING ELSE.
HE MEANS ONLY THE BEST FOR YOU. YOU KNOW THAT.
SO, WHERE IS HE?
YOU SAW THE MAN WHO KILLED MY FAMILY, DIDN'T YOU? ON THE DAY YOU ADOPTED ME.
YES.
WHAT WAS HE LIKE?

"MOSTLY, I HAD EYES FOR YOU. LET ME SEE... HE HAD DARK HAIR, VERY DARK. AND I WAS FRIGHTENED OF HIM. HE HAD A SHARP FACE. HUNGRY AND ANGRY, ALL AT ONCE, HE WAS. SILAS SAW HIM OFF."
WHY DIDN'T SILAS JUST KILL HIM? HE SHOULD HAVE JUST KILLED HIM THEN.
HE'S NOT A MONSTER, BOD.
IF SILAS HAD KILLED HIM BACK THEN, I WOULD BE SAFE NOW. I COULD GO ANYWHERE.
SILAS KNOWS MORE THAN YOU DO ABOUT ALL THIS. IT'S NOT THAT EASY.
WHAT WAS HIS NAME? THE MAN WHO KILLED THEM.
HE DIDN'T SAY IT. NOT THEN.
BUT YOU KNOW IT, DON'T YOU?
THERE'S NOTHING YOU CAN DO, BOD.
THERE IS. I CAN LEARN. I CAN LEARN EVERYTHING I NEED TO KNOW, ALL I CAN. I LEARNED ABOUT GHOUL-GATES. I LEARNED TO DREAMWALK. MISS LUPESCU TAUGHT ME HOW TO WATCH THE STARS. SILAS TAUGHT ME SILENCE. I CAN HAUNT. I CAN FADE. I KNOW EVERY INCH OF THIS GRAVEYARD.
SIGH
SILAS TOLD ME THE MAN WHO KILLED YOUR FAMILY WAS CALLED JACK. THAT'S ALL I KNOW.
MOTHER?
YES?
WHEN WILL SILAS COME BACK?
I WISH I KNEW.

SCARLETT AMBER PERKINS WAS FIFTEEN, AND, AT THAT MOMENT, SITTING ON THE UPPER DECK OF THE ELDERLY BUS, SHE WAS A MASS OF ANGRY HATE.
I HATE MY PARENTS FOR SPLITTING UP.
I HATE MY MOTHER FOR MOVING US AWAY FROM SCOTLAND.
I HATE MY FATHER.
HE DOESN'T EVEN CARE THAT I'M GONE.
I HATE THIS TOWN. IT'S NOTHING LIKE GLASGOW.
AT LEAST IN GLASGOW I HAD FRIENDS. I'LL NEVER SEE THEM AGAIN.
AT LEAST YOU'RE SOMEWHERE YOU'VE BEEN BEFORE. I MEAN WE LIVED HERE WHEN YOU WERE LITTLE.
I DON'T REMEMBER. AND IT'S NOT LIKE I STILL KNOW ANYONE. DO YOU WANT ME TO FIND MY OLD FRIENDS FROM WHEN I WAS FIVE? IS THAT WHAT YOU WANT?
WELL, I'M NOT STOPPING YOU.
SHE HATED HER SCHOOL AND SHE HATED THE WORLD, AND RIGHT NOW, SHE PARTICULARLY HATED THE TOWN BUS SERVICE.
WHEN VEHICLE IS IN MOTION.
THIS IS THE WRONG ROUTE HOME.
EXCUSE ME. I WANTED TO GO TO ACACIA AVENUE.
YOU SHOULD HAVE GOT THE 97, THEN.
BUT THIS GOES TO THE CITY CENTER.
EVENTUALLY.

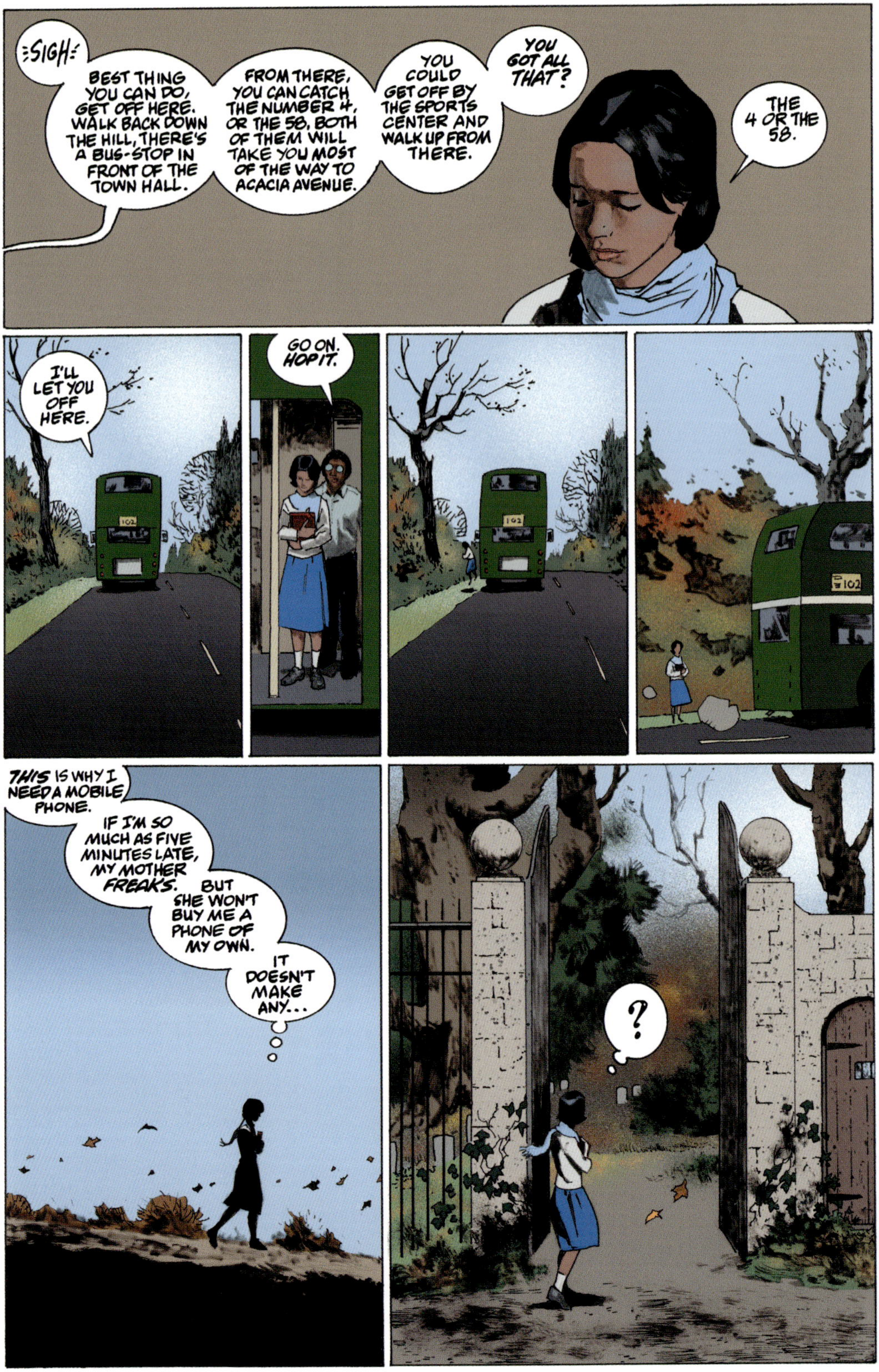
SIGH
BEST THING YOU CAN DO, GET OFF HERE. WALK BACK DOWN THE HILL, THERE'S A BUS-STOP IN FRONT OF THE TOWN HALL.
FROM THERE, YOU CAN CATCH THE NUMBER 4, OR THE 58, BOTH OF THEM WILL TAKE YOU MOST OF THE WAY TO ACACIA AVENUE.
YOU COULD GET OFF BY THE SPORTS CENTER AND WALK UP FROM THERE.
YOU GOT ALL THAT?
THE 4 OR THE 58.
I'LL LET YOU OFF HERE.
GO ON. HOP IT.
102
102
102
THIS IS WHY I NEED A MOBILE PHONE.
IF I'M SO MUCH AS FIVE MINUTES LATE, MY MOTHER FREAKS.
BUT SHE WON'T BUY ME A PHONE OF MY OWN.
IT DOESN'T MAKE ANY...
?

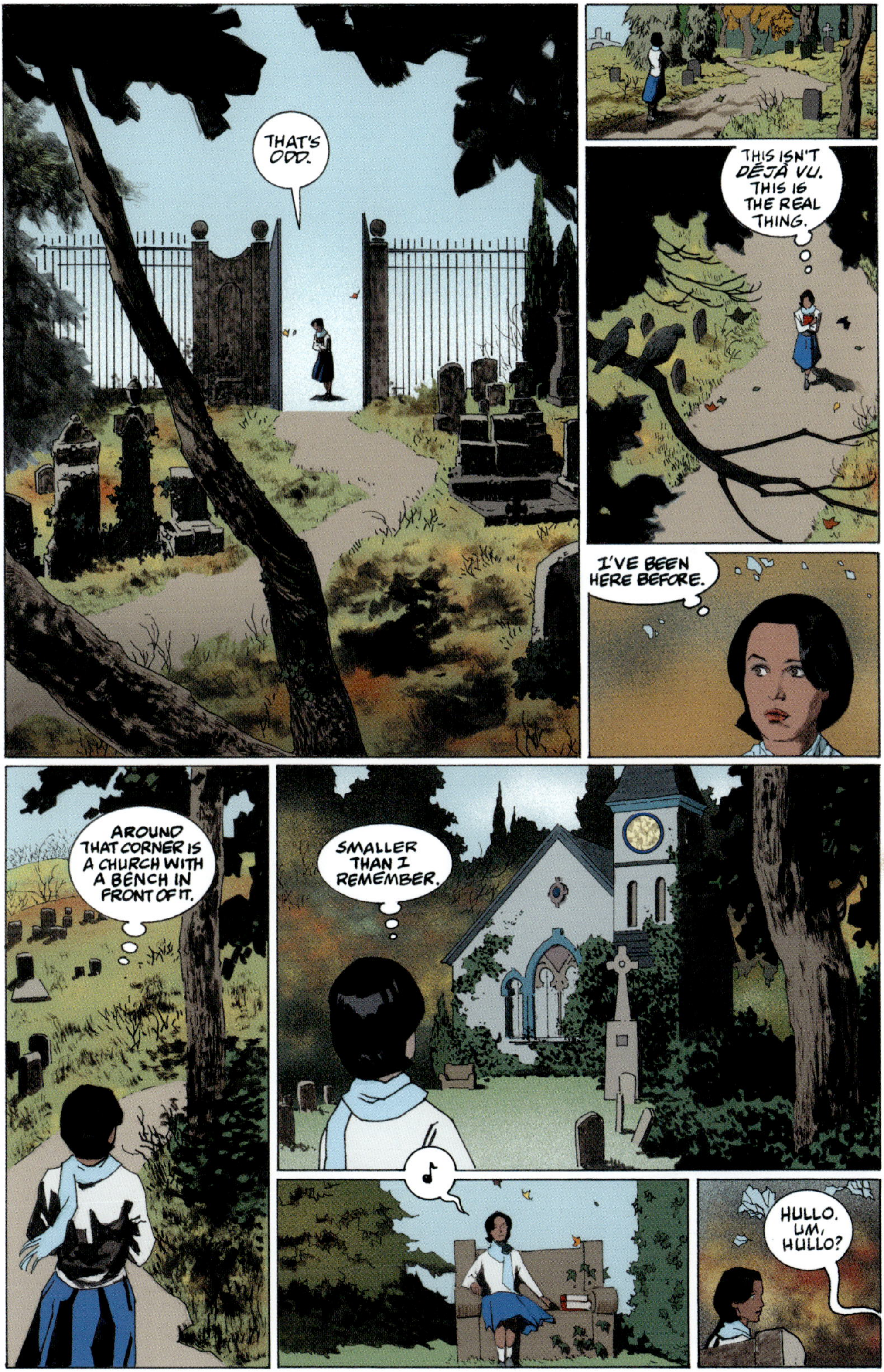
THAT'S ODD.
THIS ISN'T DÉJÀ VU. THIS IS THE REAL THING.
I'VE BEEN HERE BEFORE.
AROUND THAT CORNER IS A CHURCH WITH A BENCH IN FRONT OF IT.
SMALLER THAN I REMEMBER.
HULLO. UM, HULLO?

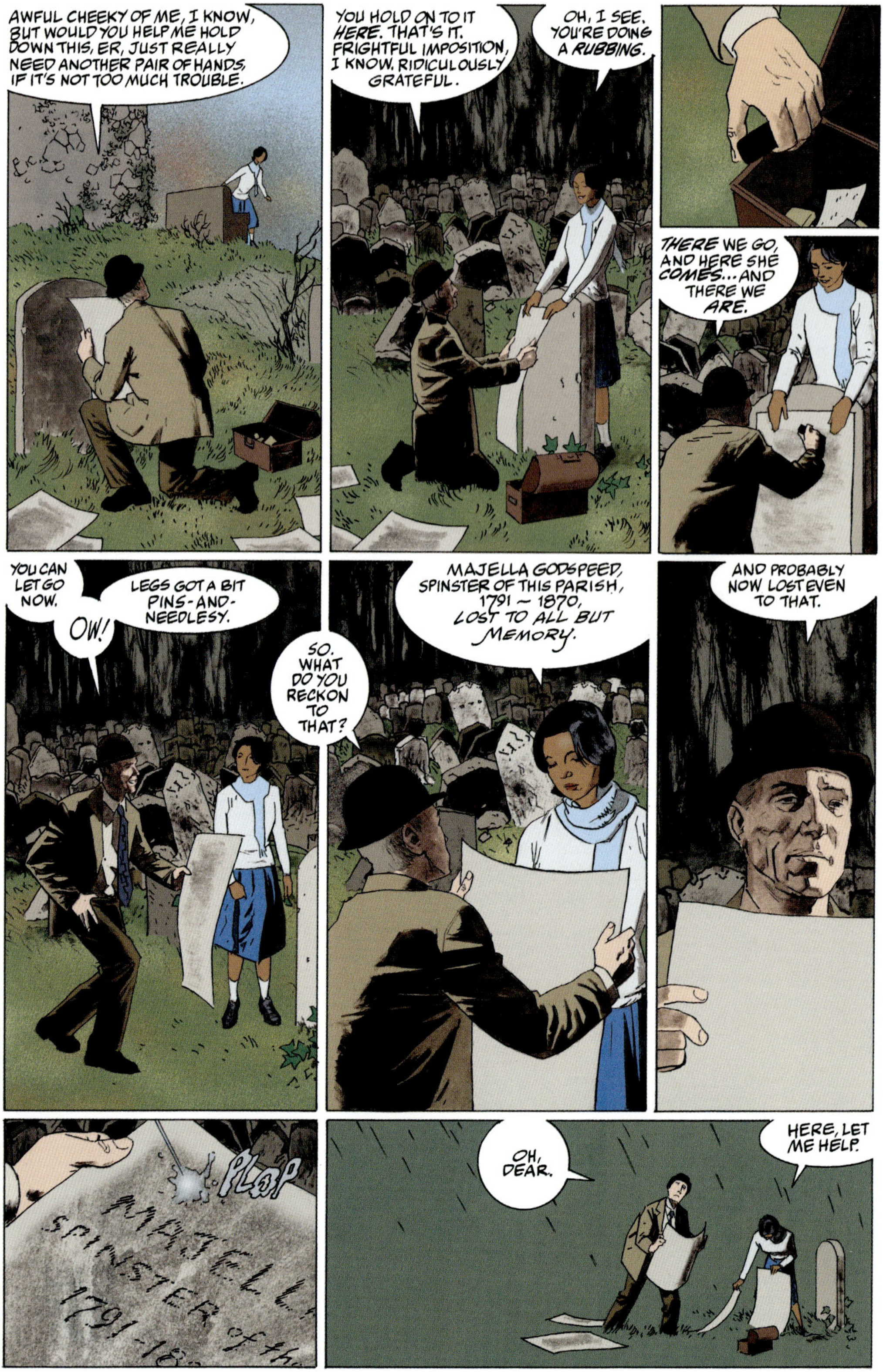
AWFUL CHEEKY OF ME, I KNOW, BUT WOULD YOU HELP ME HOLD DOWN THIS, ER, JUST REALLY NEED ANOTHER PAIR OF HANDS, IF IT'S NOT TOO MUCH TROUBLE.
YOU HOLD ON TO IT HERE. THAT'S IT. FRIGHTFUL IMPOSITION, I KNOW. RIDICULOUSLY GRATEFUL.
OH, I SEE. YOU'RE DOING A RUBBING.
THERE WE GO, AND HERE SHE COMES... AND THERE WE ARE.
YOU CAN LET GO NOW.
OW!
LEGS GOT A BIT PINS-AND-NEEDLESY.
SO. WHAT DO YOU RECKON TO THAT?
MAJELLA GODSPEED, SPINSTER OF THIS PARISH, 1791 ~ 1870, LOST TO ALL BUT MEMORY.
AND PROBABLY NOW LOST EVEN TO THAT.
PLOP
OH, DEAR.
HERE, LET ME HELP.

QUICKLY, THEN. THANK YOU SO MUCH.
I DON'T THINK IT'S REALLY GOING TO RAIN MUCH.
WEATHER FORECAST FOR THIS AFTERNOON SAID MOSTLY SUNNY.
MY MUM IS GOING TO KILL ME.
I KNOW WHAT YOU'RE THINKING.
YOU *DO?*
YOU'RE THINKING, IS THIS A CHURCH OR A FUNERAL CHAPEL? THERE WAS INDEED A SMALL CHURCH ON THIS SITE, AND THE ORIGINAL GRAVEYARD WOULD HAVE BEEN ITS CHURCHYARD.
THAT'S AS LONG AGO AS EIGHT, PERHAPS NINE HUNDRED A.D.
BUT THERE WAS A FIRE HERE IN THE 1820s, AND BY THAT TIME IT WAS ALREADY MUCH TOO SMALL FOR THE AREA, SO THEY REBUILT IT AS A FUNERAL CHAPEL.
ACTUALLY, I WAS THINKING THAT MY MUM IS GOING TO KILL ME. I GOT ON THE WRONG BUS AND I AM ALREADY SO LATE HOME.
GOOD LORD, YOU POOR THING. LOOK, I ONLY LIVE JUST DOWN THE ROAD. YOU WAIT HERE.

TOOT

COME ON. WHERE EXACTLY AM I TAKING YOU?

I DON'T TAKE RIDES FROM STRANGERS.

QUITE RIGHT TOO. BUT ONE GOOD TURN DESERVES ANOTHER AND, UM, ALL THAT.

TELL YOU WHAT. WHY DON'T YOU PHONE YOUR MOTHER— YOU CAN USE MY PHONE—AND TELL HER MY CAR'S NUMBER PLATE? YOU CAN DO IT FROM INSIDE THE CAR. YOU'RE GETTING SOAKED OUT THERE.

I COULD CALL THE POLICE TOO, COULDN'T I?
YOU CERTAINLY CAN, YES, OR YOU CAN JUST CALL YOUR MOTHER AND ASK HER TO COME AND PICK YOU UP.
WHERE DO YOU LIVE?
YOU REALLY DON'T HAVE TO. I MEAN, YOU COULD JUST TAKE ME TO THE BUS STOP.
I'LL TAKE YOU HOME. ADDRESS?
102A ACACIA AVENUE. IT'S OFF THE MAIN ROAD, A WEE BIT PAST THE BIG SPORTS CENTER.
MY! YOU ARE OUT OF YOUR WAY, AREN'T YOU?

"FRIGHTFULLY SORRY."

"I TOOK THE LIBERTY OF BRINGING YOUR DAUGHTER BACK TO YOU. OBVIOUSLY, YOU TAUGHT HER WELL, SHOULDN'T ACCEPT RIDES FROM STRANGERS."

"BUT, WELL, IT WAS RAINING, SHE TOOK THE WRONG BUS, WOUND UP ON THE OTHER SIDE OF TOWN. BIT OF A MESS ALL AROUND, REALLY."

"SAY YOU CAN FIND IT IN YOUR HEART TO FORGIVE. FORGIVE HER, AND, UM, ME."

"WELL, YOU CAN'T BE TOO CAREFUL THESE DAYS. WOULD YOU LIKE A CUP OF TEA... MISTER...?"

"FROST. BUT, PLEASE, CALL ME JAY."

"CALL ME NOONA."

"I'LL PUT THE KETTLE ON."

OVER TEA, SCARLETT TOLD HER MOTHER THE STORY OF HER WRONG BUS ADVENTURE, AND HOW SHE HAD FOUND HERSELF AT THE GRAVEYARD AND HOW SHE MET MR. FROST...

"...BY THE LITTLE CHURCH."

CLINK

... 54 ...

SORRY. STUPID.

THE GRAVEYARD ON THE HILL, IN THE OLD TOWN? THAT ONE?

I LIVE OVER THAT WAY. BEEN DOING A LOT OF GRAVE-RUBBINGS. AND YOU KNOW, IT'S TECHNICALLY A NATURE PRESERVE?

I KNOW.

THANK YOU SO MUCH FOR GIVING SCARLETT A RIDE HOME, MR. FROST. I THINK YOU SHOULD LEAVE NOW.

I SAY, THAT'S A BIT MUCH. DIDN'T MEAN TO HURT YOUR FEELINGS. WAS IT SOMETHING I SAID? THE RUBBINGS, THEY'RE FOR A LOCAL HISTORY PROJECT, IT'S NOT AS IF I'M DIGGING UP BONES OR ANYTHING.

SORRY. FAMILY HISTORY. NOT YOUR FAULT.

YOU KNOW, SCARLETT ACTUALLY USED TO PLAY IN THAT GRAVEYARD WHEN SHE WAS LITTLE. THIS IS, OH, TEN YEARS AGO. SHE HAD AN IMAGINARY FRIEND, TOO.

A LITTLE BOY CALLED NOBODY.

A GHOSTIE?

... 55 ...

NO, I DON'T THINK SO. HE JUST LIVED THERE.
"SHE EVEN POINTED OUT THE TOMB HE LIVED IN. SO I SUPPOSE HE WAS A GHOST."
DO YOU REMEMBER, LOVE?
I MUST HAVE BEEN A FUNNY KID.
I'M SURE THAT YOU WERE NOTHING OF THE, UM... YOU ARE RAISING A FINE GIRL HERE, NOONA.
WELL, LOVELY CUP OF TEA. ALWAYS A JOY TO MAKE NEW FRIENDS. I'LL BE TODDLING OFF NOW.
GOT TO MAKE MYSELF A LITTLE DINNER.
YOU'RE MAKING YOUR OWN DINNER?
WELL, DEFROSTING IT, REALLY. I'M ALSO A MASTER OF BOIL-IN-THE-BAG.
BIT OF A CRUSTY OLD BACHELOR.
JUST NEVER MET THE RIGHT WOMAN.

MR. FROST, WHY DON'T YOU COME 'ROUND FOR DINNER SATURDAY NIGHT?
YOU KNOW, I ALWAYS COOK TOO MUCH FOOD AT THE WEEKEND.
WHAT?
I WOULD LOVE TO COME AROUND FOR DINNER THIS SATURDAY NIGHT, NOONA.
LOVELY, MR. FROST.
BYE, THEN.
BYE, BYE.
YOU HATE TO COOK.
I HOPE YOU'VE DONE YOUR HOMEWORK.

I WAS IN THAT GRAVEYARD WHEN I WAS LITTLE.
THAT'S WHY EVERYTHING HAD SEEMED SO FAMILIAR.
IN HER MIND, SHE IMAGINED AND SHE REMEMBERED, AND SOMEWHERE IN THERE, SHE FELL ASLEEP.
BOY? WHAT'RE YOU DOING?
WHO SAID THAT?
OH, I CAN SEE YOU, SORT OF. ARE YOU DREAMWALKING?
I THINK I'M DREAMING.

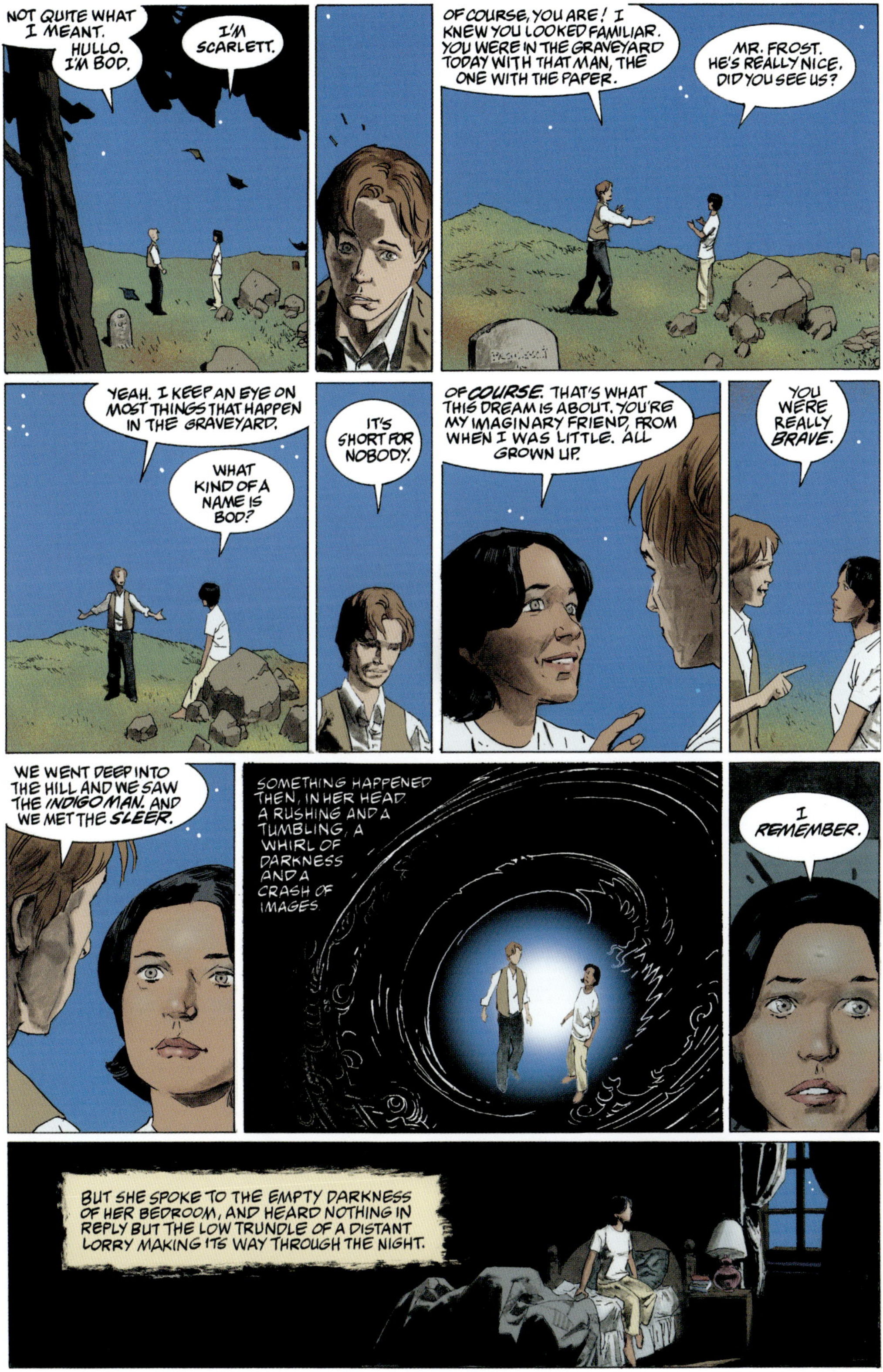
NOT QUITE WHAT I MEANT.
HULLO. I'M BOD.
I'M SCARLETT.
OF COURSE, YOU ARE! I KNEW YOU LOOKED FAMILIAR. YOU WERE IN THE GRAVEYARD TODAY WITH THAT MAN, THE ONE WITH THE PAPER.
MR. FROST. HE'S REALLY NICE. DID YOU SEE US?
YEAH. I KEEP AN EYE ON MOST THINGS THAT HAPPEN IN THE GRAVEYARD.
WHAT KIND OF A NAME IS BOD?
IT'S SHORT FOR NOBODY.
OF *COURSE*. THAT'S WHAT THIS DREAM IS ABOUT. YOU'RE MY IMAGINARY FRIEND, FROM WHEN I WAS LITTLE. ALL GROWN UP.
YOU WERE REALLY *BRAVE*.
WE WENT DEEP INTO THE HILL AND WE SAW THE *INDIGO MAN*. AND WE MET THE *SLEER*.
SOMETHING HAPPENED THEN, IN HER HEAD. A RUSHING AND A TUMBLING, A WHIRL OF DARKNESS AND A CRASH OF IMAGES.
I *REMEMBER*.
BUT SHE SPOKE TO THE EMPTY DARKNESS OF HER BEDROOM, AND HEARD NOTHING IN REPLY BUT THE LOW TRUNDLE OF A DISTANT LORRY MAKING ITS WAY THROUGH THE NIGHT.

BOD HAD STORES OF FOOD, THE KIND THAT LASTED, CACHED IN THE CRYPT. HE HAD ENOUGH TO KEEP HIM GOING FOR A COUPLE OF MONTHS. SILAS HAD MADE SURE OF THAT.

HE MISSED THE WORLD BEYOND THE GRAVEYARD GATES, BUT HE KNEW IT WAS NOT SAFE OUT THERE.

NOT YET.

THE GRAVEYARD, THOUGH, WAS HIS WORLD AND HIS DOMAIN, AND HE LOVED IT AS ONLY A FOURTEEN-YEAR-OLD BOY CAN LOVE ANYTHING.

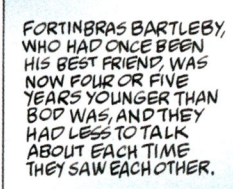

AND YET...

IN THE GRAVEYARD, NO ONE EVER CHANGED. THE LITTLE CHILDREN BOD HAD PLAYED WITH WHEN HE WAS SMALL, WERE STILL LITTLE CHILDREN.

FORTINBRAS BARTLEBY, WHO HAD ONCE BEEN HIS BEST FRIEND, WAS NOW FOUR OR FIVE YEARS YOUNGER THAN BOD WAS, AND THEY HAD LESS TO TALK ABOUT EACH TIME THEY SAW EACH OTHER.

THACKERAY PORRINGER WAS BOD'S HEIGHT AND AGE, AND SEEMED TO BE IN MUCH BETTER TEMPER WITH HIM; HE WOULD WALK WITH BOD IN THE EVENINGS, AND TELL STORIES OF UNFORTUNATE THINGS THAT HAD HAPPENED TO HIS FRIENDS.

NORMALLY, THE STORIES WOULD END IN THE FRIENDS BEING HANGED UNTIL THEY WERE DEAD FOR NO OFFENSE OF THEIRS AND BY MISTAKE.

SOMETIMES THEY WERE SIMPLY TRANSPORTED TO THE AMERICAN COLONIES AND THEY DIDN'T HAVE TO BE HANGED UNLESS THEY CAME BACK.

LIZA HEMPSTOCK, WHO HAD BEEN BOD'S FRIEND FOR SIX YEARS, WAS DIFFERENT IN ANOTHER WAY.

BOD TALKED TO MR. OWENS ABOUT THIS.

"IT'S JUST WOMEN, I RECKON."

"SHE LIKED YOU AS A BOY. PROBABLY ISN'T SURE WHO YOU ARE NOW YOU'RE A YOUNG MAN."

"I USED TO PLAY WITH ONE LITTLE GIRL DOWN BY THE DUCK-POND EVERY DAY UNTIL SHE TURNED ABOUT YOUR AGE, AND THEN SHE THREW AN APPLE AT MY HEAD AND DID NOT SAY ANOTHER WORD TO ME UNTIL I WAS SEVENTEEN."

!

... 61 ...

"IT WAS A *PEAR* I THREW."

"AND I WAS TALKING TO YOU SOON ENOUGH, FOR WE DANCED A MEASURE AT YOUR COUSIN NED'S WEDDING, AND THAT WAS BUT TWO DAYS AFTER YOUR SIXTEENTH BIRTHDAY."

"OF COURSE YOU ARE RIGHT, MY DEAR."

"SEVENTEEN."

BOD HAD ALLOWED HIMSELF NO FRIENDS AMONG THE LIVING. THAT WAY LAY ONLY TROUBLE. STILL, HE HAD REMEMBERED SCARLETT, HAD MISSED HER FOR YEARS AFTER SHE WENT AWAY, HAD LONG AGO FACED THE FACT HE WOULD NEVER SEE HER AGAIN.

AND NOW SHE HAD BEEN HERE IN HIS GRAVEYARD, AND HE HAD NOT KNOWN HER.

HE WAS WANDERING DEEPER INTO THE TANGLE OF IVY AND TREES THAT MADE THE NORTHWEST QUADRANT SO DANGEROUS. SIGNS ADVISED VISITORS TO KEEP OUT, BUT THE SIGNS WERE NOT NEEDED. NATURE HAD BEEN RECLAIMING THE GRAVEYARD FOR ALMOST A HUNDRED YEARS. PATHS WERE LOST AND IMPASSABLE.

WHEN BOD WAS NINE, HE HAD BEEN EXPLORING IN JUST THIS PART OF THE WORLD WHEN THE SOIL HAD GIVEN WAY BENEATH HIM, TUMBLING HIM INTO A HOLE ALMOST TWENTY FEET DOWN. THE GRAVE HAD BEEN DUG DEEP, TO ACCOMMODATE MANY COFFINS, BUT THERE WAS ONLY ONE COFFIN DOWN AT THE BOTTOM, CONTAINING A RATHER EXCITABLE MEDICAL GENTLEMAN NAMED CARSTAIRS.

CARSTAIRS SEEMED THRILLED BY BOD'S ARRIVAL AND INSISTED ON EXAMINING BOD'S TWISTED FOOT.

ONLY THEN COULD HE BE PERSUADED TO GO AND FETCH HELP.

BOD WAS MAKING HIS WAY THROUGH THE NORTHWEST QUADRANT, A SLUDGE OF FALLEN LEAVES, A TANGLE OF IVY, WHERE THE FOXES MADE THEIR HOMES, BECAUSE HE HAD AN URGE TO TALK TO THE POET.

HERE LIES THE MORTAL REMAINS OF NEHEMIAH TROT POET 1741 - 1774 SWANS SING BEFORE THEY DIE.

MIGHT I ASK FOR ADVICE?

... 63 ...

OF COURSE, BRAVE BOY. THE ADVICE OF POETS IS THE CORDIALITY OF KINGS! HOW MAY I SMEAR UNCTION ON YOUR, NO, NOT UNCTION, HOW MAY I GIVE BALM TO YOUR PAIN?
I'M NOT ACTUALLY IN PAIN. I JUST—WELL, THERE'S A GIRL I USED TO KNOW, AND I WASN'T SURE IF I SHOULD FIND HER AND TALK TO HER OR IF I SHOULD JUST FORGET ABOUT IT.
OH! YOU MUST GO TO HER AND IMPLORE HER. YOU MUST CALL HER YOUR TERPSICHORE.
YOU MUST WRITE POEMS FOR HER, MIGHTY ODES—I SHALL HELP YOU WRITE THEM—AND THUS—AND ONLY THUS—SHALL YOU WIN YOUR TRUE LOVE'S HEART.
I DON'T ACTUALLY NEED TO WIN HER HEART. SHE'S NOT MY TRUE LOVE. JUST SOMEONE TO TALK TO.
OF ALL THE ORGANS, THE TONGUE IS THE MOST REMARKABLE. WE UTTER WORDS BOTH SWEET AND SOUR WITH THE SAME TONGUE.
I SHOULDN'T.
YOU SHOULD, SIR! YOU MUST!
I SHALL WRITE ABOUT IT WHEN THE BATTLE'S LOST AND WON.
BUT IF I UNFADE FOR ONE PERSON, IT MAKES IT EASIER FOR OTHER PEOPLE TO SEE ME.

AH, LIST TO ME, YOUNG LEANDER, YOUNG HERO, YOUNG ALEXANDER. IF YOU DARE NOTHING, THEN WHEN THE DAY IS OVER, NOTHING IS ALL YOU WILL HAVE GAINED.
GOOD POINT.
BOD WAS PLEASED WITH HIMSELF, AND GLAD HE HAD THOUGHT OF ASKING THE POET FOR ADVICE.
REALLY, IF YOU CAN'T TRUST A POET TO OFFER SENSIBLE ADVICE, WHO CAN YOU TRUST?
WHICH REMINDED HIM...
MISTER TROT? TELL ME ABOUT REVENGE.
DISH BEST SERVED COLD.
DO NOT TAKE REVENGE IN THE HEAT OF THE MOMENT, INSTEAD, WAIT UNTIL THE HOUR IS PROPITIOUS. THERE WAS A GRUB STREET HACK NAMED O'LEARY...
AN IRISHMAN, I SHOULD ADD...
WHO HAD THE NERVE, THE CONFOUNDED CHEEK, TO WRITE OF MY FIRST SLIM VOLUME...
A NOSEGAY OF BEAUTY ASSEMBLED FOR GENTLEMEN OF QUALITY
IT IS INFERIOR DOGGEREL OF NO WORTH WHATSOEVER, AND THE PAPER IT IS WRITTEN ON WOULD BE BETTER USED TO...
NO!
LET US SIMPLY AGREE THAT IT WAS A MOST VULGAR STATEMENT.
I CANNOT SAY.
BUT YOU GOT YOUR REVENGE ON HIM?

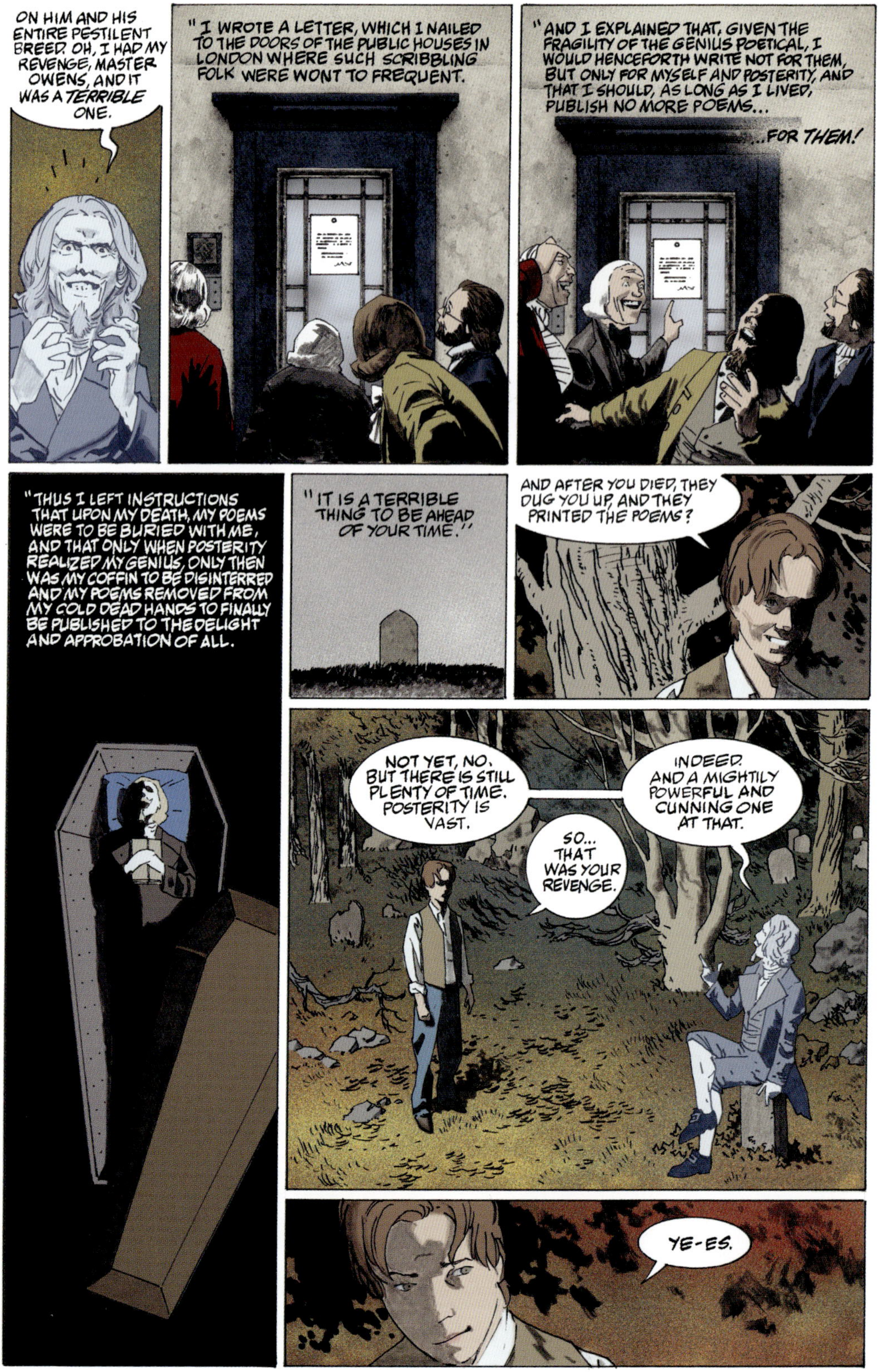

ON HIM AND HIS ENTIRE PESTILENT BREED. OH, I HAD MY REVENGE, MASTER OWENS, AND IT WAS A TERRIBLE ONE.
"I WROTE A LETTER, WHICH I NAILED TO THE DOORS OF THE PUBLIC HOUSES IN LONDON WHERE SUCH SCRIBBLING FOLK WERE WONT TO FREQUENT.
"AND I EXPLAINED THAT, GIVEN THE FRAGILITY OF THE GENIUS POETICAL, I WOULD HENCEFORTH WRITE NOT FOR THEM, BUT ONLY FOR MYSELF AND POSTERITY, AND THAT I SHOULD, AS LONG AS I LIVED, PUBLISH NO MORE POEMS...
...FOR THEM!
"THUS I LEFT INSTRUCTIONS THAT UPON MY DEATH, MY POEMS WERE TO BE BURIED WITH ME, AND THAT ONLY WHEN POSTERITY REALIZED MY GENIUS, ONLY THEN WAS MY COFFIN TO BE DISINTERRED AND MY POEMS REMOVED FROM MY COLD DEAD HANDS TO FINALLY BE PUBLISHED TO THE DELIGHT AND APPROBATION OF ALL.
"IT IS A TERRIBLE THING TO BE AHEAD OF YOUR TIME."
AND AFTER YOU DIED, THEY DUG YOU UP, AND THEY PRINTED THE POEMS?
NOT YET, NO. BUT THERE IS STILL PLENTY OF TIME. POSTERITY IS VAST.
SO... THAT WAS YOUR REVENGE.
INDEED. AND A MIGHTILY POWERFUL AND CUNNING ONE AT THAT.
YE-ES.

BEST
SERVED
COLD.
SCARLETT?
BOD FADED, BECAME A PART OF THE GRAVEYARD, NO MORE IMPORTANT THAN A SHADOW OR A TWIG.
?
BOD? IS THAT YOU?

WHY CAN YOU SEE ME?
I ALMOST COULDN'T. AT FIRST I THOUGHT YOU WERE A SHADOW OR SOMETHING. BUT YOU LOOK LIKE YOU DID IN MY DREAM. YOU SORT OF CAME INTO FOCUS.
ARE YOU... HERE ON YOUR OWN?
I HELPED MR. FROST DO SOME GRAVE-RUBBINGS AFTER SCHOOL. AND THEN I TOLD HIM I WANTED TO SIT AND THINK HERE, FOR A BIT. I PROMISED TO GO AND HAVE A CUP OF TEA WITH HIM AND HE'LL RUN ME HOME. HE DIDN'T EVEN ASK WHY.
CAN I HUG YOU?
DO YOU WANT TO?
YES.
WELL, THEN... I DON'T MIND IF YOU DO.
OW!
HA!
SORRY.
NO, IT WAS NICE. I MEAN, YOU JUST SQUEEZED MORE THAN I WAS EXPECTING.
I JUST WANTED TO KNOW IF YOU WERE REAL. ALL THESE YEARS I THOUGHT YOU WERE SOMETHING IN MY HEAD. BUT I DIDN'T MAKE YOU UP, AND YOU'RE BACK, YOU'RE IN MY HEAD, AND YOU'RE IN THE WORLD TOO.
YOU USED TO WEAR AN ORANGE COAT, AND WHENEVER I SAW THAT PARTICULAR COLOR ORANGE, I'D THINK OF YOU. I DON'T SUPPOSE YOU STILL HAVE THE COAT.
NO, NOT FOR A LONG TIME. IT WOULD BE A WEE BIT TOO SMALL FOR ME NOW.
YES, OF COURSE.

"I SHOULD GO HOME. I THOUGHT I COULD COME UP ON THE WEEKEND, THOUGH."

"I'D LIKE THAT."

"HOW WILL I FIND YOU NEXT TIME?"

"I'LL FIND YOU. DON'T WORRY. JUST BE ON YOUR OWN AND I'LL FIND YOU."

BOD SAT ATOP THE FROBISHER MAUSOLEUM, LOOKING OUT AT THE WORLD OF MOVING THINGS BEYOND THE GRAVEYARD.

AND HE REMEMBERED THE WAY THAT SCARLETT HAD HELD HIM AND HOW SAFE HE HAD FELT, IF ONLY FOR A MOMENT, AND HOW FINE IT WOULD BE TO WALK SAFELY IN THE LANDS BEYOND THE GRAVEYARD...

...AND HOW GOOD IT WAS TO BE MASTER OF HIS OWN SMALL WORLD.

TEA?
CHOCOLATE BISCUIT?
NO THANK YOU.
NO.
HONESTLY, YOU LOOK LIKE YOU'VE SEEN A GHOST. WELL, A GRAVEYARD, NOT A BAD PLACE TO SEE ONE IF YOU WERE GOING TO...
UM...
...I HAD AN AUNT ONCE WHO CLAIMED HER PARROT WAS HAUNTED.
SHE WAS A SCARLET MACAW.
THE PARROT.
THE AUNT WAS AN ARCHITECT. NEVER KNEW THE DETAILS.
I'M FINE. IT WAS JUST A LONG DAY.
I'LL SEE YOU SATURDAY. MOTHER SAID SHE'LL DROP ME OFF HERE IN THE MORNING. THEN SHE HAS TO SHOP FOR GROCERIES FOR OUR DINNER. SHE'S COOKING A ROAST CHICKEN.
DO YOU THINK THERE ARE LIKELY TO BE ROAST POTATOES?
I EXPECT SO, YES.
I WOULDN'T WANT TO PUT HER OUT OF HER WAY, I MEAN.
SHE'S LOVING IT. THANK YOU FOR GIVING ME A RIDE HOME.
MORE THAN WELCOME.

IN KRAKOW, ON WAWEL HILL, THERE ARE CAVES CALLED THE DRAGON'S DEN. THESE ARE THE CAVES THAT THE TOURISTS KNOW ABOUT. THERE ARE CAVES BENEATH THOSE CAVES THAT THE TOURISTS DO NOT KNOW AND DO NOT EVER GET TO VISIT. THEY GO DOWN A LONG WAY, AND THEY ARE INHABITED.

SILAS WENT FIRST, FOLLOWED BY MISS LUPESCU. BEHIND THEM WAS KANDAR, A BANDAGE-WRAPPED ASSYRIAN MUMMY.

KANDAR WAS CARRYING A SMALL PIG.

THERE HAD ORIGINALLY BEEN FOUR OF THEM, BUT THEY HAD LOST HAROUN WHEN THE IFRIT HAD STEPPED INTO A SPACE BOUNDED BY THREE POLISHED BRONZE MIRRORS AND HAD BEEN SWALLOWED IN A BLAZE OF LIGHT. IN MOMENTS, THE IFRIT COULD ONLY BE SEEN IN THE MIRRORS...

...AND THEN HE FADED AND WAS LOST TO THEM.

SILAS, WHO HAD NO PROBLEMS WITH MIRRORS, HAD COVERED ONE OF THEM WITH HIS CLOAK, RENDERING THE TRAP USELESS.

SO, NOW, THERE ARE ONLY THREE OF US.
AND A PIG.
WHY? WHY THE PIG?
IT'S LUCKY.
I'M NOT CONVINCED.
DID HAROUN HAVE A PIG?
HUSH.
THEY ARE COMING. FROM THE SOUND OF IT, THERE ARE MANY OF THEM.
LET THEM COME.
MISS LUPESCU SAID NOTHING, BUT SHE WAS READY FOR THEM, AND IT WAS ONLY BY AN EFFORT OF WILL THAT SHE DID NOT THROW BACK HER HEAD AND HOWL.

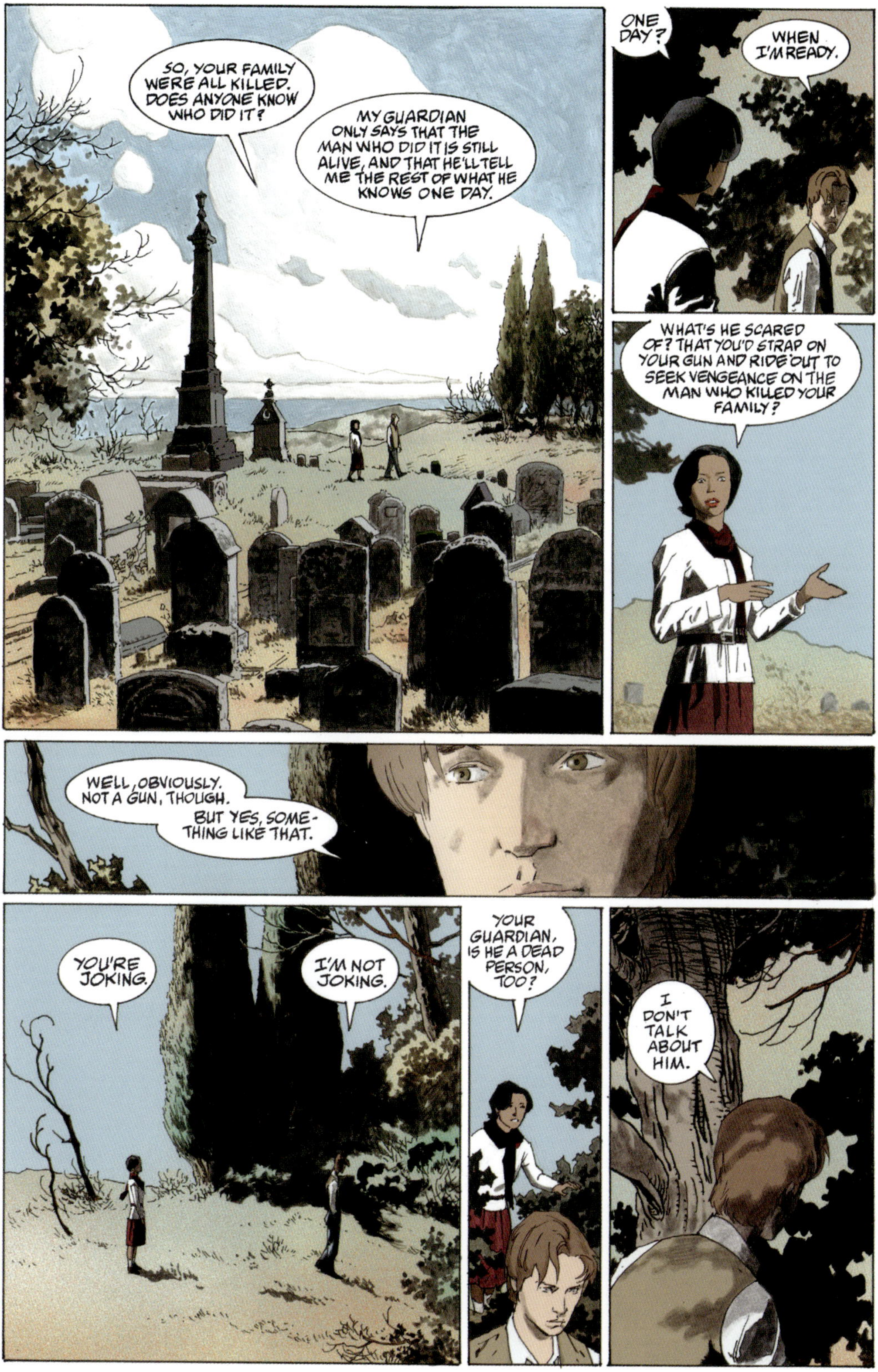

SO, YOUR FAMILY WERE ALL KILLED. DOES ANYONE KNOW WHO DID IT?
MY GUARDIAN ONLY SAYS THAT THE MAN WHO DID IT IS STILL ALIVE, AND THAT HE'LL TELL ME THE REST OF WHAT HE KNOWS ONE DAY.
ONE DAY?
WHEN I'M READY.
WHAT'S HE SCARED OF? THAT YOU'D STRAP ON YOUR GUN AND RIDE OUT TO SEEK VENGEANCE ON THE MAN WHO KILLED YOUR FAMILY?
WELL, OBVIOUSLY. NOT A GUN, THOUGH.
BUT YES, SOMETHING LIKE THAT.
YOU'RE JOKING.
I'M NOT JOKING.
YOUR GUARDIAN, IS HE A DEAD PERSON, TOO?
I DON'T TALK ABOUT HIM.

NOT EVEN TO ME?
NOT EVEN TO YOU.
WELL...
BE LIKE THAT.
LOOK, I'M SORRY. I DIDN'T MEAN—
I PROMISED MR. FROST I WOULDN'T BE TOO LONG. I'D BETTER BE GETTING BACK.
RIGHT.
LOOK AT HER! MISS HIGH AND MIGHTY!
IF YOU WANTED TO FIND OUT ABOUT A MURDER, WHERE WOULD YOU LOOK? I ALREADY TRIED THE INTERNET.
UM.
DEPENDS. WHAT KIND OF MURDER ARE WE TALKING ABOUT?

SOMETHING LOCAL, I THINK. ABOUT THIRTEEN OR FOURTEEN YEARS AGO A FAMILY WAS KILLED AROUND HERE.
CRIKEY! THIS REALLY HAPPENED?
OH YES.
ARE YOU ALL RIGHT?
NOT REALLY. BIT TOO, WELL, BIT OF A WIMP, REALLY. THINGS LIKE THAT, LOCAL TRUE CRIME, YOU DON'T LIKE TO THINK ABOUT IT. THINGS LIKE THAT HAPPENING HERE.
WHAT SET YOU OFF AFTER THIS?
OH. A BOY I KNOW. HE WAS ASKING ABOUT IT.
DEFINITELY THE LIBRARY. IT'LL BE IN THEIR NEWSPAPER FILES.
MURDER. BRR. GIVES ME THE SHIVERS.
ME TOO, A BIT.
COULD YOU, MAYBE, POSSIBLY, DROP ME OFF AT THE LIBRARY THIS AFTERNOON?
UM...
I'M SORRY. I KNOW I SHOULDN'T BE ASKING FOR RIDES EVERYWHERE.
NOT AT ALL. JUST WONDERING WHICH YOUR MOTHER WOULD PREFER, BOTTLE OF WINE OR CHOCOLATES. NOT REALLY SURE. BOTH MAYBE?
SHE LOVES CHOCOLATES. SO DO I.
CHOCOLATES IT IS, THEN.

YES?
I WANTED TO SEE SOME OLD NEWSPAPER CLIPPINGS.
IS IT FOR SCHOOL?
IT'S LOCAL HISTORY.
WE'VE GOT THE LOCAL PAPER ON MICROFICHE. ONE DAY, WE'LL HAVE IT ALL DIGITIZED. NOW, WHAT DATES ARE YOU AFTER?
ABOUT THIRTEEN OR FOURTEEN YEARS AGO. I CAN'T BE MORE SPECIFIC THAN THAT. I'LL KNOW IT WHEN I SEE IT.
COME WITH ME.
HERE.
GO WILD.
SCARLETT ASSUMED THAT THE MURDER OF A FAMILY WOULD BE FRONT PAGE NEWS BUT INSTEAD, WHEN SHE EVENTUALLY FOUND IT...
IT'S BURIED ON PAGE FIVE.
THERE WAS NO COLOR IN THE ARTICLE, NO DESCRIPTION, JUST AN UNDERSTATED LIST OF EVENTS.
ARCHITECT RONALD DORIAN, 36, HIS WIFE, CARLOTTA, 34, A PUBLISHER, AND THEIR DAUGHTER, MISTY, 7, WERE FOUND DEAD AT 33 DUNSTAN ROAD. FOUL PLAY IS SUSPECTED. A POLICE SPOKESMAN SAID THAT IT WAS TOO EARLY TO COMMENT AT THIS STAGE OF THEIR INVESTIGATIONS, BUT THAT SIGNIFICANT LEADS ARE BEING FOLLOWED.

HUNH! NO MENTION OF HOW THE FAMILY DIED. NOTHING ABOUT A MISSING BABY.

IN THE WEEKS THAT FOLLOWED— NO FOLLOW-UP.

THE POLICE NEVER COMMENTED. NOT THAT I CAN SEE.

THAT'S IT. I'M CERTAIN. 33 DUNSTAN ROAD.

I KNOW THE HOUSE. I'VE BEEN IN THERE.

THANK YOU.

HELLO? MR. FROST?

SCARLETT. EVERYTHING STILL ALL RIGHT FOR THIS EVENING? HOW'S YOUR MOTHER?
OH. IT'S ALL UNDER CONTROL.
UM, MR. FROST, HOW LONG HAVE YOU LIVED AT YOUR HOUSE?
HOW LONG? ABOUT, WELL, FOUR MONTHS, NOW.
HOW DID YOU FIND IT?
ESTATE AGENTS' WINDOW. IT WAS EMPTY AND I COULD AFFORD IT, MORE OR LESS. I WANTED SOMETHING WITHIN WALKING DISTANCE OF THE GRAVEYARD.
MR. FROST, ABOUT THIRTEEN YEARS AGO, THREE PEOPLE WERE MURDERED IN YOUR HOUSE. THE DORIAN FAMILY.
MR. FROST? ARE YOU THERE?
UM. STILL HERE, SCARLETT, SORRY.
NOT THE SORT OF THING YOU EXPECT TO HEAR. IT'S AN OLD HOUSE. I MEAN, YOU EXPECT THINGS TO HAPPEN A LONG TIME AGO. BUT NOT... WELL, WHAT HAPPENED?
THERE WAS A LITTLE PIECE ON IT IN AN OLD NEWSPAPER, IT ONLY GAVE THE ADDRESS AND NOTHING ELSE. I DON'T KNOW HOW THEY DIED OR ANYTHING.
WELL.
GOOD LORD.

THIS, YOUNG SCARLETT, IS WHERE WE LOCAL HISTORIANS COME INTO OUR OWN. LEAVE IT WITH ME. I'LL FIND OUT EVERYTHING I CAN AND REPORT BACK.
THANK YOU.
UM. I ASSUME THIS PHONE CALL IS BECAUSE IF NOONA THOUGHT THERE WERE MURDERS GOING ON IN MY HOME, YOU'D NEVER BE ALLOWED TO SEE ME OR THE GRAVEYARD AGAIN. SO, UM, SUPPOSE I WON'T MENTION IT UNLESS YOU DO.
THANK YOU, MR. FROST!
SEE YOU AT SEVEN. WITH CHOCOLATES.
DINNER WAS REMARKABLY PLEASANT. THE BURNT SMELL HAD GONE FROM THE KITCHEN, AND THE CHOCOLATES, WHICH THEY HAD FOR DESSERT WERE PERFECT. MR. FROST SAT AND TALKED WITH THEM UNTIL ABOUT 10 P.M., WHEN HE SAID THAT HE NEEDED TO GET HOME.
TIME, TIDE, AND HISTORICAL RESEARCH WAIT FOR NO MAN.
SCARLETT TRIED TO FIND BOD IN HER DREAMS THAT NIGHT, BUT WHEN SHE DID DREAM IT WAS OF WANDERING AROUND GLASGOW CITY CENTER WITH HER OLD FRIENDS. THEY WERE HUNTING FOR A SPECIFIC STREET, BUT ALL THEY FOUND WAS A SUCCESSION OF DEAD ENDS, ONE AFTER ANOTHER.

DEEP BENEATH THE HILL IN KRAKOW, IN THE DEEPEST VAULT BENEATH THE CAVES THEY CALL THE DRAGON'S DEN, MISS LUPESCU STUMBLED AND FELL.
THEY WILL COME BACK, SILAS. TOO SOON THE SUN WILL RISE.
THEN WE MUST DEAL WITH THEM BEFORE THEY ARE READY TO ATTACK. CAN YOU STAND?
DA. I AM ONE OF THE HOUNDS OF GOD. I WILL STAND.
NOW WE END THIS.

LATE ON SUNDAY AFTERNOON.
OH, HULLO, MR. FROST. FUNNY, WE WERE JUST TALKING ABOUT YOU.
NO, WE WEREN'T.
IT WAS WONDERFUL. I HAD THE BEST TIME. HONESTLY, IT WAS NO TROUBLE.
THE CHOCOLATES? THEY WERE PERFECT. JUST PERFECT.
I TOLD SCARLETT TO TELL YOU, ANYTIME YOU WANT A GOOD DINNER, YOU JUST LET ME KNOW!
SCARLETT? YES, SHE'S HERE. I'LL PUT HER ON.
SCARLETT!
I'M JUST HERE, MUM. YOU DON'T HAVE TO SHOUT.
OH.
MISTER FROST?
THE, UM... THE THING WE WERE TALKING ABOUT... THE THING THAT HAPPENED IN MY HOUSE... YOU CAN TELL YOUR FRIEND THAT I FOUND OUT- UM... LISTEN, WHEN YOU SAID, 'A FRIEND OF YOURS,' DID YOU MEAN YOU OR IS THERE A REAL PERSON - IF IT'S NOT A PERSONAL QUESTION.
I'VE GOT A REAL FRIEND THAT WANTS TO KNOW.
TELL YOUR FRIEND THAT I WAS DIGGING-NOT LITERALLY- AND I THINK I MIGHT HAVE UNEARTHED SOME VERY REAL INFORMATION.
LIKE WHAT?
LOOK... DON'T THINK I'M MAD. BUT, WELL, AS FAR AS I CAN TELL, THREE PEOPLE WERE KILLED. ONE OF THEM—THE BABY, I THINK— WASN'T. IT WASN'T A FAMILY OF THREE, IT WAS A FAMILY OF FOUR. TELL HIM TO COME AND SEE ME, YOUR FRIEND. I'LL FILL HIM IN.
I'LL TELL HIM.

OW!
IT IS THE TREASURE OF THE SLEER...
YOU'RE THE OLDEST THING HERE. I CAME TO TALK TO YOU. I WANT ADVICE.
I KNOW. BUT SILAS ISN'T HERE AND I DON'T KNOW WHO ELSE TO TALK TO.
NOTHING COMES TO THE SLEER FOR ADVICE.
THE SLEER GUARDS. THE SLEER WAITS.
NOTHING WAS SAID. JUST A SILENCE IN REPLY THAT ECHOED OF DUST AND LONELINESS.

I DON'T KNOW WHAT TO DO.
I THINK I CAN FIND OUT ABOUT WHO KILLED MY FAMILY. WHO WANTED TO KILL *ME*. IT MEANS LEAVING THE GRAVEYARD, THOUGH.
I'M NOT FRIGHTENED OF DYING. IT'S JUST, SO MANY PEOPLE I CARE FOR HAVE SPENT SO MUCH TIME KEEPING ME SAFE, TEACHING ME... PROTECTING ME.
I HAVE TO DO THIS ON MY OWN.
YES.
THAT'S ALL, THEN. SORRY I BOTHERED YOU.
THE SLEER WAS SET TO GUARD THE TREASURE UNTIL OUR MASTER RETURNED. ARE YOU OUR MASTER?
NO.
WILL YOU BE OUR MASTER?
I'M AFRAID NOT.

If you were our master, we could hold you in our coils forever. If you were our master, we would keep you safe and protect you until the end of time.
I am not your master.
No
Then find
your name
Well?
I'll do it.
Come on.

"IT'S ONLY A HOUSE, LIKE ANY OTHER."

"WELL?"

"YOU MUST BE MISS PERKINS'S MYSTERIOUS FRIEND. GOOD TO MEET YOU."

"THIS IS BOD."

"BOB?"

"BOD. WITH A D."

"BOD, THIS IS MR. FROST."

"KETTLE'S ON. WHAT SAY WE SWAP INFORMATION OVER A CUPPA?"

"THE HOUSE JUST KEEPS GOING UP. THE TOILET'S ON THE NEXT FLOOR UP, AND MY OFFICE, THEN THE BEDROOMS ABOVE THAT."

"KEEPS YOU FIT, ALL THE STAIRS."

... 85 ...

SO WHAT DID YOU FIND OUT?

WELL, YOU WERE RIGHT. I MEAN, THIS WAS THE HOUSE WHERE THOSE PEOPLE WERE KILLED. AND IT... I THINK THE CRIME WAS... WELL, NOT EXACTLY HUSHED UP, BUT FORGOTTEN ABOUT BY THE AUTHORITIES.

I DON'T UNDERSTAND. MURDERS DON'T GET SWEPT UNDER THE CARPET.

THIS ONE WAS. THERE ARE PEOPLE OUT THERE WHO HAVE INFLUENCE. IT'S THE ONLY EXPLANATION FOR THAT, AND FOR WHAT HAPPENED TO THE YOUNGEST CHILD.

AND WHAT WAS THAT?

HE LIVED. I'M SURE OF IT. BUT THERE WASN'T A MANHUNT. A MISSING TODDLER NORMALLY WOULD BE NATIONAL NEWS. BUT THEY, UM, MUST HAVE SQUASHED IT SOMEHOW.

WHO *ARE* THEY?

THE SAME PEOPLE WHO HAD THE FAMILY KILLED.

DO YOU KNOW ANYMORE THAN THAT?

YES, WELL, A LITTLE... I'M SORRY, I'M...

LOOK.

GIVEN WHAT I'VE FOUND, IT'S ALL TOO INCREDIBLE.

***WHAT* WAS? WHAT DID YOU *FIND*?**

... 86 ...

YOU'RE RIGHT. I'M SORRY. GETTING INTO KEEPING SECRETS. NOT A GOOD IDEA. HISTORIANS DON'T BURY THINGS. WE DIG THEM UP, SHOW PEOPLE.

YES.

I FOUND A LETTER. UPSTAIRS. IT WAS HIDDEN UNDER A LOOSE FLOORBOARD.

YOUNG MAN, WOULD I BE CORRECT IN ASSUMING YOUR... WELL, YOUR INTEREST IN THIS BUSINESS, THIS DREADFUL BUSINESS, IS PERSONAL?

YES.

COME ON. NOT YOU, THOUGH, SCARLETT. NOT YET. I'LL SHOW *HIM*. AND IF HE SAYS IT'S ALL RIGHT, I'LL SHOW YOU AS WELL.

DEAL?

DEAL.

WE WON'T BE LONG. COME ON, LAD.

IT'S OKAY. I'LL WAIT HERE FOR YOU.

... 87 ...

ALL THE WAY TO THE VERY TOP.
I DON'T...
WELL...
YOU DON'T HAVE TO ANSWER IF YOU DON'T WANT TO, BUT...
UM...
...YOU'RE THE BOY, AREN'T YOU?
HERE WE ARE.
CLICK
STROKE OF LUCK, REALLY.
UNDER MY NOSE, SO TO SPEAK.

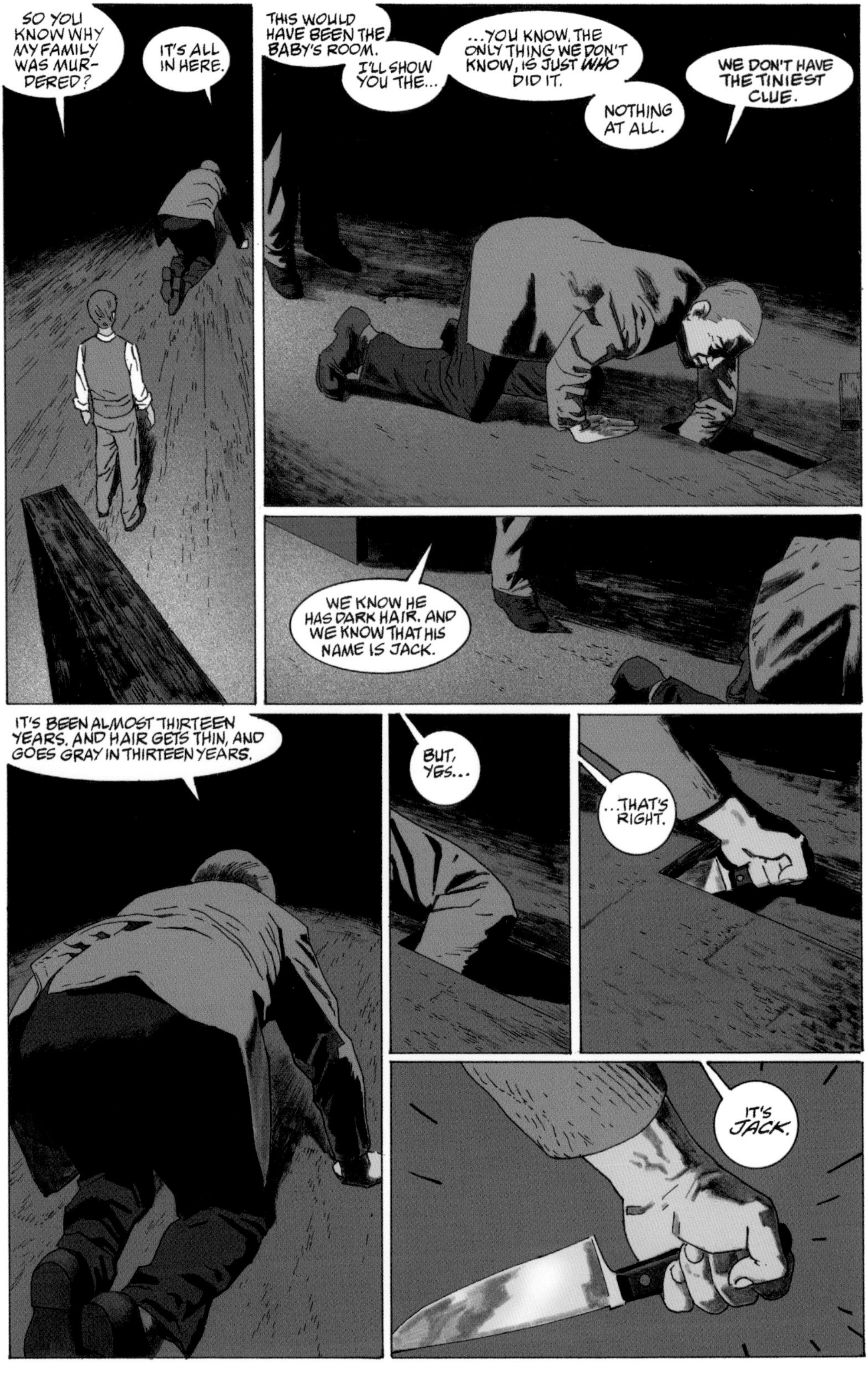

SO YOU KNOW WHY MY FAMILY WAS MURDERED?
IT'S ALL IN HERE.
THIS WOULD HAVE BEEN THE BABY'S ROOM.
I'LL SHOW YOU THE...
...YOU KNOW, THE ONLY THING WE DON'T KNOW, IS JUST WHO DID IT.
NOTHING AT ALL.
WE DON'T HAVE THE TINIEST CLUE.
WE KNOW HE HAS DARK HAIR. AND WE KNOW THAT HIS NAME IS JACK.
IT'S BEEN ALMOST THIRTEEN YEARS. AND HAIR GETS THIN, AND GOES GRAY IN THIRTEEN YEARS.
BUT, YES...
...THAT'S RIGHT.
IT'S JACK.

IT WAS AS IF MR. FROST HAD BEEN A COAT OR A HAT THE MAN HAD BEEN WEARING, THAT HE HAD NOW DISCARDED. THE AFFABLE EXTERIOR WAS GONE.
NOW, BOY. TIME TO FINISH THIS.
OH, MR. FROST!
THERE'S SOMEONE KNOCKING AT THE FRONT DOOR. SHOULD I GET IT?
EH?
I AM A VACANT DOORWAY.
?
YOU'RE HERE SOMEWHERE. I CAN SMELL YOU.
CLICK
KA-THUNK

IT BUYS YOU MOMENTS, BUT IT WON'T STOP ME, BOY.
WE HAVE UNFINISHED BUSINESS, YOU AND I.
SCARLETT!
IT'S HIM! COME ON!
IT'S WHO? WHAT ARE YOU TALKING ABOUT?
HIM! FROST.
HE'S JACK!
HE TRIED TO KILL ME.
WHAT?
BANG
BUT HE'S NICE.
NO, HE'S NOT!

BANG BANG
DON'T LOOK BACK!
FASTER, SCARLETT!
OH!
AH. GOOD EVENING, YOUNG LADY. WE ARE LOOKING FOR MR. FROST. I BELIEVE THIS IS HIS NECK OF THE WOODS.

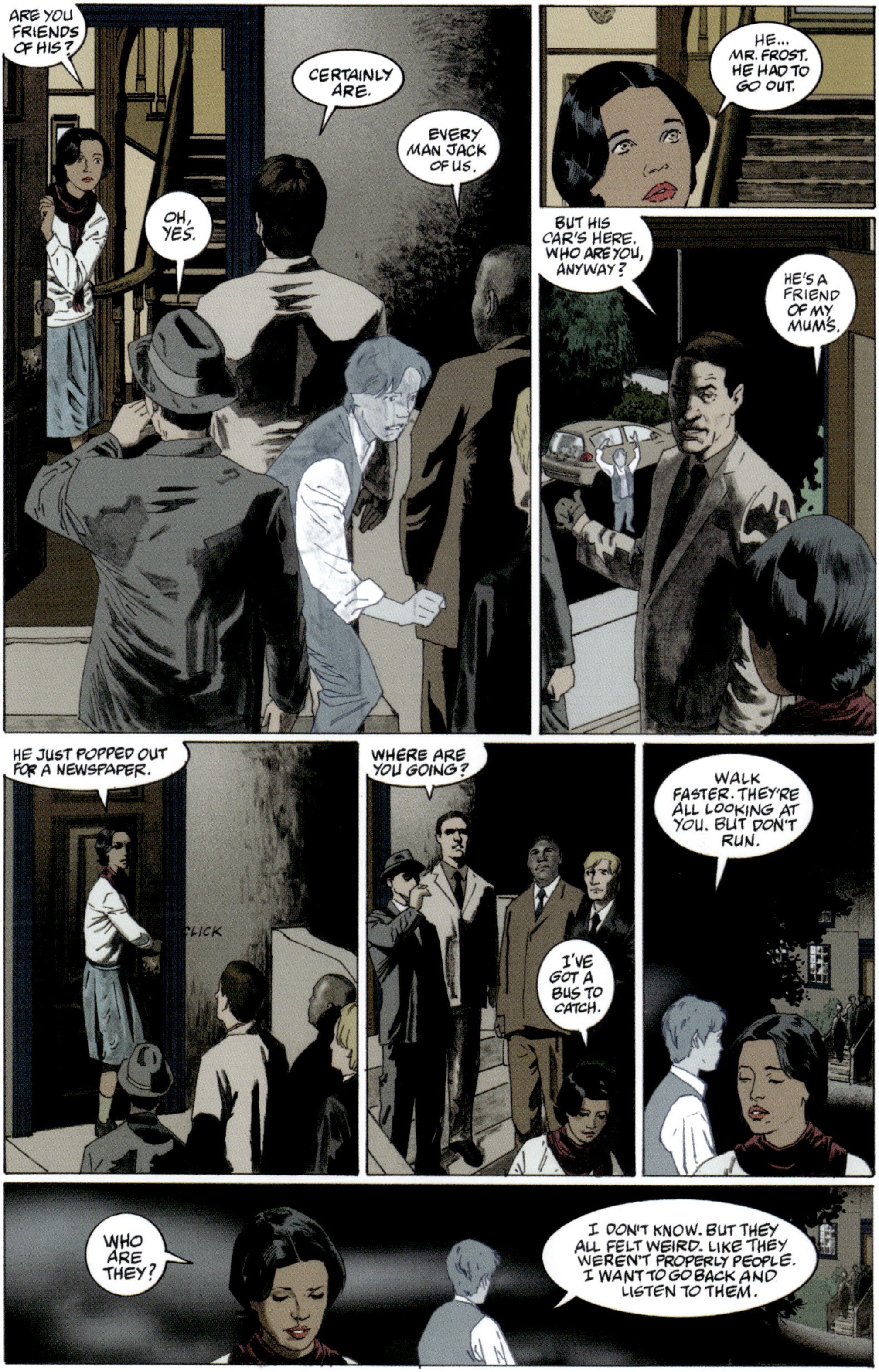
ARE YOU FRIENDS OF HIS?
CERTAINLY ARE.
EVERY MAN JACK OF US.
OH, YES.
HE... MR. FROST. HE HAD TO GO OUT.
BUT HIS CAR'S HERE. WHO ARE YOU, ANYWAY?
HE'S A FRIEND OF MY MUM'S.
HE JUST POPPED OUT FOR A NEWSPAPER.
CLICK
WHERE ARE YOU GOING?
I'VE GOT A BUS TO CATCH.
WALK FASTER. THEY'RE ALL LOOKING AT YOU. BUT DON'T RUN.
WHO ARE THEY?
I DON'T KNOW. BUT THEY ALL FELT WEIRD. LIKE THEY WEREN'T PROPERLY PEOPLE. I WANT TO GO BACK AND LISTEN TO THEM.

OF COURSE THEY'RE PEOPLE.
BOD?
I DON'T LIKE THIS.
YOU DON'T LIKE THIS, MR. TAR? NONE OF US LIKE IT. ALL WRONG. EVERYTHING'S GOING WRONG.
KRAKOW'S GONE. THEY AREN'T ANSWERING. AND AFTER MELBOURNE AND VANCOUVER...
FOR ALL WE KNOW, WE FOUR ARE ALL THAT'S LEFT.
I THINK... WE SHOULD GO AFTER HER.
QUIET.
KRAAK

I'M GOING IN. MR. TAR, YOU'RE WITH ME. NIMBLE AND KETCH, GET THAT GIRL. BRING HER BACK.
DEAD OR ALIVE?
ALIVE, YOU MORON. I WANT TO KNOW WHAT SHE KNOWS.
GET HER *NOW!*
MAYBE SHE'S ONE OF *THEM*, THE ONES WHO DONE FOR US IN VANCOUVER AND MEL-BOURNE AND...
FORCE IT.
IT'S REINFORCED. PROTECTED.
NOTHING ONE JACK CAN DO THAT ANOTHER CAN'T FIX.
GO.
NICELY DONE.

MR. DANDY!
HELLO, JACK FROST. I THOUGHT YOU HAD THE BOY.
I DID. HE GOT AWAY.
AGAIN?
ONCE IS A MISTAKE, JACK. TWICE IS A DISASTER.
WE'LL GET HIM.
THIS ENDS TONIGHT.
IT HAD BETTER.
IT WILL. THIS TIME, I KNOW EXACTLY WHERE HE'LL BE.
SNIFF

PAD-LOCKED!
BOD, THE GATES ARE CLOSED FOR THE NIGHT.
DO YOU KNOW WHERE THE KEY IS?
WE DON'T HAVE TIME. PUT YOUR ARMS AROUND ME.
WHAT?
JUST PUT YOUR ARMS AROUND ME AND CLOSE YOUR EYES.
OKAY.
I HOPE THAT MY FREEDOM OF THE GRAVEYARD MIGHT JUST POSSIBLY, JUST THIS TIME, COVER OTHER PEOPLE, TOO.

YOU CAN OPEN YOUR EYES.
HOW DID YOU DO THAT?
THIS IS MY HOME.
I CAN DO THINGS HERE.
HUL-LO.
COME ON OUT, GIRLIE. IT'S ALL RIGHT. NO ONE'S GOING TO HURT YOU.
WE JUST NEED YOU TO ANSWER SOME QUESTIONS.
WE'RE ON OFFICIAL BUSINESS.
RUN!

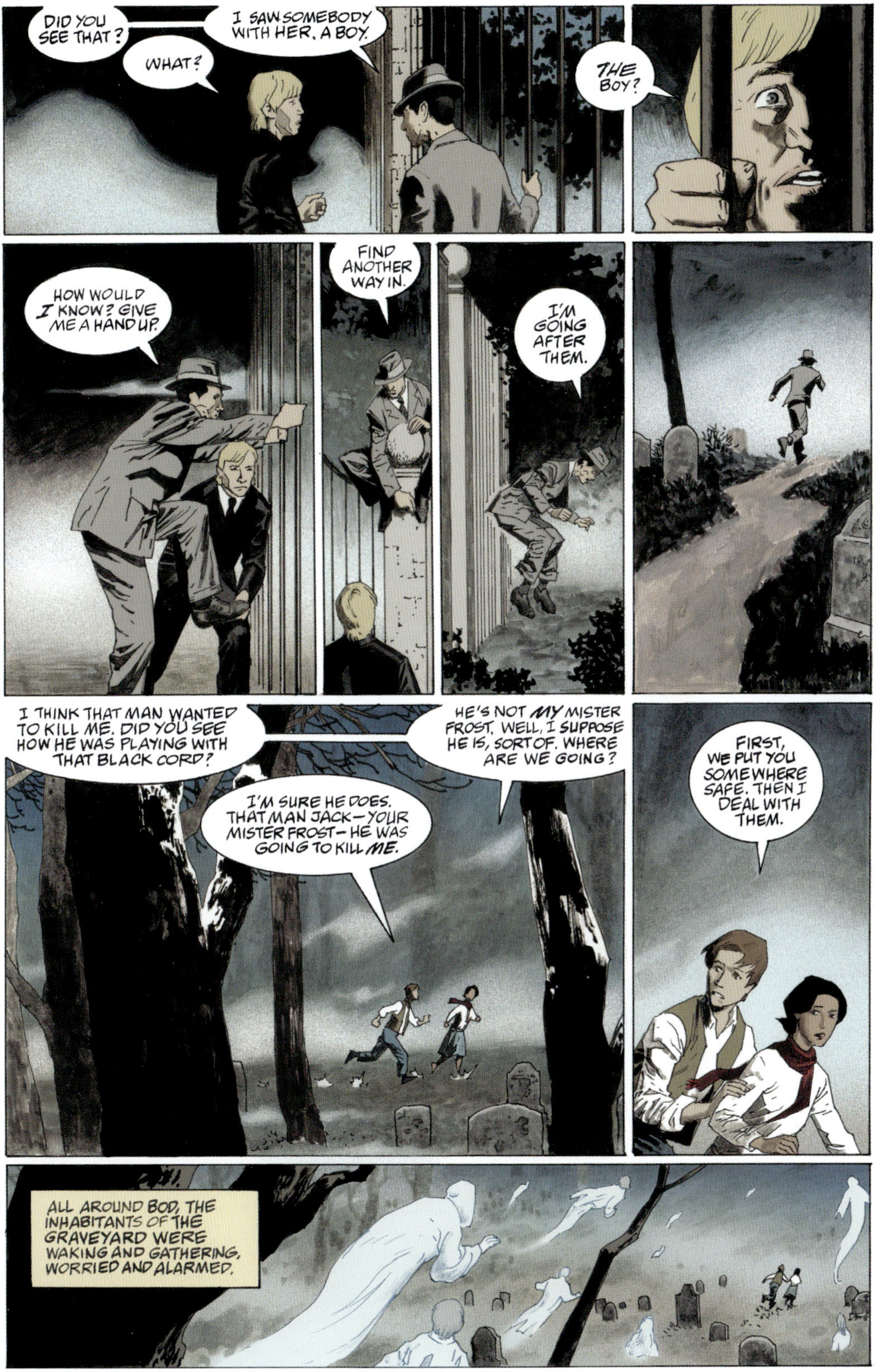
DID YOU SEE THAT?
I SAW SOMEBODY WITH HER. A BOY.
WHAT?
THE BOY?
HOW WOULD I KNOW? GIVE ME A HAND UP.
FIND ANOTHER WAY IN.
I'M GOING AFTER THEM.
I THINK THAT MAN WANTED TO KILL ME. DID YOU SEE HOW HE WAS PLAYING WITH THAT BLACK CORD?
I'M SURE HE DOES. THAT MAN JACK—YOUR MISTER FROST—HE WAS GOING TO KILL ME.
HE'S NOT MY MISTER FROST. WELL, I SUPPOSE HE IS, SORT OF. WHERE ARE WE GOING?
FIRST, WE PUT YOU SOMEWHERE SAFE. THEN I DEAL WITH THEM.
ALL AROUND BOD, THE INHABITANTS OF THE GRAVEYARD WERE WAKING AND GATHERING, WORRIED AND ALARMED.

BOD? WHAT IS HAPPENING?
BAD PEOPLE. CAN OUR LOT KEEP AN EYE ON THEM? WE HAVE TO HIDE SCARLETT. ANY IDEAS?
THE CHAPEL CRYPT?
FIRST PLACE THEY'LL LOOK.
WHO ARE YOU TALKING TO?
INSIDE THE HILL?
GOOD CALL.
SCARLETT, DO YOU REMEMBER THE PLACE WHERE WE FOUND THE INDIGO MAN?
KIND OF. A DARK PLACE. I REMEMBER THERE WASN'T ANYTHING TO BE SCARED OF.
I'M TAKING YOU UP THERE.
SCARLETT COULD TELL THAT BOD WAS TALKING TO PEOPLE AS HE WENT, BUT IT WAS LIKE HEARING SOMEONE TALK ON THE PHONE, WHICH REMINDED HER...
MY MUM'S GOING TO GO SPARE. I'M DEAD.
NO, YOU'RE NOT. NOT FOR A LONG TIME.
TWO OF THEM, NOW. TOGETHER? OKAY.
COME ON.

THE ENTRANCE IS BEHIND THE BOTTOM COFFIN ON THE LEFT. IF YOU HEAR ANYONE COMING AND IT'S NOT ME, GO STRAIGHT DOWN TO THE VERY BOTTOM... DO YOU HAVE ANYTHING TO MAKE LIGHT?
YEAH. A LITTLE LED THING ON MY KEY RING.
GOOD. AND BE CAREFUL. DON'T TRIP OR ANYTHING.
WHERE ARE YOU GOING?
THIS IS MY HOME. I'M GOING TO PROTECT IT.
I HOPE BOD KNOWS WHAT HE'S DOING.

WHERE ARE THEY NOW?
ONE FELLOW'S UP BY THE EGYPTIAN WALK, LOOKING FOR YOU. HIS FRIEND'S WAITING DOWN BY THE ALLEY WALL. THREE OTHERS ARE ON THEIR WAY OVER THE WALL.
I WISH SILAS WAS HERE. HE'D MAKE SHORT WORK OF THEM. OR MISS LUPESCU.
YOU DON'T NEED THEM.
WHERE'S MUM?
DOWN BY THE ALLEY WALL.
TELL HER I'VE HIDDEN SCARLETT IN THE BACK OF THE FROBISHER'S PLACE. ASK HER TO KEEP AN EYE ON HER IF ANYTHING HAPPENS TO ME.
BOD RAN THROUGH THE DARKENED GRAVEYARD, WHERE A LITTLE MAN WITH A BLACK SILK ROPE WAS LOOKING FOR HIM AND WANTED HIM DEAD.
I'M NOBODY OWENS.
I'M PART OF THE GRAVEYARD.
I'LL BE FINE.
HE NEARLY MISSED THE LITTLE MAN—THE JACK CALLED KETCH—AS HE HURRIED INTO THE EGYPTIAN WALK.
!

?

TINK

I'LL HAVE TO TIME THIS JUST RIGHT. TOO FAST AND THE MAN WILL LOSE ME. TOO SLOW AND I'LL FIND A BLACK SILK ROPE AROUND MY NECK.

BOD COULD FEEL THE GRAVEYARD ITSELF TRYING TO HIDE HIM, TO PROTECT HIM, TO MAKE HIM VANISH, AND HE FOUGHT IT, WORKED TO BE SEEN.

NEHEMIAH TROT!

HOLA, YOUNG BOD! I HEAR THAT EXCITEMENT IS THE MASTER OF THE HOUR, THAT YOU FLING YOURSELF THROUGH THESE DOMINIONS LIKE A COMET ACROSS THE FIRMAMENT.

WHAT'S THE GOOD WOR—

STAND THERE. JUST WHERE YOU ARE. LOOK BACK, THE WAY I CAME. TELL ME WHEN HE COMES CLOSE.

... 103 ...

BOD SKIRTED BY THE IVY-COVERED CARSTAIRS GRAVE, AND THEN HE STOOD, PANTING AS IF OUT OF BREATH, WITH HIS BACK TO HIS PURSUER.

AND HE WAITED.

HE COMES, LAD.

WOOP!

AAAAHHH

CRUNCH

... 104 ...

THAT'S ONE.
BLOODY 'ELL!
ELEGANTLY ACCOMPLISHED. I SHALL COMPOSE AN ODE. WOULD YOU LIKE TO STAY AND LISTEN?
NO TIME. WHERE ARE THE OTHER MEN?
THREE OF THEM ARE ON THE SOUTH-WESTERN PATH, HEADING UP THE HILL.
AND THERE'S ANOTHER WALKING AROUND THE CHAPEL. THE ONE WHO'S BEEN 'ROUND THE GRAVE-YARD THE PAST MONTH. BUT THERE'S SOMETHING DIFFERENT ABOUT HIM.
KEEP AN EYE ON THE MAN IN WITH MR. CARSTAIRS—AND PLEASE APOLOGIZE TO MR. CARSTAIRS FOR ME.
BOD LOPED AROUND THE HILL, ON THE PATH WHEN IT SUITED HIM, OFF THE PATHS WHEN THAT WAS QUICKER.
HE PASSED THE OLD APPLE TREE.
THERE'S FOUR OF THEM, STILL. FOUR OF THEM, AND ALL KILLERS. AND THE REST OF THEM WON'T FALL INTO OPEN GRAVES TO OBLIGE YOU.

HULLO, LIZA. I THOUGHT YOU WERE ANGRY WITH ME.
I MIGHT BE AND I MIGHTN'T. BUT I'M NOT GOING TO LET THEM CUT YOU UP, NOHOW.
THEN TRIP THEM FOR ME. CONFUSE THEM AND SLOW THEM DOWN. CAN YOU DO THAT?
WHILE YOU RUNS AWAY AGAIN? NOBODY OWENS, WHY DON'T YOU JUST FADE, AND HIDE IN YOUR MAM'S NICE TOMB, WHERE THEY'LL NEVER FIND YOU, AND SOON ENOUGH, SILAS WILL BE BACK TO TAKE CARE OF THEM.
MAYBE HE WILL AND MAYBE HE WON'T. I'LL MEET YOU BY THE LIGHTNING TREE.
I'M STILL NOT TALKING TO YOU.
ACTUALLY, YOU ARE, I MEAN, WE'RE TALKING RIGHT NOW.
ONLY DURING THIS EMERGENCY. AFTER THAT, NOT A WORD.
BOD MADE FOR THE LIGHTNING TREE.
IF ONLY I CAN REMEMBER MISS LUPESCU'S LESSONS.
YOU'VE NOT FADED. ANYONE COULD FIND YOU.
GOOD. I WANT THEM TO FIND ME.

MORE KNOW JACK FOOL THAN JACK FOOL KNOWS.
I CAN SEE HIM!
I FEEL LIKE BAIT IN A TRAP.
IT'S NOT A GOOD FEELING.
AH, THE ELUSIVE DORIAN BOY, I PRESUME. ASTONISHING. THERE'S OUR JACK FROST HUNTING THE WHOLE WORLD OVER, AND HERE YOU ARE, JUST WHERE HE LEFT YOU, THIRTEEN YEARS AGO.
THAT MAN KILLED MY FAMILY.
INDEED.
WHY?
DOES IT MATTER? YOU'RE NEVER GOING TO TELL ANYONE.
THEN IT'S NO SKIN OFF YOUR NOSE TO TELL ME, IS IT?
HAH! FUNNY BOY. WHAT I WANT TO KNOW IS, HOW HAVE YOU LIVED IN A GRAVEYARD FOR THIRTEEN YEARS WITHOUT ANYONE CATCHING WISE?
I'LL ANSWER YOUR QUESTION IF YOU ANSWER MINE.
YOU DON'T TALK TO MR. DANDY LIKE THAT, LITTLE SNOT!
HUSH, JACK TAR. ALL RIGHT. AN ANSWER FOR AN ANSWER.

WE—MY FRIENDS AND I—ARE MEMBERS OF A FRATERNAL ORGANIZATION KNOWN AS THE JACKS OF ALL TRADES, OR THE KNAVES, OR BY OTHER NAMES. WE GO BACK AN EXTREMELY LONG WAY. WE KNOW... WE REMEMBER THINGS THAT MOST PEOPLE HAVE FORGOTTEN.
THE OLD KNOWLEDGE.
MAGIC.
YOU KNOW A LITTLE MAGIC.
IF YOU WANT TO CALL IT THAT. BUT IT IS A VERY SPECIFIC SORT OF MAGIC. THERE'S A MAGIC YOU TAKE FROM DEATH. SOMETHING LEAVES THE WORLD, SOMETHING ELSE COMES INTO IT.
YOU KILLED MY FAMILY FOR—FOR WHAT? FOR MAGIC POWERS? THAT'S RIDICULOUS.
NO. WE KILLED YOU FOR PROTECTION.
"LONG TIME AGO, ONE OF OUR PEOPLE—THIS WAS BACK IN EGYPT, IN PYRAMID DAYS—HE FORESAW THAT ONE DAY, THERE WOULD BE A CHILD BORN WHO WOULD WALK THE BORDERLAND BETWEEN THE LIVING AND THE DEAD. THAT IF THIS CHILD GREW TO ADULTHOOD IT WOULD MEAN THE END OF OUR ORDER AND ALL WE STAND FOR.
"WE HAD PEOPLE CASTING NATIVITIES BEFORE LONDON WAS A VILLAGE, WE HAD YOUR FAMILY IN OUR SIGHTS BEFORE NEW AMSTERDAM BECAME NEW YORK.
"AND WE SENT WHAT WE THOUGHT WAS THE BEST AND THE SHARPEST AND THE MOST DANGEROUS OF ALL THE JACKS TO DEAL WITH YOU. TO DO IT PROPERLY, SO WE COULD TAKE ALL THE BAD JUJU AND MAKE IT WORK FOR US INSTEAD, AND KEEP EVERYTHING TICKETY-BOO FOR ANOTHER FIVE THOUSAND YEARS.
"ONLY HE DIDN'T."

SO WHERE IS HE? WHY ISN'T HE HERE?
WE CAN TAKE CARE OF YOU. HE'S GOT A GOOD NOSE ON HIM, HAS OUR JACK FROST. HE'S ON THE TRAIL OF YOUR LITTLE GIRLFRIEND. CAN'T LEAVE ANY WITNESSES. NOT TO SOMETHING LIKE THIS.
SO...
...COME AND GET ME.
I'LL SPLIT YOUR SKULL, BOY!
SKAGH! THEGH! KHAVAGAH!
HE OPENED THE GHOUL-GATE.

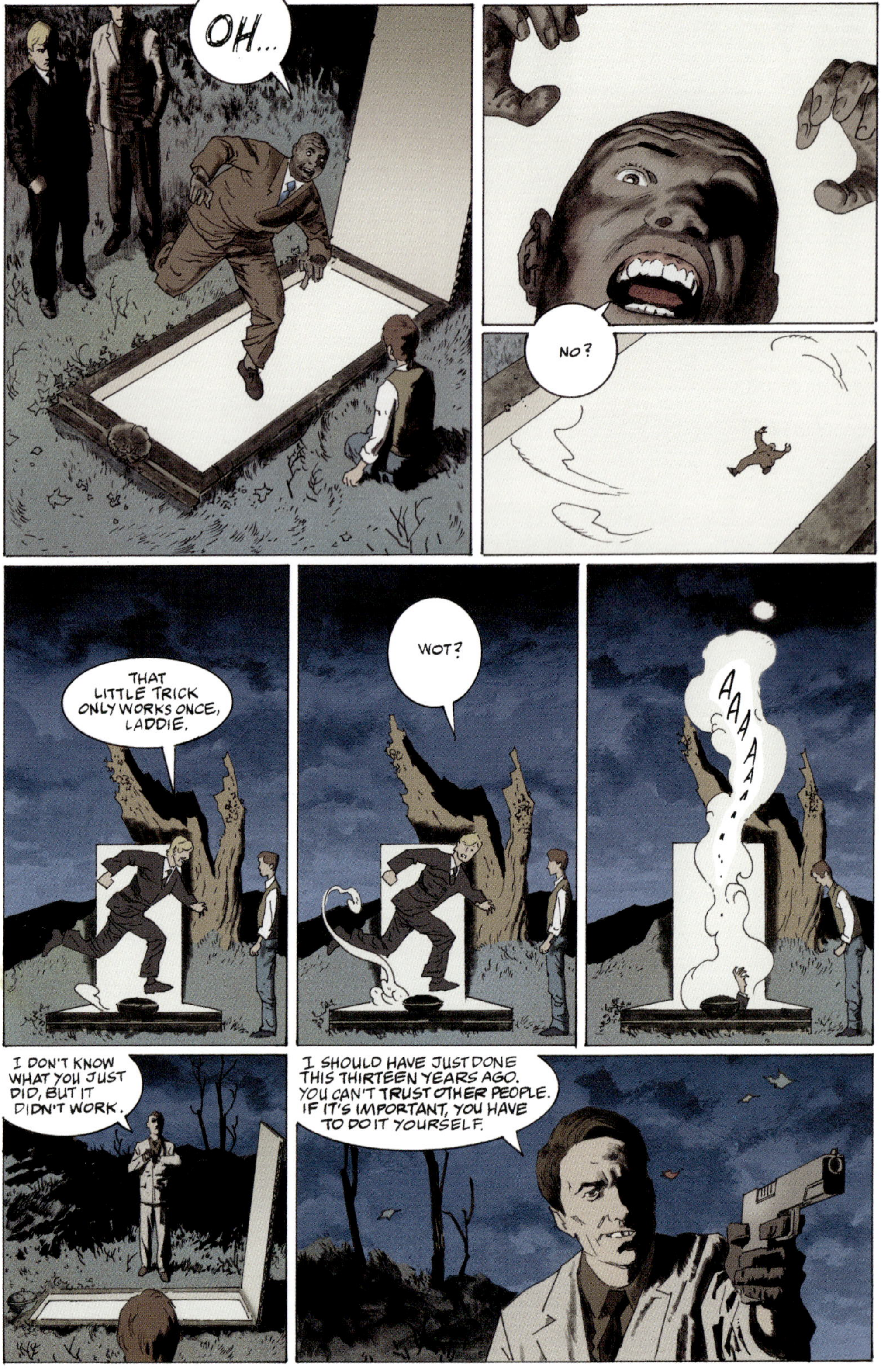
OH...
NO?
THAT LITTLE TRICK ONLY WORKS ONCE, LADDIE.
WOT?
AAAAA...
I DON'T KNOW WHAT YOU JUST DID, BUT IT DIDN'T WORK.
I SHOULD HAVE JUST DONE THIS THIRTEEN YEARS AGO. YOU CAN'T TRUST OTHER PEOPLE. IF IT'S IMPORTANT, YOU HAVE TO DO IT YOURSELF.

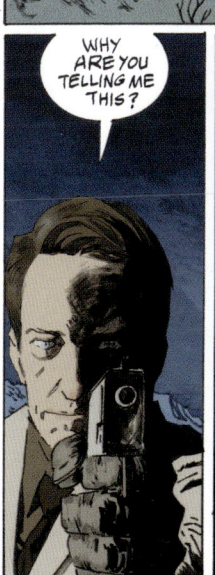

"THERE'S A DESERT DOWN THERE. IF YOU LOOK FOR WATER, YOU SHOULD FIND SOME. THERE'S THINGS TO EAT IF YOU LOOK HARD, BUT DON'T ANTAGONIZE THE NIGHT-GAUNTS."

"AVOID GHÜLHEIM."

"THE GHOULS MIGHT WIPE YOUR MEMORIES AND MAKE YOU INTO ONE OF THEM, OR THEY MIGHT WAIT UNTIL YOU'VE ROTTED DOWN, AND THEN EAT YOU."

"EITHER WAY, YOU CAN DO BETTER."

"WHY ARE YOU TELLING ME THIS?"

"BECAUSE OF *THEM*."

"THERE'S NOBOD..."

"WHERE ARE YOU? THE DEUCE TAKE YOU! *WHERE ARE YOU?*"

"GHOUL-GATES ARE MADE TO BE OPEN AND THEN CLOSED AGAIN."

"YOU CAN'T LEAVE THEM OPEN. THEY WANT TO CLOSE."

THE LIP OF THE HOLE SHUDDERED AND SHOOK. MR. DANDY HAD BEEN IN AN EARTHQUAKE ONCE, IN BANGLADESH. IT FELT LIKE THAT: THE EARTH JUDDERED...
...AND MISTER DANDY FELL.
I'M GOING TO LET THE GATE CLOSE NOW.
I THINK IF YOU KEEP HOLDING ON, IT MIGHT CLOSE ON YOU AND CRUSH YOU, OR IT MIGHT ABSORB YOU AND MAKE YOU INTO A PART OF THE GATE. DON'T KNOW. BUT I'M GIVING YOU A CHANCE, MORE THAN YOU EVER GAVE MY FAMILY.
YOU CAN'T EVER ESCAPE US. WE'RE THE JACKS OF ALL TRADES. WE'RE EVERYWHERE. IT'S NOT OVER.
IT IS FOR YOU.

THE END OF YOUR PEOPLE AND ALL YOU STAND FOR. LIKE YOUR MAN IN EGYPT PREDICTED. YOU DIDN'T KILL ME. YOU WERE EVERYWHERE.
NOW IT'S ALL OVER.
THAT'S WHAT SILAS IS DOING, ISN'T IT? THAT'S WHERE HE IS.
WEGH KHÂRADOS.

BOD!
THE MAN BY THE CHAPEL! HE'S GOING UP THE HILL.
SNIFF
CAN'T FIND THE BOY BY SCENT, NOT HERE. HE SMELLS LIKE THE GRAVEYARD.
BUT THE GIRL SMELLS LIKE HER MOTHER'S HOUSE.
LIKE THE DAB OF PERFUME SHE PUT ON THIS MORNING.
SHE SMELLS LIKE A VICTIM. LIKE FEAR-SWEAT.
LIKE MY QUARRY.
WHEREVER SHE IS, THE BOY WILL BE TOO—SOONER OR LATER.
HE WAS ALMOST AT THE TOP OF THE HILL WHEN IT OCCURRED TO HIM — A HUNCH HE KNEW WAS A TRUTH...
JACK DANDY AND THE REST OF THEM ARE GONE.
GOOD.
THERE'S ALWAYS ROOM AT THE TOP.

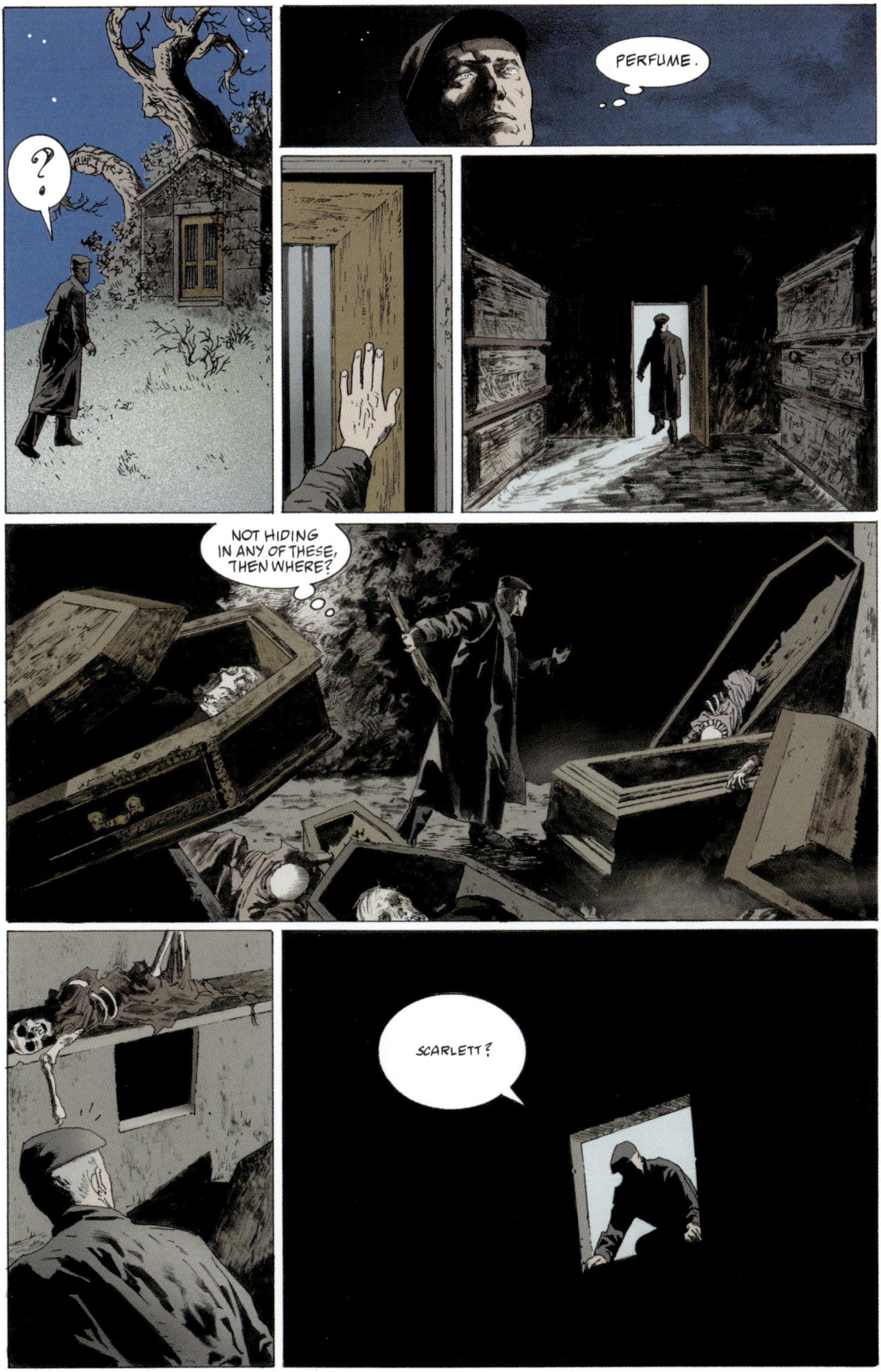
?
PERFUME.
NOT HIDING IN ANY OF THESE, THEN WHERE?
SCARLETT?

WHEN SCARLETT HEARD THE CRASHING NOISE FROM ABOVE, SHE MADE HER WAY CAREFULLY DOWN THE STEPS.
SHE MADE IT TO THE BOTTOM OF THE STONE STEPS. SHE WAS SCARED: SCARED OF NICE MR. FROST AND HIS SCARIER FRIENDS; SCARED OF THIS ROOM AND ITS MEMORIES; EVEN, IF SHE WERE HONEST, A LITTLE AFRAID OF BOD. HE WAS NO LONGER A QUIET BOY WITH A MYSTERY....
HE'S SOMETHING DIFFERENT NOW, SOMETHING NOT QUITE HUMAN.
I WONDER WHAT MUM'S THINKING RIGHT NOW?
SHE'LL BE PHONING MR. FROST'S HOUSE OVER AND OVER TO FIND OUT WHEN I'M GOING TO GET BACK.
IF I GET OUT OF THIS ALIVE, I'M GOING TO FORCE HER TO GET ME A PHONE. IT'S RIDICULOUS. I'M THE ONLY PERSON IN MY YEAR WHO DOESN'T HAVE HER OWN PHONE, PRACTICALLY.
I MISS MY MUM.
SHE HAD NOT THOUGHT ANYONE HUMAN COULD MOVE THAT SILENTLY THROUGH THE DARK...
DO ANYTHING CLEVER—DO ANYTHING AT ALL—AND I WILL CUT YOUR THROAT. DO YOU UNDERSTAND?
MM-HMM.

BOD SAW THE CHAOS ON THE FLOOR OF THE FROBISHER MAUSOLEUM. THERE WERE MANY FROBISHERS AND FROBYSHERS, AND SEVERAL PETTYFERS, ALL IN VARIOUS STATES OF UPSET AND CONFUSION.

HE IS ALREADY DOWN THERE.

THANK YOU.

BOD SAW AS THE DEAD SEE. AND WHEN HE GOT HALFWAY DOWN, HE SAW THE MAN JACK.

BOD CONCENTRATED ON HIS FADE...

EYES WILL NOT SEE ME.

...TOOK ANOTHER STEP.

HELLO, BOY.

YOU THINK I CAN'T SEE YOU. AND YOU'RE RIGHT. I CAN'T. NOT REALLY.

BUT I CAN SMELL YOUR FEAR. AND NOW THAT I KNOW ABOUT YOUR CLEVER VANISHING TRICK, I CAN *FEEL* YOU.

SAY SOMETHING NOW. SAY IT SO I CAN HEAR IT, OR I START TO CUT LITTLE PIECES OUT OF THE YOUNG LADY.

DO YOU UNDERSTAND ME?

YES, I UNDERSTAND.
GOOD.
BOD CONCENTRATED ON THE FEAR, ON RAISING THE LEVEL OF PANIC IN THE ROOM, OF MAKING THE TERROR, SOMETHING TANGIBLE.
STOP THAT! WHATEVER IT IS YOU'RE DOING. DON'T DO IT.
BOD LET IT GO.
YOU THINK THAT YOU CAN DO YOUR LITTLE MAGICS ON ME? DO YOU KNOW WHAT I AM, BOY?
YES.
YOU'RE A JACK.
YOU KILLED MY FAMILY.
AND YOU SHOULD HAVE KILLED ME.
I SHOULD HAVE KILLED YOU?
OH, YES. MR. DANDY SAID THAT IF YOU LET ME GROW TO ADULTHOOD YOUR ORDER WOULD BE DESTROYED.
I DID.
YOU FAILED AND YOU LOST.

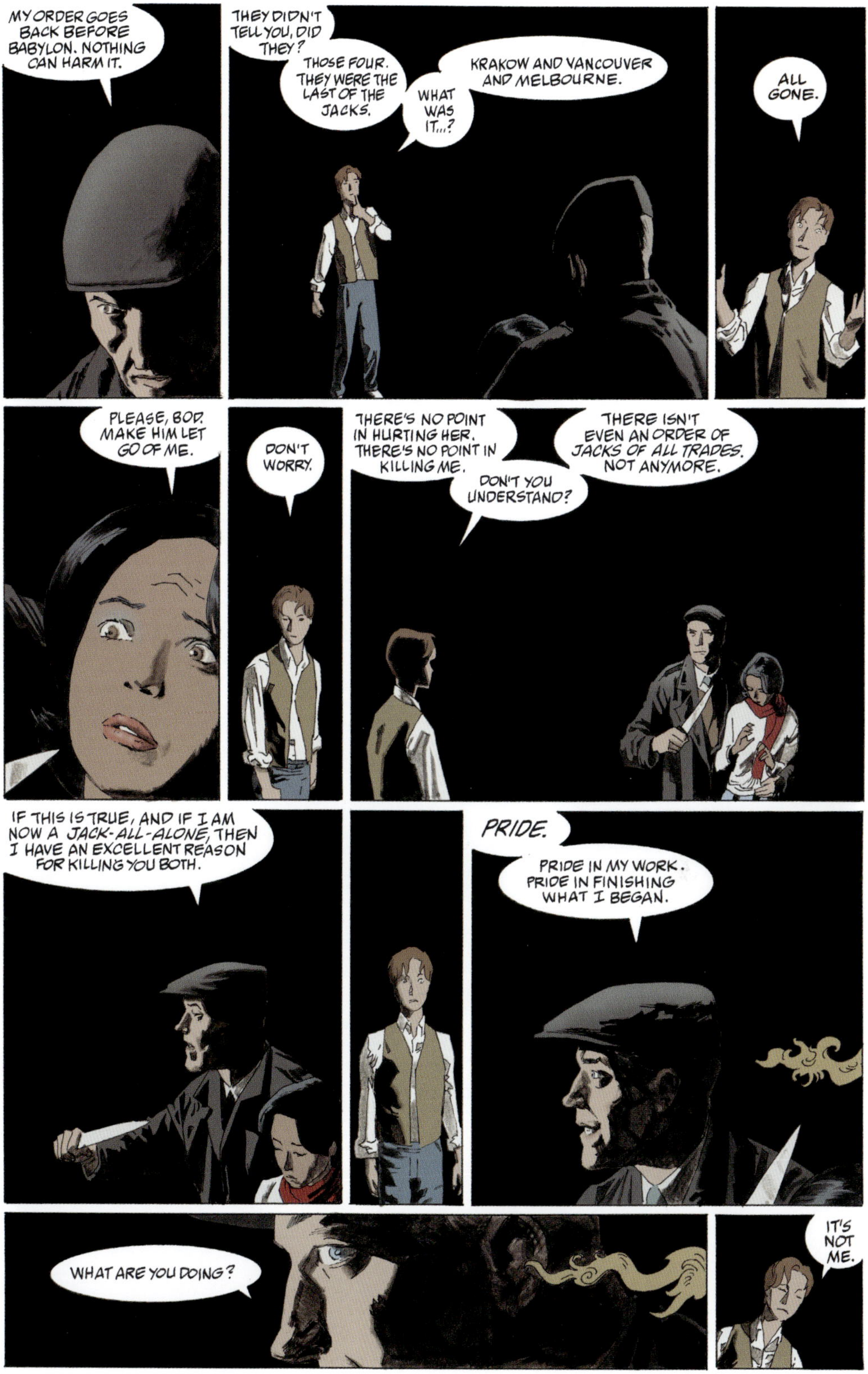
MY ORDER GOES BACK BEFORE BABYLON. NOTHING CAN HARM IT.
THEY DIDN'T TELL YOU, DID THEY?
THOSE FOUR. THEY WERE THE LAST OF THE JACKS.
WHAT WAS IT...?
KRAKOW AND VANCOUVER AND MELBOURNE.
ALL GONE.
PLEASE, BOD. MAKE HIM LET GO OF ME.
DON'T WORRY.
THERE'S NO POINT IN HURTING HER. THERE'S NO POINT IN KILLING ME.
DON'T YOU UNDERSTAND?
THERE ISN'T EVEN AN ORDER OF JACKS OF ALL TRADES. NOT ANYMORE.
IF THIS IS TRUE, AND IF I AM NOW A JACK-ALL-ALONE, THEN I HAVE AN EXCELLENT REASON FOR KILLING YOU BOTH.
PRIDE.
PRIDE IN MY WORK. PRIDE IN FINISHING WHAT I BEGAN.
WHAT ARE YOU DOING?
IT'S NOT ME.

IT'S THE SLEER. IT GUARDS THE TREASURE THAT'S BURIED HERE.
DON'T LIE!
HE'S NOT LYING. IT'S TRUE.
TRUE? BURIED TREASURE? DON'T MAKE ME—
THE SLEER GUARDS THE TREASURE FOR THE MASTER.
WHO SAID THAT?
YOU HEARD IT?
I HEARD IT. YES.
I DIDN'T HEAR ANYTHING.

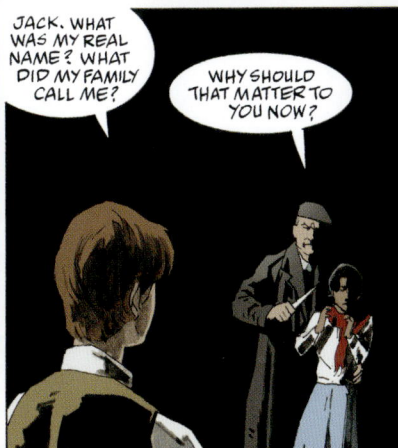

WHAT IS THIS PLACE, BOY? WHERE ARE WE?

This is the place of the treasure. This is the place of power. This is where the Sleer guards and waits for its master to return.

JACK?

IT'S GOOD TO HEAR MY NAME IN YOUR MOUTH, BOY. IF YOU'D USED IT BEFORE, I COULD HAVE FOUND YOU SOONER.

JACK. WHAT WAS MY REAL NAME? WHAT DID MY FAMILY CALL ME?

WHY SHOULD THAT MATTER TO YOU NOW?

THE SLEER TOLD ME TO FIND MY NAME. WHAT WAS IT?

LET ME SEE. WAS IT PETER? OR PAUL? OR RODERICK— YOU *LOOK* LIKE A RODERICK. MAYBE YOU WERE A STEPHEN.

... 121 ...

"YOU MIGHT AS WELL TELL ME. YOU'RE GOING TO KILL ME ANYWAY."

"OBVIOUSLY."

"I WANT YOU TO LET THE GIRL GO."

"LET SCARLETT GO."

"THAT'S AN ALTAR STONE, ISN'T IT?"

"I SUPPOSE SO."

"AND A KNIFE? AND A CUP? AND A BROOCH?"

"YES."

"HA!"

"SO THE BROTHERHOOD IS OVER AND THE CONVOCATION IS AT AN END. AND, YET, IF THERE ARE NO MORE *JACKS OF ALL TRADES* BUT ME, WHAT DOES IT MATTER? THERE CAN BE A NEW BROTHERHOOD, MORE *POWERFUL* THAN THE LAST."

POWER.

BOD COULD FEEL THE SLEER LISTENING TO JACK'S WORDS, COULD FEEL A LOW SUSURRUS OF EXCITEMENT BUILDING IN THE CHAMBER.

THIS IS *PERFECT.*

LOOK AT US. WE ARE IN A PLACE FOR WHICH MY PEOPLE HAVE HUNTED FOR THOUSANDS OF YEARS, WITH EVERYTHING NECESSARY FOR THE CEREMONY WAITING FOR US.

IT MAKES YOU BELIEVE IN PROVIDENCE, DOESN'T IT?

I AM GOING TO PUT OUT MY HAND, BOY. SCARLETT, MY KNIFE IS STILL AT YOUR THROAT— DO NOT TRY TO RUN WHEN I LET GO OF YOU.

BOY, YOU WILL PLACE THE CUP, THE KNIFE, AND THE BROOCH IN MY HAND.

THE TREASURE OF THE SLEER. IT COMES BACK. IT ALWAYS COMES BACK.

SCARLETT, I AM GOING TO RELEASE YOU. WHEN I TAKE THE KNIFE AWAY, I WANT YOU TO LIE, FACEDOWN, ON THE GROUND, WITH YOUR HANDS BEHIND YOUR HEAD. MOVE OR TRY ANYTHING, AND I WILL KILL YOU, PAINFULLY.
DO YOU UNDERSTAND?
YES.
AH!
OW.
WE ARE DEAD.
SCARLETT FELT AS IF SHE WERE WATCHING SOMETHING HAPPENING TO OTHER PEOPLE, A SURREAL DRAMA THAT HAD TURNED INTO A GAME OF MURDER IN THE DARK.
AMAZING.

TEN THOUSAND YEARS, AND THE KNIFE IS STILL SHARP.
COME HERE, BOY.
LET HER GO.
IF YOU DO EVERYTHING I SAY, I WON'T KILL HER. I WON'T EVEN HURT HER.
I DON'T BELIEVE YOU. SHE CAN IDENTIFY YOU.
NO. SHE CAN'T.
BOY, GO AND KNEEL BY THAT ALTAR STONE.
NOW!
IT HAS BEEN SO LONG.
YOU WANT TO KNOW YOUR NAME, BOY, BEFORE I SPILL YOUR BLOOD ON THE STONE?

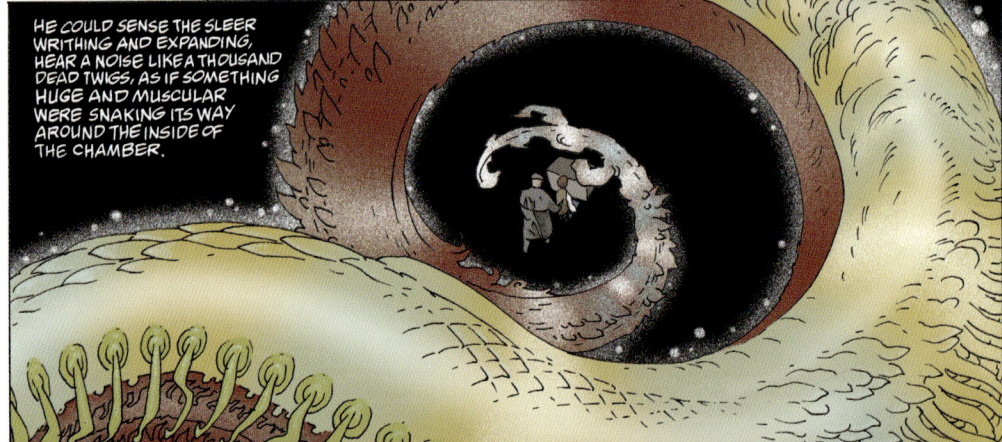

BOD FELT THE COLD OF THE KNIFE AT THE BACK OF HIS NECK, AND IN THAT MOMENT, BOD UNDERSTOOD.

EVERYTHING SLOWED. EVERYTHING CAME INTO FOCUS.

I KNOW MY NAME.

I'M NOBODY OWENS. THAT'S WHO I AM.

SLEER.

DO YOU STILL WANT A MASTER?

WELL, HAVEN'T YOU FINALLY FOUND THE MASTER YOU'VE BEEN LOOKING FOR?

THE SLEER GUARDS THE TREASURE UNTIL THE MASTER RETURNS.

HE COULD SENSE THE SLEER WRITHING AND EXPANDING, HEAR A NOISE LIKE A THOUSAND DEAD TWIGS, AS IF SOMETHING HUGE AND MUSCULAR WERE SNAKING ITS WAY AROUND THE INSIDE OF THE CHAMBER.

AND THEN, FOR THE FIRST TIME, BOD SAW THE SLEER.

AFTERWARDS, HE WAS NEVER ABLE TO DESCRIBE WHAT HE HAD SEEN.

THE FACES OF THE SLEER NUZZLED THE AIR ABOUT JACK TENTATIVELY, AS IF THEY WANTED TO STROKE OR CARESS HIM.
WHAT'S HAPPENING? WHAT IS IT? WHAT DOES IT DO?
IT'S CALLED THE SLEER. IT GUARDS THE PLACE. IT NEEDS A MASTER TO TELL IT WHAT TO DO.
BEAUTIFUL.
OF COURSE. IT'S BEEN WAITING FOR ME. AND YES. OBVIOUSLY, I AM ITS NEW MASTER!
MASTER?
MASTER.

THIRTEEN YEARS AGO I MISSED YOU, AND NOW WE ARE REUNITED. THE END OF ONE ORDER, THE BEGINNING OF ANOTHER. GOOD-BYE, BOY.
BOD.
NOT BOY.
BOD.
SLEER.
WHAT WILL YOU DO WITH YOUR NEW MASTER?
WE WILL PROTECT HIM UNTIL THE END OF TIME. THE SLEER WILL HOLD HIM IN ITS COILS FOREVER AND NEVER LET HIM ENDURE THE DANGERS OF THE WORLD.
THEN PROTECT HIM. NOW.
I AM YOUR MASTER. YOU WILL OBEY ME.
THE SLEER BEGAN TO WRAP ITS HUGE, LAZY COILS AROUND THE MAN JACK.
THE SLEER HAS WAITED SO LONG.
SO LONG A TIME.
I CAN'T SEE. WHAT IS IT DOING?

"GET BACK! KEEP AWAY FROM ME! DON'T GET ANY CLOSER!"

"SCARLETT."

"I WANT TO SEE. I WANT TO SEE WHAT'S HAPPENING."

WHAT SCARLETT SAW WAS NOT WHAT BOD SAW. SHE DID NOT SEE THE SLEER, AND THAT WAS A MERCY. SHE SAW THE MAN JACK, THOUGH.

HE WAS FLOATING IN THE AIR, FIVE, THEN TEN FEET ABOVE THE GROUND, SLASHING WILDLY AT THE AIR WITH TWO KNIVES, TRYING TO STAB SOMETHING SHE COULD NOT SEE, IN A DISPLAY THAT WAS OBVIOUSLY HAVING NO EFFECT.

SHE SAW THE FEAR ON HIS FACE, WHICH MADE HIM LOOK LIKE MR. FROST HAD ONCE LOOKED. IN HIS TERROR HE WAS ONCE MORE THE NICE MAN WHO HAD DRIVEN HER HOME.

MR. FROST, THE MAN JACK, WHOEVER HE WAS, WAS FORCED AWAY FROM THEM...

...UNTIL HE WAS SPREAD-EAGLED AGAINST THE SIDE OF THE CHAMBER WALL.

IT SEEMED TO SCARLETT THAT MR. FROST WAS BEING FORCED THROUGH THE WALL, PULLED INTO THE ROCK, WAS BEING SWALLOWED UP BY IT.

CALL IT OFF!
CALL IT OFF!
CALL IT OFF!

PLEASE.

PLEASE.

PL...

I THOUGHT YOU SAID THE SLEER COULDN'T HURT PEOPLE. I THOUGHT ALL IT COULD DO WAS FRIGHTEN US.
YES. BUT IT WANTED A MASTER TO PROTECT. IT TOLD ME SO.
YOU MEAN YOU KNEW. YOU *KNEW* THAT WOULD HAPPEN.
YES. I HOPED IT WOULD.
I'LL NEED TO CLEAN THIS ALL UP.
YOU *KNEW* THAT WOULD HAPPEN.
THIS TIME, BOD SAID NOTHING.
SO YOU KNEW THAT THE SLEER WOULD TAKE HIM.
WAS *THAT* WHY YOU HID ME DOWN THERE?
WAS IT?
WHAT WAS *I*, THEN, *BAIT*?
IT WASN'T LIKE THAT. WE'RE STILL ALIVE, AREN'T WE?
AND HE WON'T TROUBLE US ANY LONGER.

AND WHAT ABOUT THOSE OTHER MEN? DID YOU KILL THEM, TOO?
I DIDN'T KILL ANYONE.
THEN WHERE ARE THEY?
ONE OF THEM'S AT THE BOTTOM OF A DEEP GRAVE. THE OTHER THREE ARE...WELL, THEY'RE A LONG WAY AWAY.
YOU DIDN'T KILL THEM?
OF COURSE NOT.
THIS IS MY HOME. WHY WOULD I WANT THEM HANGING AROUND HERE FOR THE REST OF TIME?
LOOK, IT'S OKAY. I DEALT WITH THEM.
YOU AREN'T A PERSON. PEOPLE DON'T BEHAVE LIKE YOU. YOU'RE AS BAD AS HE WAS. YOU'RE A MONSTER.
NO. IT WASN'T LIKE THAT.
I'M AFRAID YOU DO BOD AN INJUSTICE.

BUT YOU WILL UNDOUBTEDLY BE HAPPIER IF YOU REMEMBER NONE OF THIS.
SO LET US WALK TOGETHER, YOU AND I, AND DISCUSS WHAT HAS HAPPENED TO YOU OVER THE LAST FEW DAYS, AND WHAT IT MIGHT BE WISE FOR YOU TO REMEMBER, AND WHAT IT MIGHT BE BETTER FOR YOU TO FORGET.
SILAS, YOU CAN'T. YOU CAN'T MAKE HER FORGET ME.
IT WILL BE SAFEST THAT WAY. FOR HER, IF NOT FOR ALL OF US.
DON'T— DON'T I GET A SAY IN THIS?
LOOK, IT'S OVER. I KNOW IT WAS HARD.
BUT. WE DID IT.
YOU AND ME.
WE BEAT THEM.

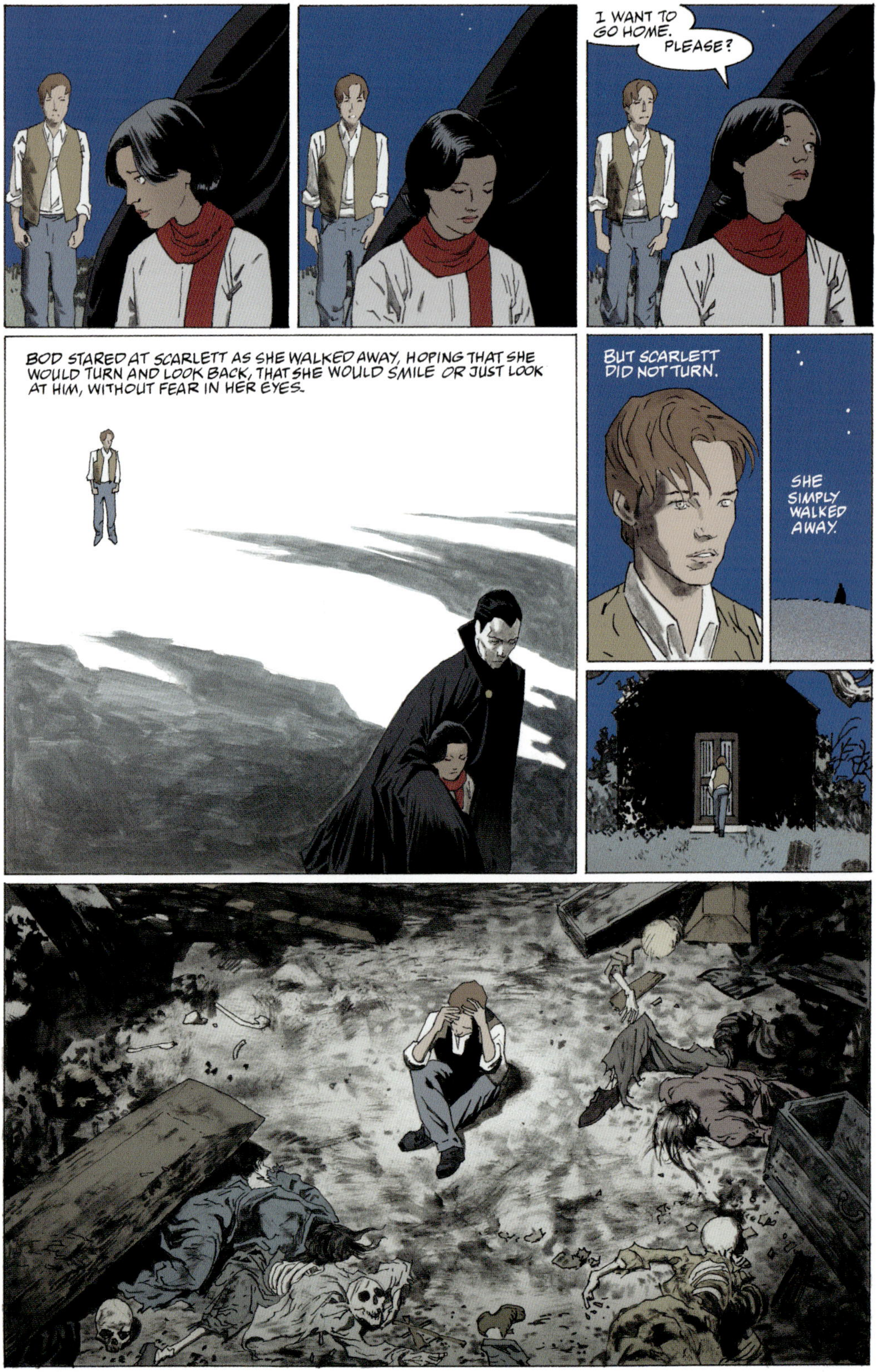
I WANT TO GO HOME. PLEASE?
BOD STARED AT SCARLETT AS SHE WALKED AWAY, HOPING THAT SHE WOULD TURN AND LOOK BACK, THAT SHE WOULD SMILE OR JUST LOOK AT HIM, WITHOUT FEAR IN HER EYES.
BUT SCARLETT DID NOT TURN.
SHE SIMPLY WALKED AWAY.

A MAN BROUGHT SCARLETT HOME.

LATER, SCARLETT'S MOTHER COULD NOT REMEMBER QUITE WHAT HE HAD TOLD HER, ALTHOUGH, DISAPPOINTINGLY, SHE HAD LEARNED...

"OH, THAT *NICE* JAY FROST."

"UNAVOIDABLY FORCED TO LEAVE TOWN."

THE MAN TALKED WITH THEM, IN THE KITCHEN, ABOUT THEIR LIVES AND DREAMS, AND BY THE END OF THEIR CONVERSATION, SCARLETT'S MOTHER HAD SOMEHOW *DECIDED* THEY WOULD BE RETURNING TO GLASGOW.

SCARLETT WOULD BE HAPPY TO BE NEAR HER FATHER, AND TO SEE HER OLD FRIENDS AGAIN.

NOONA EVEN PROMISED TO BUY SCARLETT A PHONE OF HER OWN.

SILAS LEFT THE GIRL AND HER MOTHER IN THE KITCHEN.

THEY BARELY REMEMBERED THAT SILAS HAD EVER BEEN THERE...

...WHICH WAS THE WAY HE LIKED IT.

... 135 ...

SILAS RETURNED TO THE GRAVEYARD AND FOUND BOD SITTING BY THE OBELISK, HIS FACE SET.
HOW IS SHE?
I TOOK HER MEMORIES. THEY WILL RETURN TO GLASGOW. SHE HAS FRIENDS THERE.
HOW COULD YOU MAKE HER FORGET ME?
PEOPLE WANT TO FORGET THE IMPOSSIBLE. IT MAKES THEIR WORLD SAFER.
I LIKED HER.
I'M SORRY.

"THE MEN... THEY SPOKE ABOUT TROUBLE THEY WERE HAVING IN KRAKOW AND MELBOURNE AND VANCOUVER. THAT WAS YOU, WASN'T IT?"

"I WAS NOT ALONE."

"MISS LUPESCU?"

"IS SHE ALL RIGHT?"

"SHE FOUGHT BRAVELY. SHE FOUGHT FOR YOU, BOD."

"THE SLEER HAS THE MAN JACK. THREE OF THE OTHERS WENT THROUGH THE GHOUL-GATE. THERE'S ONE INJURED BUT STILL ALIVE AT THE BOTTOM OF THE CARSTAIRS GRAVE."

"HE IS THE LAST OF THE JACKS. I WILL NEED TO TALK TO HIM, THEN, BEFORE SUNRISE."

"SHE WAS SCARED OF ME."

"YES."

"BUT WHY? I SAVED HER LIFE. I'M NOT A BAD PERSON. AND I'M JUST LIKE HER. I'M ALIVE, TOO."

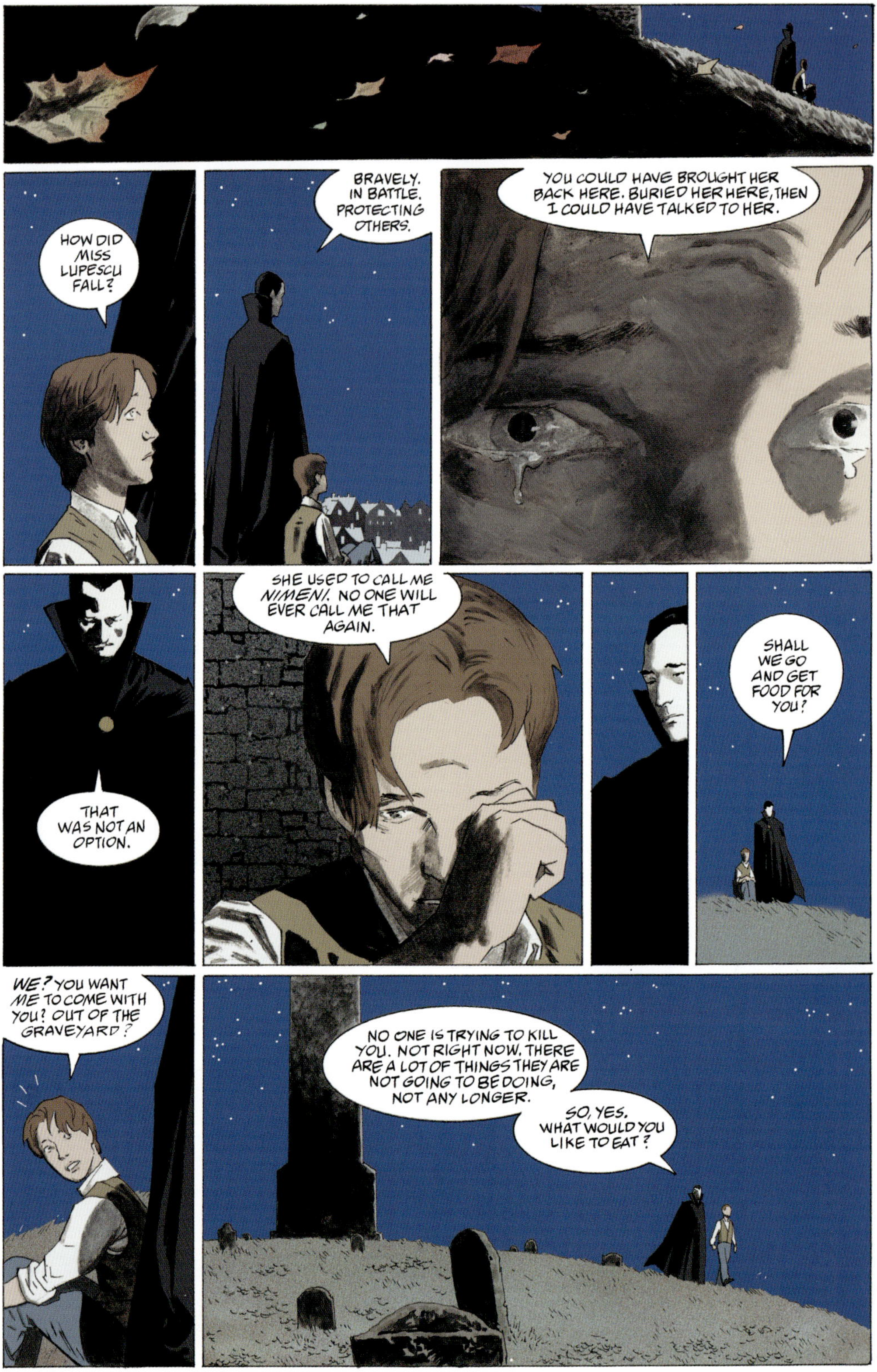
HOW DID MISS LUPESCU FALL?
BRAVELY. IN BATTLE. PROTECTING OTHERS.
YOU COULD HAVE BROUGHT HER BACK HERE. BURIED HER HERE, THEN I COULD HAVE TALKED TO HER.
THAT WAS NOT AN OPTION.
SHE USED TO CALL ME NIMENI. NO ONE WILL EVER CALL ME THAT AGAIN.
SHALL WE GO AND GET FOOD FOR YOU?
WE? YOU WANT ME TO COME WITH YOU? OUT OF THE GRAVEYARD?
NO ONE IS TRYING TO KILL YOU. NOT RIGHT NOW. THERE ARE A LOT OF THINGS THEY ARE NOT GOING TO BE DOING, NOT ANY LONGER.
SO, YES. WHAT WOULD YOU LIKE TO EAT?

BOD THOUGHT ABOUT SAYING THAT HE WASN'T HUNGRY, BUT THAT SIMPLY WAS NOT TRUE. HE FELT A LITTLE SICK AND A LITTLE LIGHT-HEADED, AND HE WAS STARVING.

PIZZA?

AS BOD WALKED, HE SAW THE INHABITANTS OF THE GRAVEYARD, BUT THEY LET THE BOY AND HIS GUARDIAN PASS AMONG THEM WITHOUT A WORD. THEY ONLY WATCHED. BOD TRIED TO THANK THEM FOR THEIR HELP, TO CALL OUT HIS GRATITUDE...

...BUT THE DEAD SAID NOTHING.

THE LIGHTS OF THE PIZZA RESTAURANT WERE BRIGHT, BRIGHTER THAN BOD WAS COMFORTABLE WITH.

SILAS SHOWED HIM HOW TO USE A MENU...

...AND HOW TO ORDER.

SILAS ORDERED A GLASS OF WATER AND A SMALL SALAD, WHICH HE PUSHED AROUND THE BOWL WITH HIS FORK BUT NEVER ACTUALLY PUT TO HIS LIPS.

BOD ATE HIS PIZZA WITH HIS FINGERS AND ENTHUSIASM. HE WOULD NOT ASK QUESTIONS. SILAS WOULD TALK IN HIS OWN TIME.

WE HAD KNOWN OF THEM... OF THE JACKS... FOR A LONG, LONG TIME.

... 140 ...

BUT WE KNEW OF THEM ONLY FROM THE RESULTS OF THEIR ACTIVITIES. WE SUSPECTED THERE WAS AN ORGANIZATION BEHIND IT, BUT THEY HID TOO WELL.

AND THEN THEY CAME AFTER YOU, AND THEY KILLED YOUR FAMILY. AND, SLOWLY, I WAS ABLE TO FOLLOW THEIR TRAIL.

IS *WE*, YOU AND MISS LUPESCU?

US AND OTHERS LIKE US.

THE HONOUR GUARD.

HOW DID YOU HEAR ABOUT—?

NO MATTER. LITTLE PITCHERS HAVE BIG EARS, AS THEY SAY.

YES, THE HONOUR GUARD.

SO...

NOW YOU'RE DONE... DONE WITH ALL THIS.

ARE YOU GOING TO STAY?

"I GAVE MY WORD. I AM HERE UNTIL YOU ARE GROWN."

"I'M GROWN."

"NO. ALMOST."

"NOT YET."

"SILAS?"

"THAT GIRL — SCARLETT. WHY WAS SHE SO SCARED OF ME?"

BUT SILAS SAID NOTHING AND THE QUESTION HUNG IN THE AIR AS THE MAN AND THE YOUTH WALKED OUT OF THE BRIGHT PIZZA RESTAURANT INTO THE WAITING DARKNESS.

AND SOON ENOUGH, THEY WERE SWALLOWED BY THE NIGHT.

8
Leavings and Partings

Illustrated by P. Craig Russell, Kevin Nowlan, and Galen Showman

SOMETIMES HE COULD NO LONGER SEE THE DEAD. IT HAD BEGUN A MONTH OR TWO PREVIOUSLY, IN APRIL OR IN MAY. AT FIRST IT HAD ONLY HAPPENED OCCASIONALLY, BUT NOW IT SEEMED TO BE HAPPENING MORE AND MORE.

THE WORLD WAS CHANGING.

!
?
ODD.
I'VE KNOWN THAT FOX SINCE IT WAS A CUB.
AND THAT CAT HAS PROWLED THROUGH THE GRAVEYARD FOR AS LONG AS I CAN REMEMBER.
THEY KNOW ME. IF THEY'RE FEELING FRIENDLY THEY EVEN LET ME PET THEM.
BOD WANDERED OVER TO THE NORTHWESTERN PART OF THE GRAVEYARD, TO THE TANGLE OF IVY THAT HUNG FROM A YEW TREE AND HALF-BLOCKED THE FAR EXIT FROM THE EGYPTIAN WALK.
HE STARTED TO SLIP THROUGH THE IVY, BUT...
MMF
ODD.

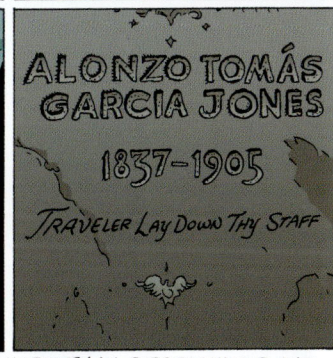

ALONZO TOMÁS
GARCIA JONES
1837-1905
TRAVELER LAY DOWN THY STAFF

BOD HAD BEEN COMING DOWN HERE FOR SEVERAL MONTHS: ALONZO JONES HAD BEEN ALL OVER THE WORLD, AND HE TOOK GREAT PLEASURE IN TELLING BOD STORIES OF HIS TRAVELS. HE WOULD BEGIN BY SAYING...

"NOTHING INTERESTING HAS EVER HAPPENED TO ME..."

"...AND I HAVE TOLD YOU ALL MY TALES."

"EXCEPT... DID I EVER TELL YOU ABOUT..."

. . . THE TIME I HAD TO ESCAPE FROM MOSCOW?
NO.
OR
. . . THE TIME I LOST AN ALASKAN GOLDMINE WORTH A FORTUNE?
NO.
OR
. . . THE CATTLE STAMPEDE ON THE PAMPAS?
NO.
BOD WOULD ALWAYS SHAKE HIS HEAD AND LOOK EXPECTANT AND SOON ENOUGH HIS HEAD WOULD BE SWIMMING WITH TALES OF DERRING-DO AND HIGH ADVENTURE.

NOW BOD WALKED OVER TO THE POINTED STONE AND HE WAITED, BUT SAW NO ONE.

ALONZO.

BOD LEANED DOWN, TO PUSH HIS HEAD INTO THE GRAVE AND CALL HIS FRIEND.

BUT INSTEAD OF HIS HEAD SLIPPING THROUGH THE SOLID MATTER LIKE A SHADOW PASSING THROUGH A DEEPER SHADOW...

BONK

OW!

ALONZO!

ODD.

... 147 ...

AWK AWK AWK

HERE, BOY! THERE'S NASTURSHALUMS GROWING WILD OVER HERE. WHY DON'T YOU PICK SOME FOR ME, AND PUT THEM OVER BY MY STONE.

SO BOD DID.

He carried them over to Mother Slaughter's headstone, so cracked and worn and weathered that all it said now was...

LAUGH

...which had puzzled local historians for over a hundred years.

YOU'RE A GOOD LAD. I DON'T KNOW WHAT WE'LL DO WITHOUT YOU.

THANK YOU.

WHERE IS EVERYONE? YOU'RE THE FIRST PERSON I'VE SEEN TONIGHT.

WHAT DID YOU DO TO YOUR FOREHEAD.

I BUMPED IT, ON MR. JONES'S GRAVE. IT WAS **SOLID**.

I...

... 148 ...

I CALLED YOU BOY, DIDN'T I? BUT TIME PASSES IN THE BLINK OF AN EYE, AND IT'S A YOUNG MAN YOU ARE NOW, ISN'T IT?
I STILL FEEL THE SAME AS I ALWAYS DID.
AND I STILL FEELS LIKE I DONE WHEN I WAS A TINY SLIP OF A THING, MAKING DAISY CHAINS IN THE OLD PASTURE. YOU'RE ALWAYS YOU, AND THAT DON'T CHANGE, AND YOU'RE ALWAYS CHANGING, AND THERE'S NOTHING YOU CAN DO ABOUT IT.
I REMEMBER THE NIGHT YOU CAME HERE, BOY.
I SAYS...
WE CAN'T LET THE LITTLE FELLOW LEAVE.
AND YOUR MOTHER AGREES, AND ALL OF THEM STARTS ARGUFYING AND WHAT-NOT UNTIL THE LADY ON THE GREY RIDES UP.
"PEOPLE OF THE GRAVEYARD..."
...SHE SAYS...
"LISTEN TO MOTHER SLAUGHTER. HAVE YOU NOT GOT ANY CHARITY IN YOUR BONES?"
AND THEN ALL OF THEM AGREED WITH ME.
THERE'S NOT MUCH HAPPENS HERE TO MAKE ONE DAY UNLIKE THE NEXT.

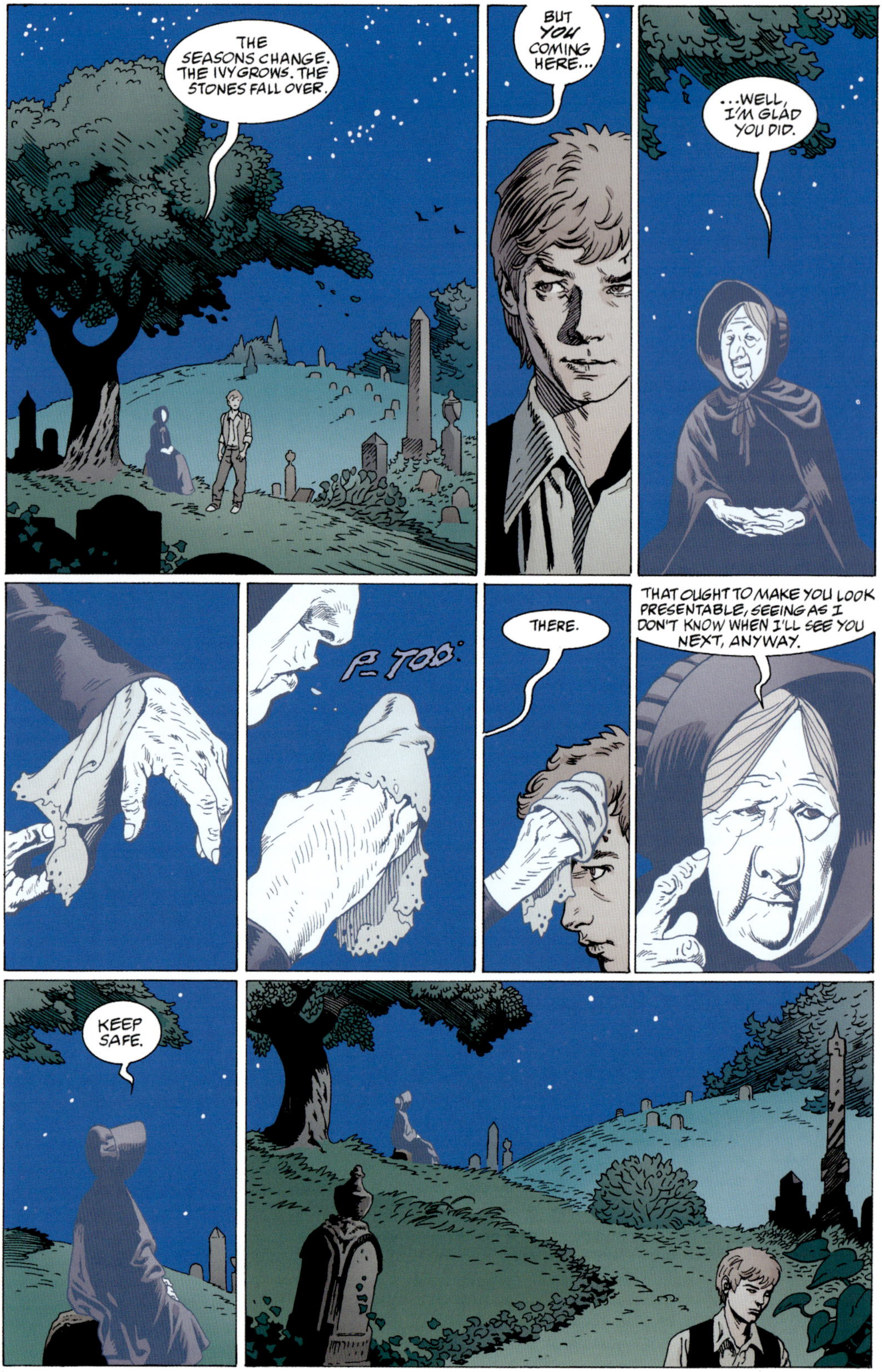
THE SEASONS CHANGE. THE IVY GROWS. THE STONES FALL OVER.
BUT YOU COMING HERE...
...WELL, I'M GLAD YOU DID.
P-TOO!
THERE.
THAT OUGHT TO MAKE YOU LOOK PRESENTABLE, SEEING AS I DON'T KNOW WHEN I'LL SEE YOU NEXT, ANYWAY.
KEEP SAFE.

FEELING DISCOMFITED IN A WAY HE COULD NOT REMEMBER HAVING FELT BEFORE, BOD MADE HIS WAY BACK TO THE OWENSES' TOMB, AND WAS PLEASED TO SEE BOTH OF HIS PARENTS WAITING FOR HIM BESIDE IT.
WHY DO THEY STAND LIKE THAT?
ODD.
OWENS
EVENING, BOD. I TRUST YOU ARE KEEPING WELL?
TOLERABLY WELL.
MISTRESS OWENS AND I SPENT OUR LIVES WISHING THAT WE HAD A CHILD. I DO NOT BELIEVE THAT WE COULD HAVE EVER HAD A BETTER YOUNG MAN THAN YOU, BOD.
WELL, YES, THANK YOU, BUT...
?
WHERE DID SHE GO?
OH, YES. AH, YOU KNOW BETSY. THERE'S THINGS, TIMES, WHEN... WELL, YOU DON'T KNOW WHAT TO SAY. YOU KNOW?
NO.
I EXPECT SILAS IS WAITING FOR YOU.
AND THEN HE WAS GONE.
OWENS

IT WAS PAST MIDNIGHT. BOD BEGAN TO WALK TOWARD THE OLD CHAPEL. THERE WAS NO SIGN OF SILAS.

SAY YOU'LL MISS ME, YOU LUMPKIN.

LIZA?

I HAVEN'T SEEN OR HEARD FROM YOU IN OVER A YEAR— NOT SINCE THE NIGHT OF THE JACKS OF ALL TRADES. WHERE HAVE YOU BEEN?

WATCHING. DOES A LADY HAVE TO TELL EVERYTHING SHE DOES?

WATCHING ME?

TRULY, LIFE IS WASTED ON THE LIVING, NOBODY OWENS, FOR ONE OF US IS TOO FOOLISH TO LIVE, AND IT IS NOT I. SAY YOU WILL MISS ME.

WHERE ARE YOU GOING?

OF COURSE I WILL MISS YOU, WHEREVER YOU GO.

TOO STUPID...

...TOO STUPID TO LIVE.

SHE KISSED HIM GENTLY AND HE WAS TOO PERPLEXED, TOO UTTERLY WRONG-FOOTED, TO KNOW WHAT TO DO.

... 152 ...

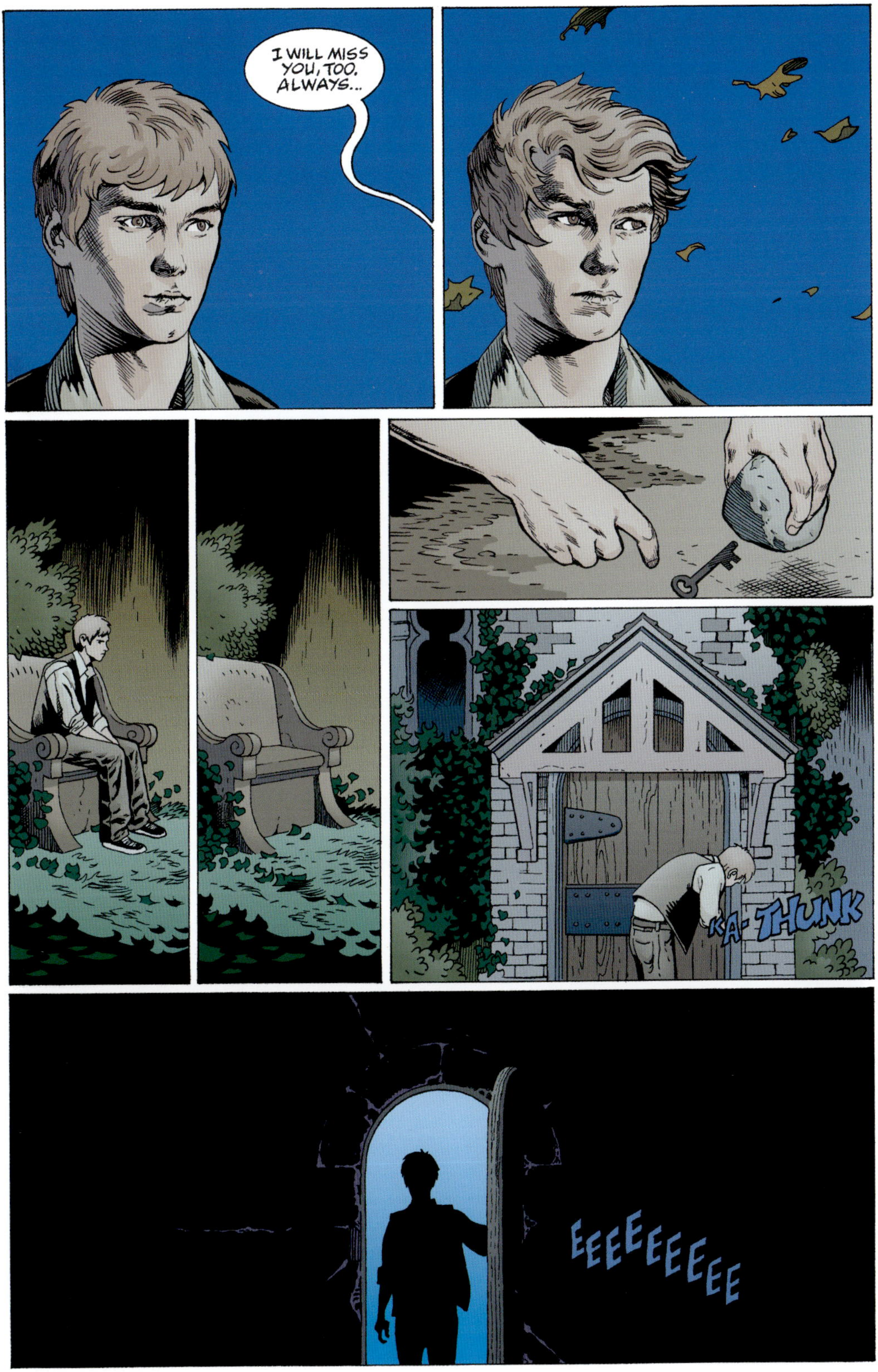
I WILL MISS YOU, TOO. ALWAYS...
KA-THUNK
EEEEEEEEE

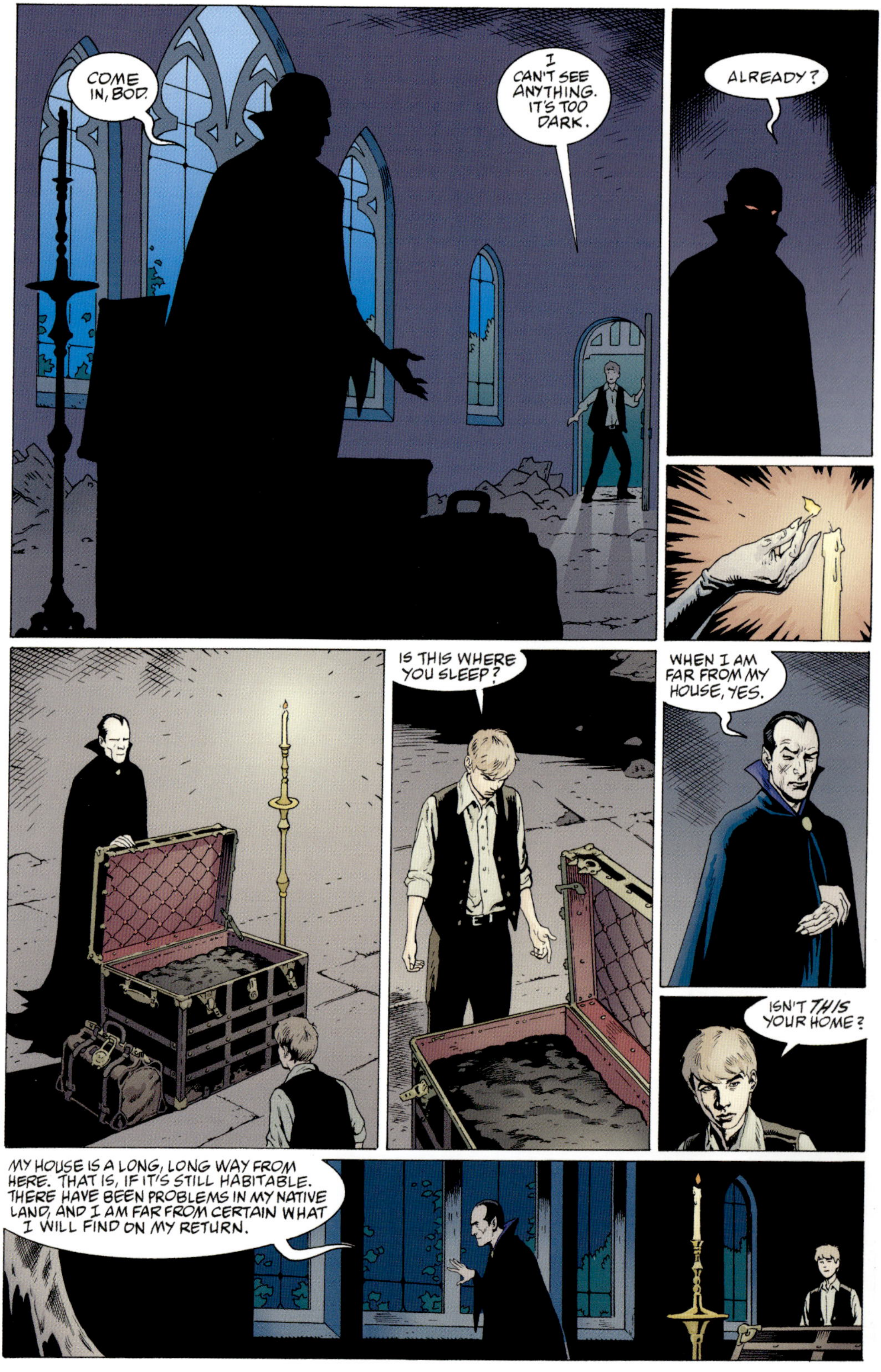
COME IN, BOD.
I CAN'T SEE ANYTHING. IT'S TOO DARK.
ALREADY?
IS THIS WHERE YOU SLEEP?
WHEN I AM FAR FROM MY HOUSE, YES.
ISN'T THIS YOUR HOME?
MY HOUSE IS A LONG, LONG WAY FROM HERE. THAT IS, IF IT'S STILL HABITABLE. THERE HAVE BEEN PROBLEMS IN MY NATIVE LAND, AND I AM FAR FROM CERTAIN WHAT I WILL FIND ON MY RETURN.

YOU'RE GOING BACK? YOU'RE REALLY LEAVING? BUT YOU'RE MY GUARDIAN.
I WAS YOUR GUARDIAN.
BUT YOU ARE OLD ENOUGH TO GUARD YOURSELF.
I HAVE OTHER THINGS TO PROTECT.
CAN'T I STAY HERE? IN THE GRAVEYARD?
YOU MUST NOT. ALL THE PEOPLE HERE HAVE HAD THEIR LIVES, BOD, EVEN IF THEY WERE SHORT ONES. NOW IT'S YOUR TURN. YOU NEED TO LIVE.
CAN I COME WITH YOU?
NO.
WILL I SEE YOU AGAIN?
PERHAPS. AND WHETHER YOU SEE ME OR NOT, I HAVE NO DOUBT THAT I WILL SEE YOU.
FOLLOW ME.
I TOOK THE LIBERTY OF PACKING A CASE FOR YOU. YOUR POSSESSIONS ARE ALL IN THERE.

TELL ME ABOUT THE HONOR GUARD, SILAS. YOU'RE IN IT. MISS LUPESCU WAS.
WHO ELSE?
ARE THERE A LOT OF YOU?
WHAT DO YOU DO?
WE DON'T DO ENOUGH, AND MOSTLY WE GUARD THE BORDERLANDS. WE PROTECT THE BORDERS OF THINGS.
YOU MEAN, LIKE STOPPING THE MAN JACK AND HIS PEOPLE?
WE DO WHAT WE HAVE TO DO.
BUT YOU DID THE RIGHT THING. I MEAN, STOPPING THE JACKS. THEY WERE TERRIBLE. THEY WERE MONSTERS.
I HAVE NOT ALWAYS DONE THE RIGHT THING. WHEN I WAS YOUNGER... I DID WORSE THINGS THAN JACK. WORSE THAN ANY OF THEM. I WAS THE MONSTER, THEN, BOD, AND WORSE THAN ANY MONSTER.
BUT YOU AREN'T THAT ANY LONGER, ARE YOU?
PEOPLE CAN CHANGE.
IT WAS AN HONOR TO BE YOUR GUARDIAN, YOUNG MAN.

THIS IS FOR YOU. TAKE IT.
IT CONTAINS MONEY. ENOUGH TO GIVE YOU A START IN THE WORLD, BUT NOTHING MORE.
I WENT TO SEE ALONZO JONES TODAY BUT HE WASN'T THERE, OR IF HE WAS I COULDN'T SEE HIM.
I WANTED HIM TO TELL ME ABOUT DISTANT PLACES HE'D VISITED. ISLANDS AND PORPOISES AND GLACIERS AND MOUNTAINS. PLACES WHERE PEOPLE DRESS AND EAT IN THE STRANGEST WAYS.
THOSE PLACES. THEY'RE STILL THERE. I MEAN, THERE'S A WHOLE WORLD OUT THERE. CAN I SEE IT? CAN I GO THERE?
THERE IS A WHOLE WORLD OUT THERE, YES. YOU HAVE A PASSPORT IN THE INNER POCKET OF YOUR SUITCASE. IT'S MADE OUT IN THE NAME OF NOBODY OWENS. AND IT WAS NOT EASY TO OBTAIN.

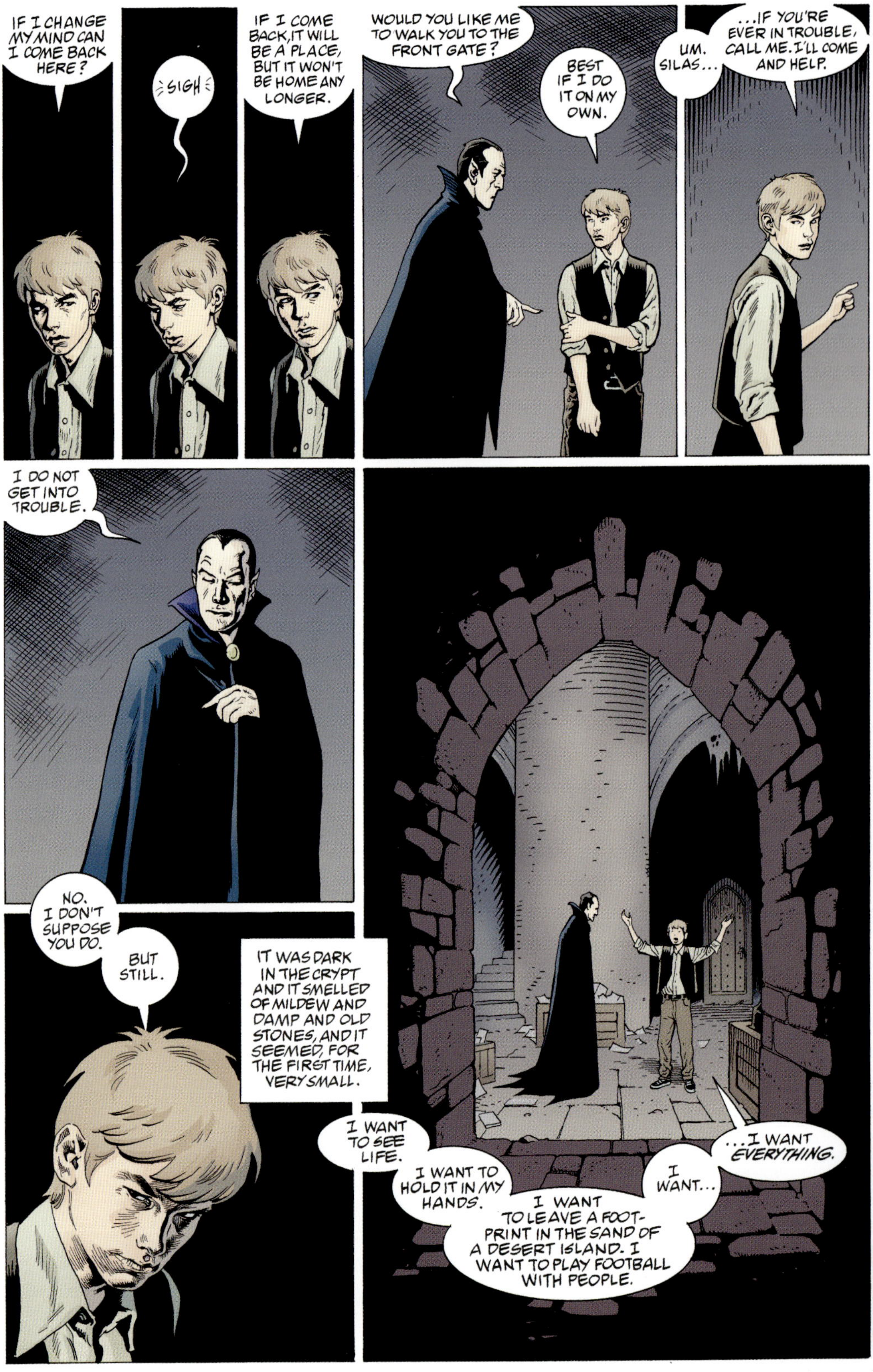
IF I CHANGE MY MIND CAN I COME BACK HERE?
SIGH
IF I COME BACK, IT WILL BE A PLACE, BUT IT WON'T BE HOME ANY LONGER.
WOULD YOU LIKE ME TO WALK YOU TO THE FRONT GATE?
BEST IF I DO IT ON MY OWN.
UM. SILAS...
...IF YOU'RE EVER IN TROUBLE, CALL ME. I'LL COME AND HELP.
I DO NOT GET INTO TROUBLE.
NO. I DON'T SUPPOSE YOU DO.
BUT STILL.
IT WAS DARK IN THE CRYPT AND IT SMELLED OF MILDEW AND DAMP AND OLD STONES, AND IT SEEMED, FOR THE FIRST TIME, VERY SMALL.
I WANT TO SEE LIFE.
I WANT TO HOLD IT IN MY HANDS.
I WANT TO LEAVE A FOOT-PRINT IN THE SAND OF A DESERT ISLAND. I WANT TO PLAY FOOTBALL WITH PEOPLE.
I WANT...
...I WANT *EVERYTHING*.

GOOD.
IF EVER IT TRANSPIRES THAT I AM IN TROUBLE, I SHALL INDEED SEND FOR YOU.
EVEN THOUGH YOU DON'T GET INTO TROUBLE.
AS YOU SAY.
GOOD-BYE, SILAS.
GOOD-BYE, NOBODY OWENS.

CLICK

"It's not yet morning. The gates will still be locked. I wonder if they will let me through? Or will I have to go back to the chapel for a key?"

But when he got to the entrance he found the small pedestrian gate was unlocked and wide open, as if it was waiting for him, as if the graveyard itself was bidding him good-bye.

"Hullo, Mother."

DO YOU KNOW WHAT YOU'RE GOING TO DO NOW?

SEE THE WORLD.

GET INTO TROUBLE.

GET OUT OF TROUBLE AGAIN.

VISIT JUNGLES AND VOLCANOES AND DESERTS AND ISLANDS.

AND PEOPLE...

...I WANT TO MEET AN AWFUL LOT OF PEOPLE.

MISTRESS OWENS MADE NO IMMEDIATE REPLY.

AND THEN SHE BEGAN TO SING A SONG THAT BOD REMEMBERED, A SONG SHE HAD USED TO LULL HIM TO SLEEP WHEN HE WAS SMALL.

"SLEEP, MY LITTLE BABBY-OH SLEEP UNTIL YOU WAKEN - WHEN YOU WAKE YOU'LL SEE THE WORLD IF I'M NOT MISTAKEN...
YOU'RE NOT.
AND I SHALL.
"KISS A LOVER DANCE A MEASURE, FIND YOUR NAME AND BURIED TREASURE . . . .
MMM
THEN THE LAST LINES OF THE SONG CAME BACK TO MISTRESS OWENS, AND SHE SANG THEM TO HER SON.
"FACE YOUR LIFE ITS PAIN, ITS PLEASURE LEAVE NO PATH UNTAKEN"
A DIFFICULT CHALLENGE, BUT I CAN TRY MY BEST.
?
MOTHER?

"I AM SO PROUD OF YOU, MY SON."

THE MIDSUMMER SKY WAS ALREADY BEGINNING TO LIGHTEN IN THE EAST, AND THAT WAS THE WAY BOD BEGAN TO WALK.

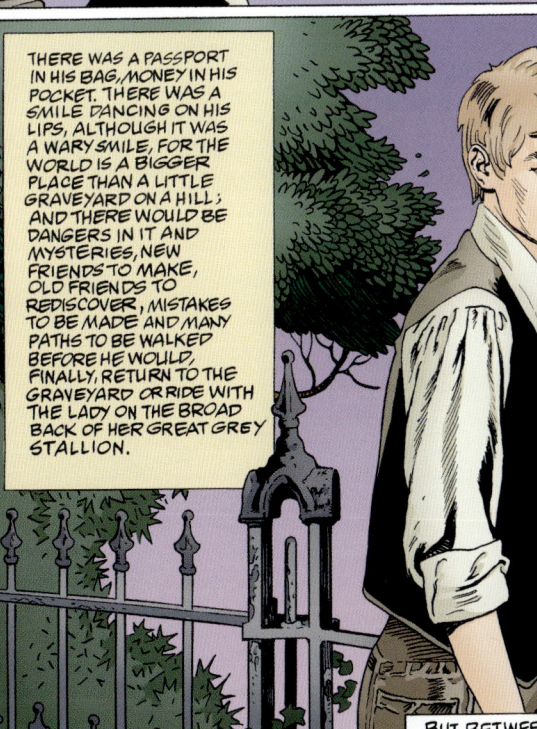

THERE WAS A PASSPORT IN HIS BAG, MONEY IN HIS POCKET. THERE WAS A SMILE DANCING ON HIS LIPS, ALTHOUGH IT WAS A WARY SMILE, FOR THE WORLD IS A BIGGER PLACE THAN A LITTLE GRAVEYARD ON A HILL; AND THERE WOULD BE DANGERS IN IT AND MYSTERIES, NEW FRIENDS TO MAKE, OLD FRIENDS TO REDISCOVER, MISTAKES TO BE MADE AND MANY PATHS TO BE WALKED BEFORE HE WOULD, FINALLY, RETURN TO THE GRAVEYARD OR RIDE WITH THE LADY ON THE BROAD BACK OF HER GREAT GREY STALLION.

BUT BETWEEN NOW AND THEN THERE WAS *LIFE*...

... 163 ...

...AND BOD WALKED INTO IT WITH HIS EYES AND HIS HEART WIDE OPEN.

NEIL GAIMAN'S
NEWBERY MEDAL WINNER
THE GRAVEYARD BOOK

THREE NEW EDITIONS

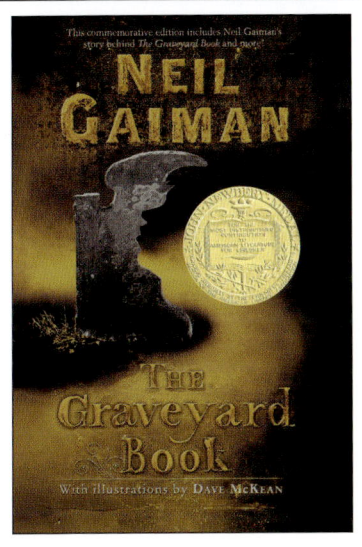

Commemorative edition paperback,
with gorgeous metallic gold cover

TWO-VOLUME GRAPHIC NOVEL ADAPTATION

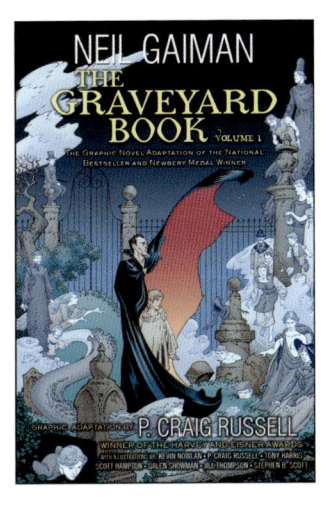

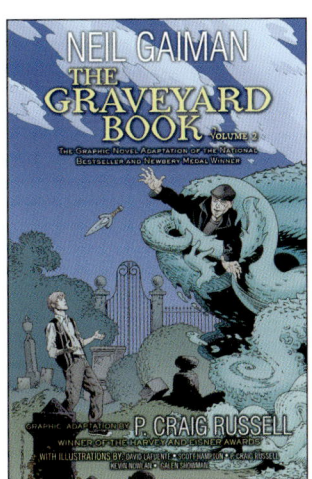

HARPER
An Imprint of HarperCollinsPublishers

www.mousecircus.com

MORE MAGICAL CLASSICS FROM BESTSELLING AUTHOR
NEIL GAIMAN

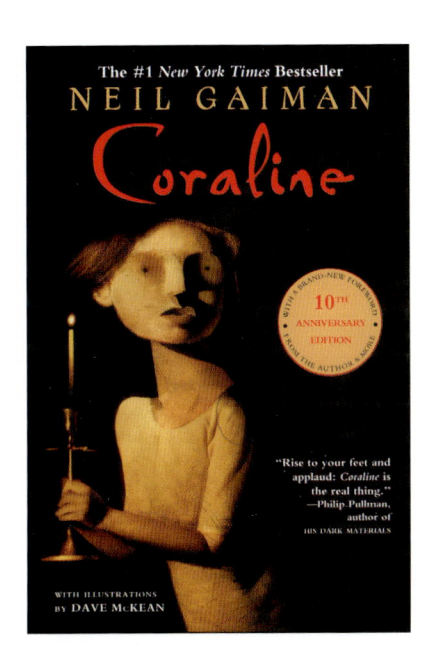

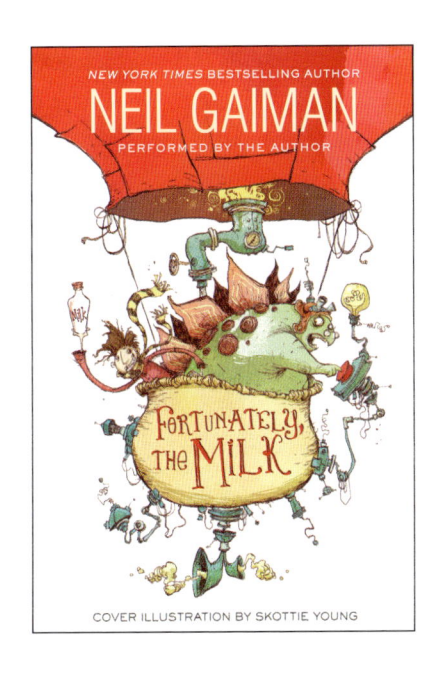

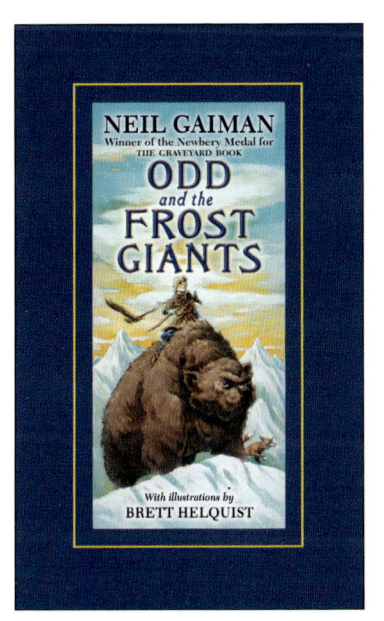

Visit
www.mousecircus.com
for exclusive
Neil Gaiman footage,
video trailers,
games, downloadables,
and more!

HARPER
An Imprint of HarperCollinsPublishers